# COUNTESS SO *Shameless*

# COUNTESS SO
## *Shameless*

*A Scandal in London Novel*

## Liana LeFey

Montlake
Romance

The characters and events portrayed in this book are fictitious.
Any similarity to real persons, living or dead, is coincidental and
not intended by the author.

Published by Montlake Romance
P.O. Box 400818
Las Vegas, NV 89140

ISBN-13: 9781612185378
ISBN-10: 1612185371

To my wonderful husband/hero, for giving me wings and encouraging me to aim for the stars.

## ACKNOWLEDGMENTS

Thanks go out to:

My parents, for their unwavering love and support and for providing the perfect example of true romance.

Sonia Lara, for being the most amazing beta reader (and friend!) on the planet.

Kim Frasier, for handing me my very first romance novel when we were fourteen—and for all the others that soon followed.

Sherry Thomas, for taking the time to mentor and encourage a scared newbie.

My fabulous agent, Barbara, for her enormous leap of faith with the girl whose "dream house" was a little stone cottage. Thank God for her sense of humor!

Lindsay Guzzardo and Krista Stroever of Montlake/Amazon, for their incredible patience and willingness to help me crest that steep learning curve and whip this story into shape.

My ARWA chapter mates, for sharing their priceless knowledge as well as their relentless enthusiasm.

Montlake/Amazon, for giving me my big break.

Thanks for believing in me. Y'all rock!

## Chapter One

### IGNORANCE IS BLISS

*Versailles, late 1744*

*SHAMELESS ROUÉ, INDEED. MAMAN WAS RIGHT ABOUT HIM.* From her concealed vantage point, Mélisande observed as Lord Alessandro Orsini, Emissary of the Holy Roman Empire, cast his spell over yet another swarm of females. Raucous laughter erupted from the man, causing heads to turn.

Her lip curled at the wave of feminine coos and titters that followed. Their display rivaled anything she'd witnessed to date. If the silly creatures batted their lashes any harder, the resulting windstorm would send the object of their affection flying across the ballroom.

Edging a bit closer to get a better view, Mélisande shook her head. Why *did* they adore him so? He wasn't at all handsome. Not like Monsieur Falloure, who caused an unbidden sigh to escape her (and every other female between the ages of twelve and the hereafter) every time she laid eyes on him.

No. Tall and whip thin, Orsini was all angles and planes. His overly large dark eyes and longish nose were topped by a mop of common, perpetually untidy, brown hair. His lips were rather on the thin side, too—although to be fair, he did have a very broad, altogether quite appealing smile. It was his one redeeming feature, this glittering grin. It lit his whole face, miraculously

1

rearranging his features into something not necessarily handsome but...*interesting.*

Another wicked chuckle burst forth from the man. Arching a suggestive brow, he leaned over to whisper into an eager ear. Seconds later, a cascade of giggles issued forth from the listener's rouged lips, her painted fan snapping up to both conceal and cool the deep flush now staining her cheeks. Orsini offered his arm, and the girl's chin lifted a fraction, her eyes gleaming with triumph—she'd just become queen bee.

"*Merde,*" Mélisande whispered, shaking her head. She'd never seen anything like it. The girl was practically panting, and they'd met only an hour ago.

She quashed a chuckle as her gaze shifted to the abandoned hive, where the new favorite's contemporaries looked on with narrowed eyes. The fools wouldn't have to wait long. Thus far, the longest *affaire* had lasted four days. He danced out of every trap they laid with all the skill of a fox evading a pack of hounds.

It was the perfect analogy. He was very like a fox, clever and quick, the chasing of chickens his chief pleasure in life. Stifling more laughter, Mélisande decided then and there to privately refer to him as *Le Renard.*

Her mother had nearly suffered an apoplectic fit upon learning of the man's presence at court. "*C'est un vrai coureur de jupons, ma fille. Ne pas aller près de lui!*" she'd admonished, promising all manner of consequences should she be caught within twenty paces of the cheerful lifter of skirts.

Which had, of course, only spurred her curiosity. She had become Orsini's shadow, and when he was not present, she lurked at the edges of his retinue. By remaining inconspicuous, she'd managed to overhear several *very* interesting conversations during which his former *amours* described in great detail (and with great relish) his skill in the bedchamber.

It was a fascinating education in the art of debauchery.

Most astounding was the discovery that the majority of his erstwhile lovers continued to regard him with fondness and affection despite having been left behind. She'd even witnessed some offering him blatant invitations to revisit their romantic relationship. One might expect a cast-off lover to bitterly mourn the end of an *affaire* or become spiteful, but certainly not to exhibit such amiable, not to mention shameless, behavior. It was beyond comprehension.

Slinking from her hiding place, Mélisande again followed his progress, mindful to stay in the periphery. He cut a dashing figure this evening, resplendent in a mint silk waistcoat trimmed with silver embroidery, jewels, and a fortune in fine lace. So opulent was his dress that had he been better groomed and less careless in his manner, he would have made a perfect dandy. But his untamed curls, mischievous eyes, and impish grin instead turned him into a perfect rogue.

Orsini was now regaling his admirers with yet another tale—of debauchery, no doubt. Flouting her mother's warning, Mélisande wandered over, staying toward the back. A little thrill of excitement mingled with trepidation ran through her, to be this close to the proverbial forbidden fruit.

Suddenly, the orator paused. "D'Alembert!"

Mélisande turned in the direction of his shout. Seeing no one, she spun back around to see mint silk and jeweled buttons. With dread in her heart, she slowly looked up to see Le Renard's warm, brown eyes staring back at her, full of wry amusement. A muffled giggle sounded to her left, and she felt the heat of a flush rising in her cheeks as she realized they were all looking at her.

"*Pardon, mademoiselle. Je m'excuse,*" he said, bowing. Sidestepping her, he whisked away to catch up with his friend.

Gone.

Speechless, Mélisande stared after him, her shoulders tingling from where he'd touched her. A slow rush of warmth spread throughout her body, fever-like, causing her to wonder briefly if she was taking ill. Irritation quickly chased away the odd sensation. The man had hardly paused! He might have run into a—a footstool rather than a person.

Disappointment pierced her. Part of her wished he'd been more solicitous after his careless blunder, despite the fact that such notice would only spell trouble for her. Sighing, she trudged back to the safety of the gallery to watch in silence.

The ball was a lovely display. Skirts swirled elegantly as the ladies danced the quadrille, their jewels glittering like star fire in soft, golden light cast from the chandeliers high above. Through it all, Le Renard made his way from flower to flower, charming all and sundry. He even paired with La Marquise de Pompadour, who laughed in delight several times during their dance.

With all her young heart, Mélisande wished herself part of the goings-on below. But she dared not. On good faith, Maman and Papa had allowed her to attend tonight's festivities, but as a spectator only. She'd given her word that she would not attract attention to herself in any way, and to break their trust would not only disappoint them but result in the further restriction of her already limited freedom.

"It is time she was told."

Mélisande awakened to hear Maman and Papa talking softly on the other side of their chambers. It was quite chilly, so she opted to remain snuggled under the warm blankets a bit longer.

A cup clinked against a saucer, the noise seeming overly loud in the quiet room.

"Are you certain it's necessary?" her father asked. "Would it not be better to simply let things remain as they are?"

"She must be made aware—for her own safety," replied her mother. "And then we will leave Versailles and *never* return."

The china clinked again, and Isabelle d'Orleans Compton, Countess of Wilmington, released a sigh of frustration. "She should not be here. *Mais, Louis a insisté*," she grated, her voice laced with bitterness. "Fool that I am, I could not refuse him, despite the danger."

Mélisande was now fully awake.

Her father's voice was gentle but firm. "Relax, Belle. We return to England in a few days. And in a couple of years she'll marry Newcastle's heir, uniting our families and lands, and none of this will matter."

*Marry David?* Mélisande could barely refrain from leaping up in protest. David was all but a brother to her. The very idea that they would consider him for a match was absurd!

"England is not far enough away to prevent a disaster, and nor will her marriage stop it, if matters here worsen—Spencer, we *must* tell her," her mother snapped. "The evidence is plain if one knows what to look for. If the wrong sort takes notice, all the lies we've so carefully planted will be for nothing."

A chair scraped back, the sound followed by footsteps. Back and forth they came and went, pacing the far side of the room.

"We cannot protect her forever," Isabelle persisted. "Things here are getting…complicated."

The pacing stopped.

Burning with curiosity, Mélisande strained to hear her mother.

"No matter how Louis ignores it, there is deep unrest here. If there is a rebellion while France is fighting a war—and I fully expect him to declare war on England, now that he has agreed to shelter Charles Stuart—the members of this court will grasp at *any* straw for their own gain. Mélisande would provide a most convenient means to an end. She must be on guard against treachery. It could mean her life. I hate this as much as you, Spencer, but it must be done."

Her father sighed, at once sounding frustrated and resigned. "When?"

"He has arranged a private audience this afternoon. You do not have to be present. I would certainly understand if—"

"No," he cut in. "She'll need both of us when she learns the truth."

Dread gripped Mélisande's heart. Her mind focused on maintaining the semblance of slumber, on holding her tongue and remaining motionless. She waited while her mother summoned Marie, waited until the noises in the room gradually changed to the normal sounds of morning preparations.

After a suitable amount of time had elapsed, Mélisande inhaled and stirred, stretching.

"*Bonjour, ma fille.* Today is a very important day. You are to be presented to His Majesty," her mother announced. "You must make a good impression—the *best* impression!" Snapping her fingers for Marie, she began pulling gowns from the wardrobe.

"Why should the king wish to see me?" Mélisande asked, sliding a leg out from beneath the covers. Easing her foot down to the floor, she winced at the contact. It was like ice, in spite of the roaring fire in the hearth.

As her mother's hands stilled momentarily in their task, Mélisande noted their trembling. That, more than anything she'd heard this morning, caused her gut to twist with fear. Not even Uncle George in a tearing rage gave her maman pause.

"I've told you of my youth here," Isabelle replied, smoothing the wrinkles out of the fabric in her hands. "The king and I are old friends, and I have written of you many times. Now, he wishes to meet you in person. It is a great honor," she finished, picking up a corset and loosening the ties with nervous little jerks. "Now, come. Your hair must be washed and restyled." She frowned, lifting a dull, lifeless hank that had worked loose from Mélisande's braid. "You cannot meet the king like this."

"*Maman*, you *made* me wear the wig and powder last night, remember? And that hideous gown!"

"*Oui*," Isabelle clipped. "It, and the gown, was appropriate for the occasion. Now, it is not." She raised a delicate brow, quelling further protest. "Marie," she called, "heat the water. And get out the green *calèche*."

As the little maid rushed to comply, Isabelle shook out a deep green silk brocade *manteau* trimmed with gold wire and picked with gold and amber Venetian glass beads. Laying it aside, she then held up and examined a matching stomacher so heavily ornamented the underlying cloth could hardly be seen. Maman would look like a queen dressed in it. Leaving it on the bed, her mother went to pour some fragrance into the washbasin.

Knowing she had nothing nearly as grand, Mélisande went and looked over the few adult dresses they'd brought along for her to wear. She selected a pale blue silk ensemble with a modest neckline. It was rather plain when compared to the green gown, but at least it wasn't ugly—unlike the monstrosity she'd worn last night. The graduated row of gossamer bows down the front was a nice touch, reminding her of Madam de Pompadour's gown the night before.

"You will not be wearing any of those," her mother announced from across the room. "You will wear this."

Mélisande's eyes widened with incredulity as she looked at the green gown. "But, *Maman*, you and Papa said you did not wish me to attract attention."

Her mother pinched the bridge of her nose, screwing her eyes shut for a moment. "Mélisande, this is the *king*. You must look your *very* best. And Papa and I will be with you every moment," she reassured. "Come, the water is ready and we must hurry if your hair is to be finished in time."

Together the women washed and dried Mélisande's long, dark hair, rubbing it with a silk cloth until the soft tresses shone. It was like finest *bistre* ink, so dark a brown as to appear nearly black. Then came the braiding, coiling, and curling.

While they worked, Mélisande ate a cold breakfast of bread and fruit. When her coiffure was finished, her mother carefully placed some jeweled pins among the curls. A silk wrapper was tied over the arrangement to preserve their work while they lightly dusted her face with powder. Then on went stockings, garters, stays, panniers, petticoats, *jupe*, stomacher, and *manteau*. *Les engageantes* were added to the cuffs of the tight, elbow-length sleeves—five layers of creamy, diaphanous lace.

Her mother clasped a thick gold chain about her neck, from which was suspended the d'Orleans crest worked in gold and rubies. The silk wrapper was removed from her coiffure, and Marie buckled on her high-heeled shoes and daubed expensive *parfum* on her wrists and throat.

When Mélisande looked in the mirror, she hardly recognized herself.

Isabelle quickly finished her own toilette, having already styled her hair in a simple chignon with a few loose curls about her lovely face. As they prepared to leave, she and Marie carefully draped the *calèche* over Mélisande's shoulders, pulling the wired hood up and over to cast her face into deep shadow.

Ladies often wore such garments in order to conceal their identities; people would merely assume she was on her way to a *rendezvous*. Still, Isabelle was concerned. The less people saw, the better. It was one thing for her daughter to appear as a young girl or to have her heavily disguised so as to be unrecognizable, as she'd been last night, but to have her look like an adult was quite different, given the circumstances.

The couple flanked their daughter as they wended their way through the palace.

"Keep your head bowed," her mother reminded her in a low whisper. "Only when we are in the presence of the king are you to raise your eyes, and *only* when I tell you."

The guards admitted them into the outer receiving room to join the others who cooled their heels awaiting the king's leisure. They did not have to wait long.

Mélisande followed them in, her stomach in knots. She kept her head bowed while the king dismissed his servants and guards, seeing only the passing of shoes and stockinged legs. At last, the door closed.

"Isabelle, Wilmington," a deep voice greeted them softly.

A rustling of silk.

"You need never bow to me, Belle."

Mélisande raised her head just enough to see a heavily beringed hand take Isabelle's fingers and raise her up. The same voice addressed her papa, and the three of them conversed for a few moments. Finally, a pair of jewel-encrusted shoes came to rest in front of her.

"This is the child?"

"Yes, your majesty," replied her mother. "I am honored to present my daughter, Mademoiselle Mélisande Esmée d'Orleans Compton. Mélisande, you may now raise your eyes."

Trembling, Mélisande did as told. Standing before her was His Majesty, Louis XV, King of France. Though she'd faced royalty many times before, for some reason, this man's presence filled her with both awe and trepidation.

Shock struck her squarely in the chest as, without preamble, he pushed back the hood of her *calèche* and calmly proceeded to untie the ribbons holding her cape closed.

It turned to outrage as his eyes fell to her exposed décolletage, drawn to the shallow swell of her left breast.

Straightening to her full height, she silently dared him to accost her person again.

At her mutinous glare, Louis's lips quirked in a smile. "I can see you've raised no coward," he said to her parents. "Good. Such courage befits her blood."

Reaching out, he laid a single, gentle fingertip on the tiny, dark mole marking the spot below which pounded Mélisande's heart.

Sucking in a breath, she jerked back and prepared to vent her spleen.

"It is as I said," Isabelle rushed, her cutting off. "She bears *la marque de la coeur*. And the other, as well, on her hip."

Mélisande flicked a startled glance at her, but her mother's eyes remained downcast and unreadable. When she looked back to the king, she saw that he still gazed at her, a queer look in his eyes.

"You have not told her anything?" he asked, seeming unable to take his eyes off her.

Mélisande's already racing heart began to beat an uneven tattoo in her chest. Something here was terribly, *terribly* wrong...

"We thought it best to wait until she was older," replied Isabelle.

"Then it is time she knew the truth."

Mélisande's stomach dropped, and the world around her took on a surreal, dreamlike quality. The conversation she'd overheard that morning suddenly made sense as she looked at the man before her, recognizing with merciless acuity the similarities between their features.

In the blink of an eye, the unthinkable became the undeniable.

Turning to her mother, she watched the blood drain from her face. Her head shook ever so slightly, her blue eyes silently pleading, begging forgiveness.

"*Ma fille—*" Isabelle began.

"*Je ne suis pas aveugle, Maman!* I have eyes—*and* ears," Mélisande snapped. "I heard you and Papa this morning. Now it all makes sense." Taking a deep breath, she turned from her mother to address the king of France—her father. "I am honored to make your acquaintance, Your Majesty." Her voice was calm and steady, as though someone else were speaking with her mouth. "I hope I give you no offense by saying that although you are my father, the man who raised me shall always hold that place in my heart."

She turned to her darling papa, who had come to stand behind her. His face was pale and drawn, but his eyes shone with love and gratitude.

Louis appeared not in the least offended by the rejection. "I would have claimed you as my own and you would have known me as your father, but I loved your mother too much to let her live the life of a courtesan raising a royal bastard." He turned to Isabelle. "She deserved better than I could give her here."

His words buzzed in her ears as if from a great distance. She just stared at him, stunned. "I only wanted her happiness," the monarch continued. "Wilmington was quite amenable when I approached him regarding the matter. He was already in love with your mother." His knowing gaze slid over to her papa. "He agreed to care for her and raise you as his own, should she consent to the arrangement. It was divine providence."

Isabelle moved forward. "What I did, I did for both of us, Mélisande." Her voice was choked with emotion, and bright tears slid down her cheeks. "I knew if I bore you here, there would be only heartache for us both in years to come. I could not remain a courtesan forever, and I had to think of your happiness as well as my own."

"*My* happiness?"

"You needed a father. I had, purely by chance, befriended your papa during his visit here. I became quite fond of his company. Enough so that when Louis offered to arrange a marriage, I chose him." Fresh tears fell as she shook her head. "I very quickly grew to love him," she continued, her voice steadying as she regained her composure. "And he has been everything I could have wished for in a father for you."

Numbness enclosed Mélisande's heart, inuring her to what she knew should have been debilitating pain, and she was grateful for it.

Louis appraised her with a wistful smile. "You have my mother's eyes," he said, brushing her cheek with the knuckles of one hand. "The mark above your heart is hers, as well," he added. "It is something we share, you and I, for I also bear it."

At his words, a peculiar emotion stirred within Mélisande's breast. *I am the daughter of a king.* Whether or not she was legitimate was of no consequence—blood was blood. A strange urge came over her, an urge to laugh hysterically and sob all at once. It took every scrap of her self-control not to give in to it and collapse into a gibbering fool.

Her eyes met the king's, and in that moment she saw into him. His face held an expression of unexpected tenderness and fierce pride. Straightening her spine, she squared her shoulders, again raising her chin.

Louis nodded almost imperceptibly in approval. "Would that you had been born under different circumstances," he said with evident regret. "Had I been unencumbered when I met your mother, I would have married her." He glanced at Isabelle. "But since that was impossible, it was better for you that your lineage remain hidden. As a result, you had a safe, happy childhood, something I could not have guaranteed here.

"No one knows you are mine," he said, "and my heart wishes that it remain so for your sake. However, I cannot deny the advantages of recognizing you—for us both. Therefore, I give you a choice."

He paused, again flicking a glance at Isabelle, whose face was beginning to register confusion. "Should you wish to remain here in Versailles, I will acknowledge you," he offered. "You will be given a title and I will arrange for a suitable marriage."

Stunned, Mélisande looked to her mother and found her astonishment mirrored.

Louis, however, was not quite finished.

"It would not be easy for you at first," he warned, his light tone belying the seriousness of his words, "but you would adjust quickly. You have courage, and your mother has boasted to me of your intelligence many times. I believe you would be an asset to my court. The choice is yours."

The sheer magnitude of the offer floored her. To live as the daughter of a king! The temptation to accept without hesitation was great, but the burdens that would come with such a change in status might be more than she cared to endure.

She was no fool; there was no relationship between herself and this king other than blood. The moment she turned fifteen, she'd be married off to whomever he wished to favor, a pawn to be sacrificed for his gain. Regardless of her illegitimacy, her hand would be a high honor to bestow on a man, an extremely useful means of ensuring his fealty and strengthening his loyalty to the crown.

She would be wealthy, titled, and live a life of pleasure and ease.

And she'd be far from home and without family—her real family.

Maman would never agree to stay. And...

Turning, she looked to her papa, seeing the fear in his eyes, the sadness. Even though it would break his heart, she knew he would allow her to choose for herself.

"I choose to return to England," she answered, her voice steady and firm. "I appreciate what you have offered me, but I do not belong here." Her mother's shoulders relaxed, and she heard her papa's breath release.

Louis's face was resigned, if a little disappointed. "I would have done my best to make you happy here, but I understand. This has not been easy for you," he added gently, looking over Mélisande's shoulder at the man who had raised his daughter, then at Isabelle, his first love. "For any of you."

Pulling a small, wooden cylinder from his pocket, he proffered it to Mélisande. "I wish you to have this," he said, placing it in her palm. "It was your grandmother's when she was a girl. Now it is yours."

Mélisande looked down at the little cylindrical box for a moment, hesitant to see what was inside it, yet curious. Twisting the top, she pulled until it came off with a soft pop. Inside the chamber nestled a delicate gold ring set with a large blood ruby cut whimsically in the shape of a heart and flanked by two bright diamonds. It was beautiful.

"There is an inscription," the king murmured, reaching out to pluck the jewel from its bed. He read aloud: " *'T'es mon coeur.'* It was a gift from her father on her thirteenth birthday, and now it is a gift from your father to you."

*You are my heart.* Her eyes began to sting again. Papa's mother had died when she was an infant and she'd never know her. Now she'd lost another grandmother without ever having known her, either. And her real father was a stranger, someone she would also never get to know. She looked at the ring in his hand and considered what it represented: a heritage she could never openly claim, a secret that would burn in her heart forever. The scarlet stone flickered at her, its shape and color ironically appropriate.

Gently, Louis slid the ring onto the third finger of her right hand. "I would have been proud to claim you as my own before all, daughter," he told her with regret, kissing her cold cheeks. "But if you must leave, then I wish you joy."

Unable to look up for the twisting pain in her chest, Mélisande could only nod in silent acknowledgment of his high compliment. Her entire life was a lie, a house built on the shifting sand of a falsehood that had been laid down before she was even born. *Who am I?*

Louis nodded to Isabelle. "You may take her back to her chambers. Wilmington will remain, and we will discuss the matter of Charles Stuart. Come back once she is settled, if you wish, Belle," he added softly. "You know I have ever valued your opinion in all matters."

The manner of Louis's speech shook Mélisande to the core. It was the same way her parents spoke to each other when in private. Warm, familiar, completely trusting—*intimate.* To hear another man speaking to her mother that way was a shock, even though she knew now that Maman and he had once been...

She could not even think it without feeling ill. How horrible her poor papa must feel! Her gaze flicked to his face, but she could read nothing there.

"Take her up, Isabelle," Wilmington commanded. Nothing in his voice or demeanor betrayed emotional unrest, but when he turned to Mélisande, his eyes were filled with tenderness for the child he'd raised as his own. "We'll talk later, poppet. I know you have many questions, including those about David, but they will have to wait."

Desperate to flee this place, Mélisande nodded. Stepping away from her mother's light hold, she again faced the king. "Again, I thank you, Your Majesty, for both your kind offer and your gift." She looked down at the ring, the stone glittering like a drop of bright blood against her pale skin. *Blood of my blood. A queen once wore this ring. My grandmother.* "I pray your reign is long, prosperous, and peaceful, and I bid you fond farewell."

Taking her hand, Louis pressed it between his own. "Go with God's blessing, my child. And though you must never speak of it, never forget you are a Bourbon."

His eyes were fierce and hard as he stared into her and spoke these last words. Something intangible passed between them, and again her heart leapt with a strange sense of pride. She'd always been proud to be a Compton, but this was somewhat else.

*I am the daughter of a king.*

The fact kept repeating in her thoughts as her mind turned it over and over, examining it from all angles. Though she had no way of knowing how it would affect her in years to come—if it would even make a difference at all, now that she'd chosen to return to her life in England—she knew her place in the world had just been forever altered.

Dipping one final curtsy, she quickly but calmly walked to the door, opened it, and swept through with her head held high.

After a moment's stunned hesitation, her mother followed, but Mélisande's longer legs and faster pace quickly outstripped her. Dignity would not permit Maman to run after anyone in public, not even her own daughter; thus, all she required was to get out of sight and then find an adequate hiding place.

Passing into the Hall of Mirrors, Mélisande plunged into the milling throng. In her haste, she'd forgotten the *calèche*, and people stared at the newcomer in curiosity as she passed.

*Out. I must get out!*

The wide doors leading to the palace gardens tempted her not at all. She wanted to be alone, and the gardens here would afford her no privacy whatsoever. Too many people frolicked along the paths and hid in the manicured groves—and it was the first place Maman would look for her.

No, she knew exactly where to go to avoid capture.

Rounding a corner, Mélisande slipped down a servants' corridor she'd found in a previous exploration. Ducking in, she took a number of turns that eventually dead-ended at a door. Filled with trepidation, she paused, listening for the sound of voices. Hearing nothing, she opened it a crack and peeked out into a deserted hall.

There, through the windows, she saw solitude. Across a lush green lawn nestled a little wood that was, like everything else here, an artificial construct. No matter. It was unlikely to be inhabited, and that was all that was important.

The moment fresh air hit her face, Mélisande's feet began moving faster and faster. By the time she reached the edge of the wood, her breath came in great gulps and the landscape swam before her. Blinded by rage and grief, she ran beneath the shade of the trees at full tilt.

# Chapter Two

## INNOCENCE MEETS WITH A MISHAP

THE IMPACT KNOCKED HIM SPRAWLING TO THE GROUND. Alessandro let out a grunt of pain with what little breath was left him as he broke his assailant's fall. Bracing her hands on his chest, the girl clumsily propped herself up.

"*You!*" Her expression was one of acute dismay.

Considering he'd just likely saved her from smashing into a tree, it was a bit unflattering to be looked upon with such horror. He gazed up at her with interest. Most young ladies regarded him with at least a modicum of admiration, if not downright lust.

"*Dio,*" he uttered in a reverent whisper, taking in her face. The woman atop him had wide eyes so deep a green beneath the sweep of her dark lashes that they put him in mind of a shaded wood.

And the rest of her was just as delightful. From his vantage point he could see almost the entire expanse of her glorious décolletage. The faint, pink blush of areolae peeked just above the edge of her neckline as her breasts strained against the fabric of her gown. Slowly, his gaze traveled from those creamy swells to the curve of her long, white neck. His arms tightened involuntarily around her tiny waist as he gazed into her fabulous eyes once more.

Eyes shimmering with tears.

He could not bear to see a woman weep. It didn't hurt that she was by far the most beautiful woman he'd ever laid eyes on. Or hands. The feel of her was pure heaven.

"I believe you have the advantage of me, mademoiselle," he breathed, reverting to French.

The girl only continued to stare at him with saucer eyes. It was gratifying to see he was having an effect on her, but her silence did nothing to satisfy his curiosity.

*Patience.*

He waited, and as they lay there panting together, the trepidation in her eyes slowly ebbed away, replaced by something else. Something infinitely more dangerous. Slowly, he stretched up toward her.

Their lips very nearly touched, mouths hovering less than a breath away from each other, when, squeaking in dismay, she shoved against his chest with all her might, staggering back to catch herself on a tree.

Slowly, he rose and dusted off his rump, looking ruefully at his once-pristine cream silk jacket with its embroidered violets. *Ah, well.* Straightening his coat and cravat, he came to stand before her. "Alessandro Vicino Orsini at your service," he announced, sketching his most elegant bow.

The apparition curtsied, a dark curl escaping its confines to fall across one eye. "Lady Mélisande...d'Orleans."

Taking the hand she offered, Alessandro brushed it with his lips. The gentle touch of his mouth on her bare flesh caused her to flinch and her cheeks to pink. With a half smile, he released her. "It is my pleasure to make your acquaintance, Mademoiselle d'Orleans. Please accept my humble apology for being so inconveniently placed in your path."

"The fault was mine entirely. I was not looking ahead as I should," she replied, seeming embarrassed.

"Is there someone pursuing you?" He looked about, as if expecting her assailant to leap out from behind one of the trees.

She shook her head, looking down. "No, my lord."

"Then, if I may ask"—he hesitated, torn between wishing to be polite and showing concern—"if you were not fleeing pursuit, then what cause for such haste?"

"It is of no importance."

Reaching out, he removed a forgotten tear from her cheek. "A woman's tears are never a trivial matter. Tell me, what were you running away from, *tesoro*?"

A silent debate played across her delicate features, and Alessandro held his breath. Slowly, her shoulders relaxed. He smiled. Curiosity was the undoing of every female he'd ever encountered.

"I simply wished to be alone."

He sauntered a little closer, and her eyes whipped up, instantly wary. Leaning back against a tree trunk, he arched a brow. "Is that all? You were in such distress that I thought perhaps you'd caught your lover in flagrante delicto with another. Although I cannot imagine the fool who would do such a thing," he added, looking her up and down with bold admiration.

"It is a matter I do not wish to discuss with a stranger," she replied, her tone firm in spite of the little smile now quirking her lips.

He took the point. "Ah. Then, since I'm not permitted to lend a sympathetic ear, may I at least offer you the solace of my excellent company, mademoiselle? In the hope that you will soon consider me a friend rather than a stranger."

The look with which she favored him as he offered his arm was much the same as one might give a Gypsy horse trader offering a "bargain."

Alessandro remained patient, for in truth, he had nothing better to do than await the lady's leisure. He watched as her curiosity again defeated caution. After a long moment, she took his arm and allowed him to lead her farther into the wood.

Knowing that it was usually best to keep quiet when Fate worked in one's favor, lest one muck up one's own good fortune, he remained silent as they walked.

Only a short distance through the trees, a charming copse peppered with seemingly random clumps of wildflowers was revealed. The little green was graced with a small bench.

In a show of just how nervous she really was, Mademoiselle d'Orleans immediately disengaged herself and sat, leaving just enough space beside her. Her startled glance as he seated himself at her side told him her invitation had been an unwitting one. Giving her an innocent smile, he folded his hands in his lap and again waited.

Her fingers curled and bunched the fabric of her gown. In an effort to ease her anxiety, Alessandro leaned back and looked up at the bit of sky peeking from between the leaves. "Do you intend to speak, or do you prefer silent companionship?" he teased.

"I'm sorry, my lord. I suppose I'm still a bit embarrassed." She flicked a worried glance at him. "About knocking you over, I mean."

"It will forever be our secret," he promised, his smile broadening. "The secret of how we met." A soft laugh escaped her, and Alessandro's breath stilled. Her gentle smile transformed an already beautiful face into something worthy of a master's brushstroke.

*Brushstroke...*

A vague memory teased the edges of his thoughts, just out of reach.

"This is not the first time we've met, my lord," she informed him, still chuckling. "We met last night during the ball, quite by accident. You probably don't even remember me."

She was wrong. The dappled sunlight caught in her eyes, sparking their depths with emerald fire, and Alessandro bit back an oath as it all came back in a rush: the unattractive gown, the ridiculous powdered hair—and the impossible eyes.

*Da tutto che è santo!* The creature he'd run into last night had been a disaster. The woman before him now was so beautiful that it was difficult to believe she was even the same person. But the eyes, they were the same.

Impossible emerald eyes.

The memory that had been tickling his subconscious finally surfaced. He'd seen those eyes *before* last night's encounter…

*Brushstrokes.*

A portrait hung in Louis's private chambers—a portrait of his mother.

Astonishment rendered him mute. Her odd disguise, her reluctance to speak—it all suddenly made sense. If she was who he thought she was, then…

*Madre di Dio…I must be very careful here. If she knows who she is, I risk the king's wrath, and if she does not…*

In the eye blink that had passed while these thoughts raced through Alessandro's mind, the lady's expression had turned rueful.

"I admit I was not at my best last night," she muttered, coloring a little.

Shaking off a strange feeling of premonition, he forced himself to stop staring and answer her. "Well, you have certainly made up for it today," he murmured. He must act as though he knew nothing. Which was only true, actually, for he had no way of proving his theory. Yet. "But why hide your beauty behind—if you will please pardon my rudeness—such an ill-appearing disguise? You would have outshone every other woman present at last night's fête."

One corner of her full, ripe lips curled. Lips that had come so very close to his only moments ago.

"I thank you for the compliment, monsieur, but you should know that your reputation precedes you. I am well aware of your habits where women are concerned."

The chit was a strange mixture of woman and girl, one moment innocent and fresh, the next as wary and cynical as any jade. Alessandro decided not to bring up the matter of her disguise again, since she'd chosen to evade his question. Her frank admission of knowledge regarding his pursuits was far more interesting, anyway.

"If you are aware of my proclivities, then why did you choose to come here alone with me?"

The air between them became charged as the silence stretched, as she groped for an answer. He could tell part of her wanted to run away, while another part, the curious, rebellious part, wished to stay.

"I think you know as well as I that a reputation is often a poor reflection of a person," he chided. "People say many things about me. It is up to you to determine whether you believe the good or the bad. I would, however, hope that you form your opinion of me based upon your own experience. As you can see, mademoiselle, I have refrained from leaping upon you like a wild beast, though I admit it has been terribly difficult," he teased, lightening the mood.

"That you have, monsieur," she granted with a grudging smile.

"Then trust the instinct that brought you here. Tell me what sent you fleeing to this place. Perhaps I can help?"

After a long hesitation, she finally relented. "A match has been arranged for me with someone I do not wish to marry."

Inexplicable disappointment filled Alessandro. "Have you told them of your objection to their choice?"

"I have not, as I came by this information through another means. My desires matter not, in any case. Regardless of my opinion, I know they will insist upon the marriage."

"They?"

"My parents."

"I see. What is so bad about this prospective husband?"

"Nothing," she snapped. "He is a good man, and already a great friend of mine."

"Then I am afraid don't see the problem." *Damn.* If she'd told him the man was abusive or indifferent, he might have had a chance.

"I *cannot* marry him! The idea is repugnant!"

The vehemence of her protest surprised him. "Is he deformed?" he asked, confused.

A sad little laugh escaped her. "No. In truth, he is considered quite handsome."

"Yet *you* feel no desire for him." It was a statement, not a question, for the answer was clear in the grim set of her mouth. Who was this man? It could not be anyone in his circle or he would surely have heard about this woman. "Does the gentleman share your lack of sentiment?"

"We have known each other since I was born. He is a brother to me in all but blood, and I am certain he feels the same."

Looking at her now, Alessandro doubted the man would continue to feel brotherly for very long. "Perhaps in time you will learn to desire him?"

She shot him a withering stare.

"I see," he mumbled. "Surely, you can convince—"

"There is nothing to be done," she interrupted. "My father has already said that upon our return home, the agreement between our families will be formalized. There is no alternative for someone like me. Whether I want it or not, I must accept it."

*My father. Our families. Someone like me...* A royal cuckoo. It was the only explanation. "If there is no alternative, then you can only try to view your circumstance with optimism. At least you are amiable toward one another." The lie tasted sour in his mouth. Nothing good would come of forcing this woman to marry a man she did not want. After a moment's pause, he cocked his head and peered at her. "Or is it that you have already given your heart to someone else?"

An indelicate snort of derision was her only answer.

*Molto bene.* At least her heart was not taken—yet.

"Indulge me for a moment, mademoiselle," he continued, taking on the tone of a trusted counselor. "I have helped many a friend escape an undesirable marriage. What if you were to *tell* your parents that you have fallen in love with someone else? Would that not make them reconsider the match?"

She shook her head. "Such a lie would never work."

"Why not?"

"Because he is one of only two unmarried gentlemen in my acquaintance. And I have even less desire to marry the other."

"There is a third option," he whispered, giving her a sidelong look. "You could always say you were corrupted by a mysterious stranger. Someone with a reputation black enough to deter his parents' interest in you as a prospective bride." Leaning back, he quirked a brow.

"But I would be ruined!"

"*Sciocchezze!*" he scoffed. "There would be a little scandal, just enough to rid you of your unwanted bridegroom. Then, next year you can return to court and find someone more to your liking. I can assure you that such a tiny incident will be *nothing* to a man in love. Especially when he discovers your innocence on your wedding night."

A furious blush stole into her cheeks, making her eyes appear even greener. "And I suppose you're offering to be the scapegoat?" she asked, eyeing him dubiously.

"I've played the sacrificial lamb countless times," he whispered, his grin widening.

"And when my parents go to the king to force you to marry me, what then?" she retorted, laughter in her voice. "Will you go to the slaughter on behalf of a woman you do not even know?"

"Mademoiselle, you underestimate my skills at evasion," he said in a wounded tone. "You see, I am not a citizen of France. No one here can force me to marry unless it is my wish to do so."

"Ah, so you would jilt me?" she said, eyes lighting with merriment. "I would simply be another of the unfortunate women left crying in your wake. Another casualty of your charm."

Unruffled by her sarcasm, Alessandro accepted the backhanded compliment with aplomb. "Not to seem immodest, but I have done this before with great success. My monstrous reputation can be used to your advantage, if you will allow me to help you."

Mélisande considered the shameless seducer beside her. She had no illusions regarding his motives—but his idea was inspiring. Had she been a Frenchwoman facing an untenable marriage to another Frenchman, she would have leapt at his offer. But as she was returning to England soon, it was not a feasible solution.

She opened her mouth, fully intending to thank Lord Orsini for his "kind" offer and then politely excuse herself. Maman was looking for her, and...

*Maman.* Anger sat in her chest like a burning-hot coal. Papa wasn't to blame. After all, he'd only been kind enough to give both his name and love to another man's get. *He probably wants to marry me off to David as quickly as possible to protect me and make certain no one finds out I'm a...*

She couldn't even think the word without her throat tightening.

Something stirred within Mélisande then, a recklessness born of hurt and rage. The circumstances of her birth, her impending marriage, all the pain she felt now—*everything* was her mother's fault.

And here she was, alone with a man whose very name represented everything her mother wanted her to stay away from.

The sun shone on Orsini's hair, infusing it with warm russet lights. His brown eyes gleamed, full of the promise of pleasures she could only begin to imagine—and probably several she couldn't.

With a shock, Mélisande realized she *wanted* him to kiss her. She wanted him to take her in his arms again, hold her as he'd done when she'd knocked him to the ground, and kiss her.

She'd never been kissed before, not really. David didn't count. She'd been only ten years old at the time, and it had been on a dare. And it had been disgusting.

*Kissing this man would be quite different.*

A wild, feverish heat ignited in Mélisande's belly. Somehow, her desire must have communicated itself to the man beside her, for his warm, brown eyes deepened to nearly black and, only a moment later, he leaned in and captured her mouth.

She flinched at the initial contact but did not retreat. She couldn't have even if she'd wanted to—her body simply would not allow it. She knew she ought to have delivered a stinging slap in reward for his presumption, but instead, she reveled in the turbulent sensations raging through her as her lips clung to his.

Her eyes drifted shut as his hands rose, one to clasp her waist, the other to lightly caress the nape of her neck. Gooseflesh rose all over her body, and she sighed into his mouth, softening, melting into him.

Every nerve in her body was alive, drowning in an ocean of touch, smell, and taste. He felt so wonderfully solid against her, all lean muscle beneath his clothes. His kiss was infused with the sweet, heady flavor of brandy, and the clean scent of soap and leather clung to his warm skin. Her hands began to roam, first clutching his shoulders, then traveling up to twine about his neck, where her fingers curled into his soft, dark hair.

He tasted her as though savoring a sweet, and she responded instinctively by grazing the corner of his mouth with her tongue. At that delicate, hesitant touch, he shuddered and pressed his palm hard into the curve of her spine, deepening the contact.

The only coherent thought left in Mélisande's mind was: *more.*

At her unconscious urging, he gently caressed the side of one silk-clad breast, his thumb grazing the very edge of her nipple through the thin fabric.

She gasped as the hardening bud began to itch and ache, longing for something infinitely more satisfying. He touched her again, and liquid heat built down below, coalescing into a molten fire that made her yearn for him to touch her there, to touch her everywhere. Her body thrummed like a plucked harp string, responding to his caresses with a violent joy that resonated throughout her.

*Laughter.*

Harsh and unwelcome, it intruded into Alessandro's awareness, dragging him back to the earthly realm. It had originated at the outer edge of the wood—and it was moving closer. The sweetness in his arms was oblivious to the danger, but he was not.

With regret bordering on physical pain, he pulled away. She resisted, making a small sound of protest.

"My lady!" he whispered, startled at the unsteadiness of his own voice. The dark fringes of her lashes lifted, revealing emerald slits glazed with unmitigated lust. His mouth went dry and the muscles of his arms trembled.

The sound of voices drew closer, and her gaze shifted away, sweeping the little glade in confusion. When she turned back, he saw the entire scene as it must look through her eyes: her wrists held prisoner in his hands. His hair, mussed from the restless meanderings of *her* fingers.

A high-pitched squeal from the trees nearby caused them both to start in alarm.

Helpless, Alessandro watched the emotions flicker across her face. In that instant, he knew without a doubt she was an innocent. It hit him like a cannonball in the gut. He wondered if this had been her very first kiss. To his amazement, his loins tightened unbearably at the idea. He was no seducer of virgins, yet he wanted this one with a ferocity that overrode every other desire he'd ever experienced.

The interlopers drew closer, and before he could so much as open his mouth to speak, she broke free and bolted.

"Wait!" He took off after her, swearing. But it was too late. By the time he made it to the edge of the wood, she was already far ahead, flying across the green toward the palace.

He stopped. If he were seen chasing after her, it would result in her ruination and quite possibly the king's wrath.

A wry grin creased his lips. If she *was* ruined, would Louis allow her to marry him instead of her "family's" choice?

The thought surprised him. That a green girl could make him contemplate abandoning the life of debauchery he'd so enjoyed was ridiculous. The minx could be no more than sixteen or seventeen! Marriage was out of the question.

But he could make her his mistress.

It might be nice to have a steady mistress. Given what she'd told him, it was unlikely that her groom-to-be would object.

The more he thought about it, the more sense it made. She was a natural-born sensualist, like himself. She'd be quick to learn and just as uninhibited, given the right encouragement. Innocent she might be, but she was no fool. Their conversation had revealed much. She was intelligent and canny, possessing wit and humor.

She was his perfect match.

Yes. He would find Lady Mélisande d'Orleans and make the arrangements. With these thoughts, Alessandro settled against the bole of a tree to wait until enough time had elapsed before following his soon-to-be lover.

# Chapter Three

## THE NOT SO TENDER TRAP

*Warwickshire, England, early spring 1747*

RAIN PELTED THE CROWN GLASS WINDOWS OF THE PARlor, echoing Mélisande's dark mood as she looked across the room at David Pelham, nineteen-year-old heir to the dukedom of Newcastle. Any woman should have been ecstatic at the prospect of becoming not only the wife of a duke but the wife of a dear friend.

Her current state, however, was one of irritation and despair. Since his introduction to Society, women had made fools of themselves over David on a constant basis, but when she looked at him, Mélisande was distinctly uninspired. He was David. The closest thing to a brother she had on this earth. Love him, yes; but *want* him, no.

"We could do worse, I suppose," he announced with a faint grimace of distaste. "We know each other, at least, and our lands adjoin, so you'd be close to your home and your parents."

She looked at him as if he were mad. "It doesn't matter how *convenient* it would be, David! There is no point in even having this ridiculous conversation. We'd both be absolutely miserable, and you know it!" Exasperated, she flopped into a chair.

They'd both argued vociferously against the marriage since her discovery of the arrangement, but to no avail. As children, they'd been promised to each other for the good of both families, and wed they would. Nothing could persuade their parents otherwise.

David had done his best, ignoring his father's summons for the past year. He'd been brought to heel only when the duke himself had come to fetch his son—along with several burly "footmen."

Now, the unwillingly betrothed pair had been locked in an upstairs parlor in the hope that confinement together would bring them to reason. After all, they'd not actually laid eyes on each other in almost four years, and both had changed a great deal. Their parents assumed that a handsome young couple put in such a situation would be unable to resist the lure of nature's impulses.

They were wrong.

David chuckled, lounging against the mantelpiece. "I never imagined they would go as far as this."

Mélisande made an unladylike noise.

He shook his head and laughed. "You've not changed at all."

"They will be livid. This marriage is the culmination of generations of planning." Sighing, she rubbed her tired eyes. "I find it ironic that I'm even held to this agreement at all, given the circumstances. If your father knew…"

He came and sat next to her. "But he doesn't. As far as he or anyone else knows, you're the first female born to the Compton line in almost a century and the last of that line. You're also Wilmington's last hope. If he hadn't claimed you as his own, he would have no heir and the land would revert to the Crown upon his death. He knows what he's doing. As for my father, I don't think he'd care about the blood in your veins, if you want to know the truth, so long as our lands are joined."

"Thanks. I feel so much better for knowing that," she said with sarcasm. "Regardless, we'll be lucky if they don't disown us both for this."

"They'll get over it," he told her, rising. "Life is full of disappointments. I'm my father's biggest, and he hasn't disowned me yet."

She couldn't help but smile. David had, as she'd always known he would, grown into an absolute terror. Indeed, his latest *affaire* had been with a married woman, resulting in the crossing of blades and near imprisonment that had, in turn, caused his father to insist that he marry her immediately in order to prevent further scandal.

"How can we keep them from forcing us to the altar?"

Casting her a mischievous look, David stalked over to the window and eased it open.

Mélisande shook her head. "You *know* those ruffians your father hired are just waiting for you to try something like that. You'll never even make it to the village."

"Don't bet on it," he muttered. "Just make it sound as though we're still talking for as long as possible, and I'll borrow one of your father's horses and disappear for a while. I've plenty of friends in France who'd welcome a long visit."

"I'll just bet you do, you scoundrel. Am I to play the jilted fiancée, then?" she inquired with just a touch of acid. "You know what people will say if they find you've climbed out of a window rather than marry me. *You* might not wish to wed until you're thirty, but I have other plans."

His face fell, then brightened. "Why not marry Reggie? The Stantons' lands also adjoin yours. We could pose it as a possible solution—more of a delay, rather than a total loss. Perhaps our children will be more amenable to the idea of a marriage?"

Mélisande allowed her expression to tell him her opinion of his suggestion.

"It was just an idea," he grumbled. "I thought perhaps he might not repulse you as much as I apparently do. My poor, bruised ego is much gratified to know I'm not the only one you've blacklisted, truthfully," he laughed. Sighing, he walked over to stand before her, all traces of humor gone. "Then our only choice is to refuse, no matter the consequences. I already know what's in store for me, and I'm prepared."

Mélisande gazed at the floor, thinking how much she hated to disappoint her parents, especially Papa. But she simply could *not* marry David. "Let us get it over with, shall we?"

David went to the door and knocked. "Tell them we're ready to talk," he ordered the footman guarding it. Turning back to Mélisande, he gave her a hard stare. "Melly, we could always have an arrangement. I wouldn't care, and it would be an easy way out of this whole sticky mess with our parents."

She shook her head vehemently. "I've had enough of 'arrangements,' thank you! And we've already agreed we'd be miserable living that lie. They would expect us to eventually have children, and though the rest of the females in the world might view such a task with joyful anticipation, I *don't*. And neither do *you*," she stressed, jabbing a finger at his chest.

The lock rattled, making them both jump, and the door opened, admitting their parents.

"I presume you've both come to your senses?" the old duke rumbled as he filed in behind Mélisande's parents.

"Father, I cannot and will not marry Melly," David immediately announced, ignoring his father's thunderous expression. "You can't force me to marry a woman I don't want, and I certainly won't marry one who doesn't want me."

Mélisande spoke before David's spluttering, purple-faced father could gather his wits enough to respond. "David is like a brother to me. I would never be able to share a bed with him without feeling as if I were committing a—a mortal sin. I cannot marry him," she finished, feeling her cheeks flush with embarrassment.

Aghast at hearing such words from a young, supposedly innocent girl, the duke's mouth opened and closed soundlessly, like that of a fish, for several seconds before he broke the silence with a bellow that was likely heard all the way in the village. "By *God*, girl, you *will* marry him! No more delays, no more prevaricating! You'll marry, and there's an end to it!"

"You cannot make me!" Mélisande shouted back. He was an intimidating figure, but she would *not* back down, she would not show fear. "I don't want him, and he doesn't want me!"

"Don't be ridiculous, girl!" the duke scoffed, slamming a fist on a tea table, rattling the delicate figurines adorning it. "You don't know *what* you want! Now stop this foolishness!" He turned to the earl and countess. "Wilmington, make her see sense!"

"Now, Melly, you know your mother and I are only interested in what's b—"

"I swear by all that is holy, if you force me to the altar, the union will never be consummated." Her voice shook, but her gaze was hard as she met that of the furious duke. "You will *never* have an heir—at least not a legitimate one!"

"And what the devil is *that* supposed to mean?" the duke snapped menacingly, taking a step toward her.

Isabelle calmly stepped between the two and faced her daughter. "Enough of this! Mélisande, you'll do as you're told. I promise you'll feel differently once you are married, *ma petite*," she said smoothly, reaching out to straighten the lace on her child's gown.

"*No, Maman!*" Mélisande said, jerking back. "I've never felt that way about David, and I never will!" Switching to French, she continued. "You think me so naïve, but I'm no innocent. I tasted desire in Versailles. I know what passion is, and I know I will *never* feel it for David. You could tie us together naked and my blood would not stir. I will *never* marry a man for whom I feel nothing but sisterly affection!"

Isabelle's face had grown ashen, and her voice was chill as she responded in the same language. "Who? Who dared?"

"The one you warned me of, the Italian," Mélisande replied, defiant.

"Impossible!" Isabelle half laughed. "I cannot believe such a thing—you were never left alone long enough."

Mélisande's mouth twisted, the remembrance of her stolen kiss with Le Renard bringing a tremor of longing into her voice. "I met Lord Orsini several times," she fibbed. "In the library, the gardens, on the night of the ball, and again just after our audience with the king. He showed me a world of pleasure that I never knew was possible. It was magnificent."

It was *mostly* truth, though somewhat skewed in the telling. Her mother's stricken face made her wish she had not added that last bit, but she had no choice now. She had to persist. "I came *alive* in his arms, Maman, and I will never settle for anything less when I choose a husband." Silence filled the room as mother and daughter stared at one another, as everyone else stared at them.

Mélisande's eyes flicked to David, marking his faint smile. He knew she was deliberately misleading them, for she'd told him the whole story via letters using the secret code they'd created as children. Her true lineage, their parents' plans for them, her encounter with Orsini.

Her papa, who also spoke French, stood with his mouth hanging open in shock. If there was anything Mélisande regretted in all this, it was hurting him.

The duke did not speak the language and was quite obviously annoyed at being unable to understand the conversation. "What the devil are you people saying?" he roared, turning helplessly from person to person. "Speak English, for God's sake! And will someone have the decency to tell me what the hell is going on?"

No one answered him.

"*Mon Dieu*," Isabelle whispered. "You are compromised, then?" she demanded, still speaking in French, her blue eyes turning hard.

Anger stiffened Mélisande's spine. *Hypocrite!* "Though I've wished otherwise since, I did not allow him full liberties. I valued *my* honor, Maman," she flung back, her voice just as cold. Her mother flinched at the verbal slap. "But it changes nothing. Punish me if you like, but there will be no match between us. Ever."

Isabelle stared at her with a veiled expression for a long moment before turning to her husband. A look passed between them, and he nodded.

Lord Wilmington turned and addressed the Duke of Newcastle. "I'm afraid our children are not properly suited for marriage," he stated, his tone brooking no argument. "As such, I request the betrothal contract be voided without penalty, as both are unwilling to fulfill the terms."

The duke's face paled, his eyes bulging with fury as he turned on his son. "You put her up to this, didn't you?"

Unperturbed, David smiled. "Though she and I are in agreement, Melly made her own decision to oppose this farcical arrangement. But even if I felt differently, Father, I would still respect her wishes. I want a wife who is *happy* to share my bed."

Knowing fully the hidden meaning behind his words, Mélisande winced. Damn David's quick tongue! Why did he feel the need to constantly provoke his father?

"Worthless spawn!" the duke spat. "I would disown you this minute were you not my only living heir! By George, I may still do so, and damn the succession! You'll receive no further funds from the estate until the day you marry, and until that day arrives, I want you gone from my sight! And do not think to appeal to your mother!" he shouted, shaking his fist.

Something dangerous sparked in David's eyes. "Though I may frequently be found under them, I've never been one to hide behind a woman's skirts, Father," he quipped in a deceptively mild voice. "And I've no need of an allowance, as you well know. I'm quite content to *continue* making my own way in the world."

The lines bracketing his father's mouth went white, but before the duke could act, David departed.

Less than an hour later, a soft knock sounded at Mélisande's door. Preparing for another battle, she bade her mother enter.

Sitting on the edge of the bed, her mother looked her in the eyes. "I knew you were changed after our visit to Versailles, but I attributed it to the shock of learning your true lineage. Now I know differently. I should have seen this coming. After all, you are the child of a man who is completely uninhibited in his passion and a woman who was reckless enough to follow her own desires to the very brink of ruin."

"Maman, I—"

"I know what you experienced in Versailles," her mother cut her off. "The same passion once overwhelmed me, and it has cost me much. I do not wish you to suffer as I have."

She looked sad and tired, and for the first time Mélisande noticed the fine network of lines at the corners of her mouth and eyes.

"You would do well to marry David," her mother advised, holding up a hand to forestall protest. "I know you find it an undesirable prospect now, but I ask you to trust me when I say that a marriage of this kind will save you from the sort of pain I have endured. Passion is made much of by the poets and romantics of this world, *ma fille*, but it is an unreliable guarantee of happiness."

Mélisande's brow crinkled in consternation at her mother's bitter tone. To all appearances, her mother led a happy, contented life.

"I have no desire to break your heart, but I must save you from yourself," her mother murmured sadly. "I am extremely fond of your—" She took a deep breath. "Of Spencer. He has been very good to me, and we have had many wonderful years together. But you already know that I once loved another, Mélisande. In truth, I have never stopped loving him, and I never will."

She paused to wipe away her tears. "I adore your papa, Mélisande—truly I do—but I've never loved him in that way. I wanted to, but I simply cannot. You must understand: though I had been groomed as a young woman to become the king's mistress for my family's gain, I *knew* I could never truly have him for my own. But it did not matter. Louis took my heart the moment I met him, and he has never given it back," she whispered, her mouth twisting. "I loved him so desperately. For a courtesan, that is the ultimate folly."

Mélisande's world tipped once again. *A courtesan?* So her involvement with Louis had not even been by chance, but a deliberate thing. She'd been *trained* to seduce him. *My mother was a...*

"I was a very lucky fool," her mother continued, ignorant of the tumult she'd caused. Your papa married me knowing I carried another man's child because he was in love with me. Madly so. He still is."

"Does he know?" Mélisande whispered.

Her mother looked at her with sorrow. "He learned the truth in Versailles. I could not hide it from him there, though I tried. You must know that I had no wish to wound him in this way. If I could have prevented it, I would have done. I regret that visit to France with all my heart, and wish now that we had kept you ignorant of the truth. There would have been a danger in it for you, but it would have been better than this."

With these words, all of Mélisande's happy illusions shattered. Everything was a lie. Not only was her own identity founded on secrets and lies, but her parents' marriage was a falsehood as well. How could she do it? Even though he'd been willing, how could her mother have *used* Papa like that?

"Now you understand," Isabelle muttered, her voice hollow, her eyes lifeless. "My heart has been divided all these years. I was parted from the man I loved more than life itself and married to another who loved me enough to overlook it. And he has been so good to me, so very kind. I have no better friend in all the world, and I know it. But there is a vast difference between loving someone and being *in* love with them, *chérie*. How I wish I'd met Spencer first! Then I might have loved him the way he deserved."

Her lovely face darkened with sudden fury. "And how I wish you'd never met that Italian *cochon*!" she hissed, making Mélisande flinch. "Had it not been for that, that horrid *roué*, you would have married David, had children, and been content! But now—now your tainted blood has been awakened."

"Maman—"

"It is my fault, and I accept the blame," said Isabelle, again cutting her off. "Unfortunately, you now pay the price for my sins. And David with you." Taking a deep breath, she returned to her intended topic of discussion. "Mélisande, now that you are aware of your proclivity for passion, you must learn to control it, to master your own desires, for your own sake."

Her eyes glimmered with unshed tears as she gently held Mélisande's face between her palms. "Spencer and I would not have you marry without the possibility of happiness—we *love* you, Mélisande. But, like David's father, we expect you to marry someone of similar social standing. If you find yourself attracted to someone either beneath your station or beyond your reach, you *must* not let your passions drive you, as I did!"

"I understand, Maman," Mélisande said, wanting this uncomfortable conversation to end. "I will be careful."

"Caution is not enough to sway passion from its course, *chérie*," her mother murmured after a moment, gracing her with a wry smile as she released her. "Guard your heart well. Hold it and your passion prisoner until you find someone deserving of such gifts."

Her expression grew calm. "The hour grows late. I must go now and prepare for dinner," she announced as if nothing more than polite conversation had just passed. "Will you come down, or shall I have a tray sent up?"

# Chapter Four

## THE PRICE OF FREEDOM

ALESSANDRO'S STOMACH TIGHTENED WITH UNEASE AS HE walked the halls of his childhood home. He'd bravely faced men in battle many times, in both war and single combat, but this was different. Beyond the heavy doors at the end of this hall sat the only man on earth with the power to make him feel insignificant, which in his opinion was far worse than death.

Bracing himself, Alessandro forced a careless smile to his lips as he opened the doors and strode into his father's study.

The Duke of Gravina looked up from his desk, impaling him with accusing eyes. "Ah, the prodigal son, at last. What took you so long?" the querulous old man snapped, a disapproving frown creasing his leathery face. "I summoned you nearly two months ago!"

"My journey was delayed by a foul-tempered monarch and equally ill-tempered weather. Do not ask me to name the worse, for I would be unable to distinguish between man and nature by the behavior of either," Alessandro answered with levity. "But Italy has welcomed me back with gentle arms. I'd almost forgotten how lovely it is here in spring. The countryside is so peaceful and refreshing after years spent serving the Empire in cold, noisy, filth-ridden cities like Paris and Petersburg."

His father glowered from beneath bushy, grey brows. "Serving? Pah! Do not provoke me with your impertinence! I have been kept informed regarding your reprehensible behavior while you are supposed to be acting as a representative of Rome. If you have served anyone, it has been yourself."

"It was not my intent to be impertinent, father," Alessandro countered, maintaining a benign expression. He'd accomplished every assignment given him, achieved every goal set by his superiors. How he spent his personal time was no one's business but his own. He let it go for the sake of peace. "I was merely trying to be pleasant."

"Now is not the time for pleasantries." His father's chin quivered for a moment as he paused to draw a shaky breath. "I have brought you here because Pietro has died."

The blood drained from Alessandro's face with an abruptness that matched his father's announcement. "How?" was the only word he could get past the constriction in his throat.

"He was thrown from his horse while riding. They brought him to me still alive, but..."

Alessandro watched as his father seemed to sag beneath the weight of the unspoken words. The same crushing weight bore down on his own heart. "Father, I—"

"His wife was with child, and we had hoped...but the boy was stillborn. Thus, *you* are now my heir," the duke pronounced bitterly, his voice cracking. "I know you've never coveted your brother's place and that you view any responsibility an onerous burden, but in this, you have no choice. Neither of us does. Be it for good or for ill, you are my successor now."

The grizzled old man appraised his elaborately decorated garments with open disgust. "I expect you to don proper mourning at once, at least while you are here. What you do when you leave here is beyond my control, but in *this* house, you will behave with proper decorum and respect."

"Of course, Father." An odd sensation spread slowly across Alessandro's skin, like cold fingers trailing over it. *Does he not think that I grieve, too?*

"I will allow you to stay for a time to comfort your mother, for it was at *her* request you were summoned. Had it not been for her, I would have simply informed you of Pietro's passing in the letter and bid you remain in Petersburg until it became necessary to bring you home to assume your duties."

As though he couldn't bear the sight of him any longer, his father bent his silvered head, focusing instead on the ledger before him. "It is out of care for her that I have held my tongue about your degeneracy abroad and kept it from my superiors. See to it that you bring no disgrace upon yourself while you are in this house, for if you cause her even a moment's additional pain through your lack of self-control, I will strip you of your allowance and have you excommunicated."

"I would *never* deliberately—"

"You already have," his father cut in, looking up.

Alessandro flinched beneath his piercing gaze, feeling just as he had when, as a boy, he'd been caught fondling one of the housemaids.

"When I was forced to send you away, it cut her to the heart," the old man muttered through his teeth. "Pietro as well, for he loved you also and did not wish to be parted from you. You abandoned *them* when you abandoned your honor. I tell you now, if I could have prevented you from ever having been born, I would have done so and saved them that pain."

Concealing his hurt, Alessandro kept a neutral face. He deserved this. He'd never been the son or brother he should have been. Always it'd been Pietro who had shouldered the burden for them both. *And now he is gone.*

"I now find myself in the untenable position of having *you* as my heir," his father continued, the chill creeping back into his voice as he closed the tome with a thump. "Whether it be Fate or God that has commanded it, this is our lot, though neither of us desires it."

Standing, the Duke of Gravina crossed to the window and looked out at the gentle, vine-covered hills that had belonged to his family for generations. Alessandro marked how stooped his once-strong shoulders were, how frail he now looked. It struck him that with Pietro's death, his father's pride and vitality had been stripped. He was a toothless old lion still trying to roar as if he were dangerous.

The fear Alessandro had once felt in his father's presence drained away, replaced by pity. Unfortunately, it did nothing to dispel the old pain, the thought of what might have been had the old bastard spared a little tenderness for his second son.

"From this point forward, I expect you to at least *act* as though you are worthy of your family's great name—and of the love your mother holds for you," his father went on, "though God knows you are undeserving of it in every way. It is *her* grace that has saved you from my wrath these many years, and it is her grace that has brought you here now. She would drown in her grief, were it not for the prospect of seeing you. Leave me now. Go to her, and be of some use to me by bringing *her* joy."

It was as though a door had shut between them.

Heart stinging from fresh wounds dealt atop old scars he'd wrongly thought healed, Alessandro left. A shiver ran down his neck as he paused before Pietro's portrait hanging on the wall above the entrance to the great hall. He stared into his brother's eyes, emotions swelling in his chest until he felt it would burst. The artist had captured him in an appropriately pensive moment, his expression most solemn indeed, as befitted the heir to the dukedom.

The loss of Pietro was a pain as keen as any blade that had ever parted his flesh. All the talks they'd never had because he'd been sent away in disgrace. Now they would never have them. All the joys they'd never shared, all the grief. The past was lost, and now the future would never be.

*Why did you have to die? Why did you have to leave him with only me, the son he never wanted?*

He would never receive an answer.

"Alessandro."

Turning, he beheld his mother, the Lady Sophia Orsini, Duchess of Gravina. Though she was still beautiful and looked far younger than her nearly sixty years, sadness had put its stamp upon her. A sadness he now shared. He moved into her outstretched arms.

"Mama. I'm so sorry it took me so long to come back. If only I'd been here, perhaps I could have—"

"No, Alessandro," she interrupted. "You would have been with him, but you could not have prevented his death. It was God's will that he should join Him in heaven." She smoothed back a wayward lock of his hair. "I take it you've already been to see your father," she said with a faint smile, linking her arm with his and steering him away from Pietro's portrait.

"Yes."

Her sharp eyes assessed him. "Worry not, my son. You will make a fine duke, when the time comes."

"Father does not share your opinion. He would rather have someone else, *any*one else, follow him."

"Give him time, Alessandro. You have changed, and he does not know you anymore."

"He did not know me before, and he never wanted to," Alessandro muttered. "What makes you think he will wish to do so now? He will never see me as anything but a failure, no matter how much time passes."

"I do not believe that to be true. He will soon see that you have grown and matured into a worthy man," his mother insisted. Her eyes were filled with hope. "He will soften, once his own pain has eased."

Alessandro doubted it. If the pain he was experiencing now was any indication, he wouldn't expect such a miracle anytime soon. If ever. *Pietro...*

"Come. Let me show you the new roses in my garden," she told him, changing the subject. "Much has changed since you were last here."

*Indeed.*

"Another ghastly proposal," Mélisande grumbled, crumpling the parchment and tossing it aside. Men had flocked to her when she debuted. The combination of her fortune and beauty had assured instant success, and before her first Season was half over, she'd received proposals from more than a dozen ardent admirers.

She'd accepted none.

"Surely there must be at least one man in the world who pleases you, *cherie*," her mother commented, eyeing with disappointment the wadded missive on the floor.

Turning away, Mélisande allowed herself a wistful smile. There *had* been one. But he'd probably married by now. The thought evoked a wave of melancholy. *Stop it*, she told herself. There was no sense pining over what could never have been in the first place. She'd find someone like him, someone who made her feel the way he had. Eventually.

And when she did, she'd marry him.

"I'm certain he exists, Maman. Until he appears, I will keep waiting."

"Do not wait *too* long. Each year passes more quickly than the one before, and old age can be most unkind to an unmarried woman," her mother muttered, shooting a pointed glance at her.

Early that autumn, the earl was stricken with a debilitating paralysis in his legs. It spread with alarming swiftness, mystifying the physicians who were called in one after another. Though they examined him and did their best, nothing could prevent the inevitable. Three weeks later, Lord Spencer Compton, Earl of Wilmington, died peacefully in his sleep, leaving his widow to hold his lands in trust until Mélisande married.

"It is too soon—even if I wanted to, Maman, I *cannot!*" an appalled Mélisande objected upon discovering her mother making plans to attend the London Season.

"You will," Isabelle insisted. "It is imperative that you marry soon, Mélisande, and you will never find a husband here. You must go to London."

"You wish me to seek a husband while in mourning? I'll be ostracized!"

Her mother's lips compressed. "The king is aware of our situation, Mélisande. The land needs a lord. George's blessing will protect us from censure. I know it is hard, *ma fille*. I also have no desire for London, but we simply cannot afford to miss a Season."

"Given my fortune, I could be as old as Methuselah and have warts on my nose, and still they would pursue me," Mélisande groused. "One year will hardly matter."

But it would. Though she hid it well, Isabelle's health was failing, and Mélisande knew it. The ache she evinced upon drawing more than shallow breath told her that time was growing perilously short.

"When your father realized he was dying, he requested that I do this, and I shall respect his wishes. You will go to London, and that is final."

And so, albeit unwillingly, Mélisande donned the muted mauve and grey of half mourning and went. Drifting among her peers, she neither smiled nor cried, feeling little save the empty hole in her heart and the bitterness of disappointment regarding her would-be suitors.

A reunion with her other childhood friend, Reginald Stanton III, finally drew her out of her darkness. Back at last from the Grand Tour, Reggie's return to Society caused despair among her admirers, but the easy familiarity engendered by their long association soothed Mélisande's sore heart.

As it had been when they were children, she, David, and Reggie once more became an inseparable trio. David cheerfully provided her entrée into his set, which included some of the most influential people in England—politicians, musicians, writers, artists, scientists, and philosophers. Many of these same individuals also exhibited an alarming lack of propriety, according to her mother.

This, more than anything, pleased Mélisande.

Thanks to her new friends, she discovered a natural aptitude for gaming. Not long after, she began spending less time dancing at balls and more time whiling away the hours playing chess and Bragg. It was her small way of rebelling against being trotted out on display when all she wanted was to go home.

And, as long as she behaved herself, Maman could not really object, either; for if it was of the utmost importance that she marry, then her new pastime did more by far to keep her in the company of eligible gentlemen than any amount of dancing.

The parlors where she now held court were filled with talk of politics and intrigue, art, science, music, and literature, all of which served to challenge and satisfy her sharp young mind. During those blissful hours, Mélisande not only forgot her sadness, but learned to win with grace and laugh at defeat.

In short order, she began to garner a certain celebrity of her own. Acquaintances began bringing visitors to meet the unconventional young woman; thus, she befriended many men of renown, including the famed chess master Philip Stamma and the American scientist Mr. Benjamin Franklin, among many others.

Everywhere Mélisande went she caused a stir; people began referring to her as not only "original" but "eçcentric"—a dangerous term for an unwed woman. But despite her growing reputation for strangeness, she remained one of the most sought-after heiresses in England.

To her mother's despair, however, not a single spousal candidate passed muster. The Season closed without a wedding.

Isabelle's health deteriorated rapidly that winter. As it had been with her husband, doctors were brought in one after another and every possible remedy was tried, but none could cure her malady. The first true cold snap was without mercy, and by the time the snow ended, her constant coughing had stopped as well.

Mélisande would never forget that long night. She had stayed with her mother, listening to the soft, terrifying bubbling as her chest rose and fell with each shallow breath.

Awakening in the early dawn, Maman had smiled at her and squeezed her hand. "I was wrong," she had announced, her voice thin and weary, her eyes glazed with a pain that went far deeper than her chest. "I loved him more than I knew. I only wish I had told him before it was too late."

"I'm sure he knew, Maman," Mélisande had reassured her. "Now rest, and don't concern yourself with such things."

No matter what her mother had said about not being in love with her husband, her true feelings had become evident during his last days. Watching her care for him tenderly night and day, Mélisande had seen her hold on to each moment with a ferocity that defied death to take him from her side. Her mother had fought the battle along with him, and as he'd faded, so had she.

"I am so very tired, *cherie*," Maman had whispered, pausing to take a sip from the cup her daughter held to her lips. "I wish I could stay and watch over you, but such is not my fate. I pray you find as good a husband as my Spencer. A man who will care for you the way he did for me. You must marry, Mélisande."

"I will, Maman. I promise. Now rest, please." Mélisande's heart had broken all over again for what was lost, and for all that would *be* lost with her mother's passing. Unable to bear thoughts of a future without her mother, her mind had retreated into the immediate, focusing only on what was needed at that moment.

*Is she warm enough?*

*Make sure her lips are kept moist.*

*Listen for the next breath.*

Everything else would come in its own time, far sooner than she wanted.

Half an hour later, her mother's blue eyes had opened wide, looking through Mélisande to fix upon some distant point. A radiant smile had lit her pale, drawn features, making her beautiful once more as she released her last, trembling breath in an exhalation of joy.

*"Chèr ami..."*

The bitter cold of winter held England in its icy grip as Mélisande arrived at Kensington House in answer to the royal summons. After settling in her chambers, she wandered the grounds she knew so well from summers spent here with her parents, wondering what would become of her.

The fact that George happened to be her godfather would not prevent him from using her to his advantage. The Jacobites had been subdued, but Charles still stirred the pot from his exile in France. The earldom was just waiting to be bestowed upon some lucky courtier whose loyalty he wanted to secure. The most she could hope for was a decent man with a tolerable disposition. She prayed he would elevate a man of lower rank so she would at least be able to remain in her home. Papa had always taken care of their farmers, laborers, and household servants. Hopefully, she'd be allowed to continue the tradition in his stead.

But who would His Majesty name as her husband-to-be? She prayed it wouldn't be Beaufort. Though he had a great deal of influence at court and had expressed keen interest in her, the man was an utter lackwit.

And definitely not Lord Herrington. She shuddered with distaste. She'd sooner marry Beaufort's favorite hound than *that* horrid brute.

The next morning, she received the summons.

George smiled at her with visible pleasure as she sank into a deep curtsy. "Who is this vision I see before me? Where is the mischief-making imp who used to run my halls? It's good to see you again, Melly. I only wish the circumstances were different."

Looking down, Mélisande blinked away the stinging in her eyes, surprised to find herself capable of producing any more tears. "I would have arrived sooner, Your Majesty, but the weather did not permit it."

"Entirely understandable," he said, waving away her apology. "As it is, I disliked disturbing you so soon, but there is important business to be addressed, and it must be done quickly. I shall come right to the point. You are aware your father had no male heirs, of course. After his death, your mother held everything in his stead at my behest, in the hope that you would marry and the title be given to your husband and his heirs through you."

Steeling herself, Mélisande closed her eyes and nodded.

"In her final correspondence, your mother made a request regarding the issue of your marital state, or rather the lack thereof," George announced. "We have chosen to honor this request, in memory of our long friendship with your family."

The subtle shift in his manner of speech was not lost on Mélisande. It was as she'd feared. He was no longer acting as her "Uncle George" or her godfather; he was her king. And *he* hadn't arranged her marriage—her *mother* had. By his hand, Maman would enforce her will from the grave, knowing that though her daughter had defied her in life, she could not disobey the king's command.

David would be wroth.

"Isabelle asked that we *not* arrange a marriage for you," George continued, the corner of his mouth lifting in a knowing smile.

Mélisande's heart leapt from the pit of her stomach to lodge squarely in her throat. "She did?"

"Indeed. She was most adamant that you be allowed to select your own husband," he stated. "She also made us aware that you assisted Wilmington a great deal in the oversight of the estate during the last two years of his life, and that after his death you managed the business of the earldom almost entirely yourself. Is it true you dismissed your steward for thievery?"

Still bewildered, she nodded. *If he isn't marrying me off, then why have I been summoned to court?* "Yes, Your Majesty," she answered. "After Papa died, I grew suspicious when the cost of certain items sharply increased, but when I asked the steward about it, he told me it was no business of mine. I inquired of the merchants shortly thereafter and discovered his dishonesty. I would have brought him to justice, but he learned of my inquiries and escaped before I could have him detained."

"Well, should he be found, you have our full permission to have him hanged for his crimes," George growled, eyes flashing. "Now," he said, settling himself once again, "we have verified that the estate has been well run and productive in your care, and as long as it remains thus, we are quite happy for things to continue as they are. Of course, we should much *prefer* it if you married," he said pointedly, "but should you choose to remain unwed and childless, the earldom will simply revert to the Crown upon your death."

Mélisande stared, unbelieving. If nothing else, she'd expected a command to find a husband within a certain amount of time. "I may remain unwed?"

"The choice is yours," he confirmed. "There is one condition. Should you decide to take a husband, he must meet with my approval prior to the nuptials. Your mother entrusted me to see to it no scoundrel takes advantage of you; thus, I have determined your husband shall have no claim to the title, but that it shall instead pass to your eldest son immediately upon his coming of age. We have, as such, created you the new Countess of Wilmington."

It was almost too much to fathom. *I'm free...*

On impulse, she went to him and kissed his cheek. "Oh, Uncle George, *thank* you!" she whispered, tears of relief filling her eyes.

"There now," he said gruffly, patting her back. "I expect you'll find a suitable husband soon enough. You're a pretty thing, even in mourning, and should have no trouble at all in that regard. You'll smile at him and be married within the year."

Mélisande disagreed. No man would ever inspire her to give up her autonomy, now that it was hers. The only one with any chance of convincing her otherwise was long gone and far away, but she didn't dare break Uncle George's jovial mood by saying it. Keeping her contrary notions to herself, she departed, feeling light for the first time in almost a year.

Sweeping into her chambers triumphantly, she lifted her skirts and tore off her panniers, vowing to never again wear the beastly things. "Burn them, Marie," she commanded her startled maid, giving the metal baskets a good shake before dumping them on the floor. "I never want to see them again."

Immediately, she began writing letters. The first was a cheerful missive to David. The second was to her dressmaker.

*This Season is going to be very different.*

The following week, Mélisande sipped her tea and waited—delightfully unchaperoned—in David's townhouse parlor.

"Congratulations on escaping the noose," David said from the doorway. "I anticipate a general uproar when it becomes public knowledge. No doubt there'll be some strong protest at court."

"I don't see why there should be," she grumbled. "Female autonomy is certainly nothing new. After all, was there not an unwed woman on England's *throne* more than a century ago? And like that illustrious queen, I also plan to announce that I have no intention of ever marrying."

"Then let us hope the number of suicides among your admirers does not forever earn the enmity of your fellow sex," he quipped, taking a scone from the tray. "Though I expect you've earned that already. I also expect you know your announcement will do nothing to dissuade fortune-hunting males from pursuit. Your wealth and title are simply too enticing a lure."

"I'm well aware of the wolves wearing sheep's wool, thanks to you," she scolded without rancor, waiting for him to take a bite before continuing. "But I didn't come to discuss them. I came to ask the name of your mistress's mantua-maker."

The fit of coughing and cursing that followed her request was well worth the trip across town.

"I beg your pardon?" David asked, his voice a full octave higher than before. His brows lowered. "Melly, what have you done?"

"Your concern is touching," she said, flicking a stray bit of crumpet off her sleeve. "But I've 'done' nothing untoward.

I merely want a new wardrobe for the Season, and my current mantua-maker has refused to outfit me." At his dubious look, she elaborated. "Apparently, she has very definite opinions on what an unmarried lady ought to wear."

His bark of laughter brought a frown to her face. "I fail to see the humor. As I'm not planning to marry, I don't see why I should refrain from dressing as I please. And it's not as if I asked her to put me in anything inappropriate. It's just that my design ideas are not precisely in step with current fashion. She won't do what I want for fear of losing her other customers. Neither will any of the other mantua-makers of my acquaintance. I need someone willing to be a little adventurous."

"I see. Rebelling against the institution of marriage isn't enough for you. Now you must take on fashion as well."

Arching a brow in answer, she waited.

"Very well," he sighed after a moment. "I've sent my, erm, female friends to Madame de Favriele on Bond Street for the past two years. Hers is a small establishment compared to some of the more popular ones, and she is not yet well known in London, but she is a most excellent mantua-maker nonetheless. And she won't refuse the commission, no matter how *outré* your ideas."

"I *knew* you would have a solution! Thank you, David!" Mélisande cheered, smiling again.

"Don't thank me until after you've gotten the bill," he answered. "Her shop may be small, but her services are not, I fear, inexpensive."

The new Countess of Wilmington set Society on its ear that Season. As soon as the deep mourning period ended, Mélisande began wearing the new gowns she herself had helped design— gowns in rich, bright silks and brocades, gowns shockingly *sans panniers.* She played chess, whist, and Bragg to her heart's content, and when she danced, she enjoyed herself thoroughly, uncaring of the black looks from those displeased by her bold conduct.

"Life is far too short to waste appeasing people I care nothing about," she explained to a concerned Reggie after a particularly scandalous incident involving the Duke of Devonshire.

"You played chess with a married man—*alone*—until nearly dawn to determine whether or not you would agree to breed a bloody horse!"

The unpleasant prickle of anger heated Mélisande's cheeks. "If I choose to discuss the future of *my* racing stock with another breeder, it is no business of yours! And we were *not* alone!"

"You might as well have been." Reggie raised one finger. "A footman. A single footman! It'll be a miracle if Lady Devonshire hasn't already begun demanding that her friends ostracize you."

"Lady Devonshire knew of our whereabouts the entire time. It was *her* footman," she replied, bored of his harranguing. "And since when did you appoint yourself my chaperone?"

"That's not nearly the half of it," he continued, igoring her. "Your personal war with Herrington must also end. You will stop provoking him immediately."

A sigh of irritation escaped her.

"I mean it, Melly! You took my pipe *and blew it out in his face*—in front of an entire roomful of people at Tynwick's. I've never seen him so enraged. You went too far!"

For a moment, Mélisande had difficulty containing her laughter. Never would she forget the look on her *bête noire*'s face.

"Damn it, this is no time for jests," he growled. "I intervened before he could commit some unforgivable offense, but what if I hadn't been present?"

"I should have handled it myself, of course," she answered, shrugging a careless shoulder. "Reggie, you were there, you *heard* the man insult me in front of everyone. He practically *begged* for retaliation. I merely returned his insult. And I don't see why you're making such a fuss, anyway. You dislike him as much as I."

"That isn't the point!"

"Then what *is* the point, pray tell?" she demanded, exasperated. "You've become such a prig of late! You used to enjoy tweaking his nose right along with me."

"Yes, well, that was before nearly having to challenge him to a duel on your behalf. As fond of you as I am, I've no desire to die defending your honor. And neither does Pelham. And yes, he and I are in complete agreement regarding the matter."

"You've spoken with David about this?" she demanded, scowling.

"I have," he clipped. "About this and many other things involving your recent behavior. He's very concerned that you draw too much attention to yourself, attention that could be to your detriment."

Apprehension quickened her pulse. *Did David tell him? Does he know?* Searching Reggie's eyes, however, she saw no condemnation, no disgust. Only worry. Her secret was still safe, then.

"I see. It appears I have not one but *two* self-appointed chaperones." Settling herself in a chair, she peered up at him. "One a known rakehell and the other fast becoming a degenerate right along with him. Yet, with me, you behave as though you belong in a cassock. If you're not careful, I'm going to start calling you Father Stanton."

Crossing the room, Reggie sat opposite and stared soberly into her eyes. "Melly, I know you've been given the title in your own right, but that won't stop King George from marrying you off, should you become troublesome. You may be his godchild, but that does not make you immune to his wrath or his will."

Though she did not like it, Mélisande knew he was right. It wasn't worth the risk. "Very well. You may tell your fellow curate that I shall endeavor to use more discretion." Her lips quirked upward. "When next I see him, I shall ask David to say a prayer of petition to the Almighty to keep Herrington out of my path for the remainder of the Season."

# Chapter Five

## THE DEVIL YOU KNOW

*London, 1750*

*STAMMA IS COMING BACK!* FOLDING THE LETTER, MÉLISANDE immediately set forth to arrange another one of her now famous parties.

*I'll invite that fellow from Germany...Kesselman. He played an excellent match at the Sheffields' ball last June. Georgiana just told me he's a guest of Lord and Lady Renquist.*

It would be just the thing to snap her friend out of his morose mood.

After Stamma's demoralizing chess defeat at the hands of that upstart François-André Philidor, he'd left for the Continent to lick his wounds, depriving her of his company. It had been a sore blow, for she had few enough true friends these days. Having him back would be a delight.

As would having another female in the house. Reggie's sister Charlotte would be here tomorrow. With Lord Stanton away overseas, his stepmother expecting another child any day now, and his only other female relatives a pair of ancient aunts currently living in Bath, Reggie had asked her to oversee the girl's debut.

It surprised her how much she found herself looking forward to the task.

And it was with great anticipation that she also looked to the first ball of the Season, to be held in just three days. Her wardrobe was practically bursting with glorious new gowns. There was one in particular she could hardly wait to wear. The mere thought of it made her chuckle wickedly.

On impulse, she walked over to the wardrobe, flung open its doors, and fingered the midnight silk. The first ball would *definitely* set the tone for the rest of the Season.

*Reggie'd better have practiced the steps while moldering away in the country*, she thought. *I'll skewer him alive if he bungles it.*

The road was clogged with coaches wending their slow way to Hawthorne Manor. Mélisande waited impatiently, fidgeting with excitement as they inched closer.

David eyed her busy hands and tapping feet with a droll expression. "For someone determined never to wed, you certainly seem eager to rejoin the fray. Have you decided to participate in the husband hunt, then?"

Mélisande looked back at him with unconcealed irritation. "You of all people know I've no intention of doing any such thing. I refuse to parade myself before a gaggle of fortune-seeking imbeciles with the purpose of bagging one of them and dragging his mercenary hide to the altar."

"No, but you're perfectly happy to bait the poor 'fortune-seeking imbeciles,' aren't you?" He chuckled. "Rather like dangling a piece of raw beef before a pack of hungry dogs without ever intending to actually feed them. Just be careful you don't get bitten."

She made to protest, but he cut her off with a wave of his hand, grinning.

"I know you far too well, Melly. For you, the thrill is in the chase and in being chased, not in the catch. Relax. I know when a battle is lost, and this is one of those times. You, my dear, are a lost cause. Thus, I concede. Gracefully." His salute was indeed graceful—and purely mocking.

"Well, at least you know when to give up." She sniffed. Relaxing back against the cushioned seat, she winked at her fellow conspirator, Charlotte, who sat listening to their banter with round, sparkling eyes. "Unlike some," she added, arching a brow at Reggie.

Though Reggie held his tongue, she knew he objected mightily. Especially the part involving Charlotte. Any moment now, he would try to convince her to—

"I'm still not entirely certain this is a good idea," Reggie ventured weakly, interrupting her thoughts. "It's Charlotte's debut, after all. The dance is too provocative. I just don't think it's worth the risk."

"We've been over this." Mélisande rolled her eyes. "You'll be right there alongside her to act as chaperone. It's an excellent strategy to ensure she stands out from the rest of the debutantes. And you watch—she'll skim off the cream of the eligibles all for herself. You'll see. It'll work perfectly!"

The carriage finally rolled to a stop, and Mélisande stepped down. Smiling, she carefully arranged her skirts, ignoring the startled murmurs of the lookers-on. The moment she'd laid eyes on the finished gown, she'd known it would cause a sensation.

The garment boasted only a hint of padding at the hips instead of the enormous *panniers* favored this Season, and rather than the typical front lacing, it was held together by a row of tiny silver buttons at the back. There was nothing to mask her natural silhouette—no stomacher and no shoulder pleats. The midnight-blue silk hugged her every curve before flaring out into fullness at the hips. Filmy layers of *les engageantes* fluttered at her elbows, and tiny diamonds sewn into the fabric of her ensemble glittered in the torchlight like stars in a clear night sky.

Raising her chin, she gazed out at the crowd, surveying the field of battle.

When Charlotte alighted, she presented a startling contrast dressed in palest mauve and pearls, her honey-blonde hair arranged in a profusion of riotous curls. She was a delightful confection, all rosy cheeks and bright eyes. Her naïveté shone so brightly that it must surely be visible from a good league away. It made Mélisande smile to think she'd once been thus.

"Melly, my dear! So good of you to come!" Lord Ludley boomed, beaming from ear to ear as they approached.

She cast her host a glittering smile. "I wouldn't miss this for the world, Luddy. It would require last rites being read for me to be anywhere but here." She inclined her head politely to Lady Ludley, who smiled in welcome.

"Pelham, Stanton," Ludley addressed the young men. He stopped when he saw Charlotte, his brows lifting. "Surely this is not your little sister!" he exclaimed, looking to Reggie with mock amazement. "She looks far too angelic to be related to *you*, you young rascal!"

Charlotte curtsied, a faint blush of pleasure tinting her cheeks.

Reggie's chest puffed out. "This is indeed my youngest sister, Miss Charlotte Stanton."

"Miss Stanton," Ludley murmured, bowing, "it is an honor to have you as our guest."

"The honor is mine," the girl replied.

Mélisande longed to get the social niceties over with as quickly as possible. A good round of chess or perhaps a few hands of Bragg was what she needed to settle the nerves and pass the time until the waltz.

Catching sight of a familiar face, she barely refrained from making an audible sound of displeasure.

Herrington's odd, amber eyes bored into her. Even at this distance, she felt the disapproval radiating from him. Memory took her back to when she'd first met her *bête noire*. She'd been minding her own business, playing cards with friends, when he'd rudely interrupted their game.

His arrogant words still stuck in her craw: *An earl's daughter should be in the ballroom dancing with a proper gentleman, not associating with this lot of devils.*

Heart still aching over her father's recent death, her response had been cutting: *If I prefer to associate with devils, it is because I find the company of prudish clergymen uninspiring and tedious. I suggest you preach elsewhere, for I'm neither your wife nor daughter to correct.*

Red-faced, Herrington had departed with indignant haste.

But that had not been the end of it. Oh, no. On every possible occasion thereafter, the ill-mannered brute had haunted her steps, harassing her with critical comments regarding her behavior. He'd become the proverbial burr beneath her saddle, souring many an evening's good pleasure.

In return, she did her best to shock and annoy her priggish detractor whenever the opportunity presented itself.

Mélisande turned away. This was one evening he wouldn't spoil.

Champagne in hand, Alessandro wandered aimlessly, listening to snatches of conversation, looking for someone worthy of his attention. Ludley had made it clear that he expected him to live up to his reputation, and he did not want to disappoint his host.

A woman's laughter reached his ears from a few yards away, and a feathery finger tickled down his spine at the sound of it, stopping him dead in his tracks. Rich and throaty, it was a siren's call, utterly irresistible. Turning, he sought out the owner of that marvelous laugh.

To his disappointment, he saw only her back—but it was a very lovely back. The gleaming mass of her dark hair was swept high and smoothly bound into a twist, leaving her neck exposed, save for the sapphires and diamonds that graced it. He noted her delicious silhouette was conspicuously devoid of *panniers*.

*Not afraid to defy convention.*

His gaze dropped to her left hand. She wore no wedding ring. *Benissimo.*

Fascinated, he observed as she turned to touch the arm of the gentleman standing beside her. Her narrow waist twisted slightly, and with a shock he realized that, in addition to wearing no wedding ring, the lady was also wearing no corset.

Now *that* was absolutely intriguing.

Taking the arm offered by her obedient escort, she bade fond farewells to her friends and then swept away. As though tied to the mysterious woman by some invisible tether, Alessandro followed as she meandered through the throng. Something about the woman's voice had tugged strangely at his innards. He strained to hear her speak again as she greeted friends in passing, but all he could catch were bits and pieces, a word here, a husky laugh there.

"Ah, Gravina! There you are. I've been looking everywhere for you."

Concealing his annoyance at the untimely intervention, Alessandro turned to greet his host.

Lord Ludley eyed his infamous guest. "Thought you'd be surrounded by a group of rabid females by now," he boomed, and then lowered his voice. "Not losing your touch, are you? Perhaps I ought to have announced your presence here instead of keeping you a surprise."

Alessandro clamped his teeth on a nasty riposte. Damn it all, she was getting away! "Luddy, that woman, the one in the dark blue just there—who is she?"

Ludley chuckled. "I expected you might take notice of *that* one," he rumbled approvingly. "Too bloody beautiful not to, eh? A true *objet d'art*. A man would have to be stone blind not to appreciate God's brushstroke, there. Even at my age."

Fixing him with a gimlet stare, Alessandro waited.

Ludley colored slightly and coughed. "Ah, yes. Well. Countess of Wilmington. Delightful gel. Chock-full of good mischief, too!" he added with a wink, his good humor quickly restored. "But I should warn you—she's formidable. Not to be trifled with, if you know what I mean," he said a little too regretfully.

"Is that her husband with her?" Alessandro inquired, indicating the man upon whose arm the countess was draped. The casual familiarity between the pair evidenced a long, comfortable acquaintance. "I saw no ring, but…"

"What, him? Good Lord, no!" Ludley laughed. "Hellion's got the title all to herself and announced she'll never marry—so you're out of luck if it's a rich wife you're after, old boy. Dozens have tried and failed."

Alessandro's smile returned. "Ah, so he's her lover, then." Much easier to get rid of. If the gentleman objected to his seduction of the lady, well, his skill with a blade was almost as lauded as his talent in the bedchamber.

"No, no." Ludley frowned. "That's only young Pelham. Needn't be concerned with him. They *were* cradle 'trothed, but they broke off the engagement years ago. Parents were furious! They're friends, or cohorts in crime some might call them, but never lovers."

"Does she *have* a lover?" Maybe if he was more direct, he'd get an answer that was of use.

"That one? Not likely," sniffed Ludley. "You won't catch *her* stealing kisses in the garden grotto. Hiding in the library is more her style, poking about on a chessboard or engaged in philosophical rattle or some such nonsense."

Alessandro felt like a cat that'd just been told there was an unguarded dish of cream waiting round the corner. "Thank you, Luddy," he said absently, watching his quarry disappear into the crowd. "Why don't you introduce me to some of your other friends?" he asked, turning away. Now that he had a name, he could take his time and make a proper entrance.

As he played the dutiful guest, he thought about the woman Ludley had described as "formidable" and "not to be trifled with." But he'd also revealed her antipathy toward marriage.

So she was not impossible; she was merely a challenge.

And he never backed down from a challenge. Especially one presented in delectable female form. She was a woman, and if there was anything he knew how to do well, it was gain a woman's confidence. Earn her trust and friendship first, and then the seduction. He hadn't even seen her face, but already he knew he wanted her. Her laugh alone was enough to make him feel a desire he had not thought to experience ever again.

By the time he entered the library, the Countess of Wilmington was indeed thoroughly engrossed in a game of chess—with none other than his good friend Stamma.

Drifting closer, Alessandro viewed the board over her shoulder. She had the upper hand and looked to win, which surprised him. He was no slouch, himself, but when Stamma had visited him in Italy several years ago, he'd lost every single game to the master. It reaffirmed his assumption of her intelligence, for Stamma was not the type to play false, no matter how beautiful his opponent.

"Melly, my dear, you've improved." Stamma chuckled, pulling at his neat goatee and taking a moment to contemplate his next move. He scooted his queen out of danger, keeping an eye on her bishop.

"I certainly hope so," she replied. "I've sharpened my skills on every willing opponent in England, as well as a few visiting countries, in your absence."

Alessandro heard the smile in her response and wondered at its warmth. Stamma was an old man, a *married* man. And he'd mentioned nothing of a beautiful English mistress during his visit.

"Consider me duly impressed," Stamma answered, sounding pleased. "At this rate, it shan't be long before you surpass me. You'll be challenging Philidor next," he quipped, eyes twinkling as he watched her make her move, an aggressive one that put him in retreat.

"Oh, I certainly hope so," she murmured. "The man is an ass, and I should like nothing better than to wipe the smug expression off his face with a sound drubbing."

The stillness that followed her statement was palpable.

It might as well have been an invitation to duel, only the battle would be waged on a chessboard rather than a grassy field.

Alessandro knew Philidor. Chance had placed the man at his father's house the year prior, shortly after his famous match with Stamma. The braggart had reveled in his triumph ad nauseam, coming across as a swaggering idiot.

His smile deepened. It was always to one's benefit to have something in common with one's prey. The enemy of my enemy is my friend, the saying went.

"I heard you've already put him in his place quite neatly, my dear," Stamma said, glancing up at her. "News of your little disagreement followed me all the way to the Continent. It is all but legend. The 'slap heard across the channel,' so to speak.

Everyone in Europe knows you refused him. His behavior was appalling, if you ask me, and he deserved far worse than a slap," he snapped, chin jutting pugnaciously. "Even so, Melly, I don't want you picking a fight with him," he added in a stern voice, moving his piece. "You've no need to prove anything to anyone. Certainly not to him."

"All the same, I fear I crave a match," she replied. Her teasing tone fooled none of her observers. "I shall play him for the sheer entertainment of the thing. It will help stave off the *ennui*," she added as she made her countermove. "Check."

Stamma frowned at the board. "Bloody hell. I'm mated in two moves." Looking up, he began to laugh. "You little minx, you *have* improved. That'll teach me to give away all my secrets to beguiling young women. I concede and congratulate you. What forfeit do you claim, then?"

The countess sat back in her chair and tapped her fan against its arm, contemplating. "I believe I shall claim a dance," she announced. "Right now!"

Just as she began to rise, Stamma looked up and exclaimed in delight, "Orsini, you young devil! What a smashing surprise— but I thought you were in Russia?"

Mélisande's stomach clenched as the floor dropped from beneath her.

*It cannot be!*

"I was in St. Petersburg for a while," the newcomer laughed. "Court was certainly warm enough, but I found the rest of the climate inhospitable. Damned frigid place. Miserable. And it's Gravina now, not that it makes any difference. My father has gone to his eternal reward."

Though the Italian's voice was a shade deeper than Mélisande remembered, and tinged with an unfamiliar bitterness, there could be no doubt. Still, her mind refused to believe what her eyes had not yet seen.

Rising slowly, she turned, grasping the back of the chair to steady herself as her heart lurched back into motion.

It was him.

Her eyes devoured him as she waited for her pulse to settle its chaotic rush. Five years had refined his appearance. Though still tall and slender, he could no longer be called skinny. Broad shoulders and well-muscled legs had replaced the lankiness of youth, lending him a solidity that had not been present when last she'd seen him. Time had done nothing to soften his angular face, however, but had continued to sculpt his features into almost predatory sharpness.

In a departure from his previous bright silks, laces, and dandified frippery, he wore black trimmed with elegant silver embroidery. But instead of making him look severe, the simple, dark attire complemented his warm complexion. He'd been kissed by the sun, and his skin glowed with a deep, golden hue that set him apart from everyone else in the room.

*His skin.* Her fingers remembered the texture of it: warm and dry; cheeks slightly scratchy; soft, silken lips. She stilled in shock, mind and body possessed by the memory of their kiss. A tendril of heat uncurled deep in her belly, followed by a clangor in her head as good sense screamed at her to slip away undetected.

Too late.

Stamma turned toward her, beaming. "Melly! Allow me to introduce you to a friend of mine, His Grace, the Duke of Gravina. We met during my travels. Gravina, this is Lady Compton, Countess of Wilmington."

Alessandro turned, the smile vanishing from his face, replaced by the shock of recognition. "You!"

With monumental effort, Mélisande maintained outward composure. Assuming a cool expression, she politely inclined her head. "I believe His Grace and I have already had the pleasure."

# *Chapter Six*

## AND THE DEEP BLUE SEA

STONISHMENT REVERBERATED THROUGH ALESSANDRO'S entire being at the sight before him. His unbelieving gaze flicked to her décolletage, and there it was, the same little mark above the heart.

*Lady Compton.*

Yet she wore no ring—had she been widowed?

"Indeed, my lady," he responded haltingly, somehow managing to get the words out past a sudden dryness of the mouth. "It is an unexpected pleasure to see you again after so many years."

"You already know each other? How delightful!" Stamma boomed heartily.

Alessandro watched as Pelham drifted over to stand behind Mélisande.

Taking in the other man's cold eyes and clenched jaw, he thought perhaps Luddy might have been mistaken about their association.

A corner of the lady's sensuous mouth lifted. "Your Grace, may I introduce you to some of my other friends?" She tilted her head back toward her self-appointed bodyguard without bothering to actually look at him. "This is Lord Pelham, and this," she indicated another gentleman who'd just entered the room, "is Mr. Stanton."

Alessandro nodded to each. "A pleasure." The Stanton fellow appeared friendly enough, or at least neutral, but Pelham fairly bristled with hostility. *Too bad.* Dismissing them from his thoughts for the moment, he turned his full attention back to Mélisande. "So many years have passed that we shall have to become reacquainted all over again, my lady. May I escort you back to the ballroom?"

"I should very much like to become reacquainted, Your Grace," she told him, her cool tone belying the words, "but I'm afraid it will have to wait. I've just won a dance with Monsieur Stamma and I'm loath to delay claiming my prize, as he so rarely deigns to dance these days." She moved to Stamma's side, ignoring her friend's bewildered look. "But perhaps later?"

"I should like that very much," Alessandro responded sincerely, watching Pelham's already thunderous expression grow even more threatening. The man looked ready to commit murder. He'd seen the look too many times not to recognize it.

And it didn't matter in the least. *I've found her.* And he wasn't letting her get away again, even if it meant he had to remove an unwanted rival. "If I may be so bold, my lady, I would be most honored if you would allow me the dance immediately following—if you are not already obligated," he ventured. He stared into her eyes, willing her to accept.

Everyone waited to hear her answer.

Mélisande hesitated only a moment. "I'd be delighted." Turning to Stamma, she took his arm. "Shall we?"

Stamma patted her hand in fatherly fashion. "Of course! And afterward I shall fetch us some champagne and we shall all retire to a quiet corner where you can tell me how the two of you met."

Alessandro saw that her cool façade was just that. Her control was superb, but he knew better—he'd seen the telltale flare of her delicate nostrils and the way her eyes had widened slightly at Stamma's suggestion. She was completely terrified of revealing the circumstances of their acquaintance.

"My lady, before you go, tell me, do you still dance as gracefully as I remember?" he interjected, his tone deliberately mischievous. "I remember a very determined young lady practicing in Louis's garden. My toes remember it as well," he laughed, inviting her to pick up the thread.

A delicate brow arched as she grabbed the rope he'd tossed her. "You *and* your toes will be pleased to know that my skills have greatly improved since our last encounter." Her grin was saucy as she turned away. "Until our dance, Your Grace," she threw over her shoulder as she passed through the door.

In the stunned silence following her departure, a bemused smirk crept across Alessandro's face. *Formidable indeed.* The young lady he'd kissed in the grove had been no more than a precocious girl on the cusp of womanhood recklessly testing her wings. But the girl had grown into a seductive temptress, one quite aware of her power over men, he suspected.

He needed information. It would only be to his advantage to learn more about her and her odd assortment of friends. And the best place to obtain that sort of information was among the womenfolk.

Returning to the ballroom, he found what he was searching for: a pair of pretty young magpies chattering away.

"I cannot *believe* she's dancing with him," chirped the owner of a towering pile of flame-red curls.

Alessandro followed her gaze and saw she was staring at Mélisande and Stamma.

"It's indecent the way she dotes on him," the girl continued. "He's a married man! Ever since she became countess, she's shown a complete lack of regard for her reputation." Her fan snapped open and she began fluttering it violently. "Look at her. No *panniers*, hair barely dressed, and my sister Daphne said she rides *astride*. Swears she saw it with her own eyes last year. Disgraceful!"

The golden-haired girl beside her let out a delicate squeak of shock. "Ride astride? Oh, I could never do such a thing. Papa would disown me—if I didn't break my neck first. But I suppose she *is* a countess," she added wistfully. "I wish I were a countess so I could do as I liked."

"Catch an earl or a duke, and you can," said the redhead. "But Her Foolishness is unwed and should have better care for her reputation. What little she has left, that is. Hanging about the likes of that rakehell Pelham and his *appalling* friends, it's no wonder she's without decency!" Her voice sank to a loud whisper, clearly intended to be heard at least five feet away. "I've heard he maintains several mistresses at once. It wouldn't surprise me if *she* was one of them."

"Oh, Lydia! Everyone knows that isn't true," the blonde said, plainly horrified. "And not *all* of her friends are scoundrels. At least one of them is quite nice."

Alessandro followed her wistful gaze and saw that it was fastened on Stanton, standing just a few paces away.

"Don't tell me you want to be a countess and then swoon over a mere viscount's son in the next breath, Angelica," Lydia sniped, rapping her friend's elbow with her fan to shift her attention away from the apparently unsuitable Mr. Stanton. "You were the toast of the Season even *before* your coming out. You have it within your power to catch a duke, you silly goose! I saw the way Herrington looked at you tonight."

"I suppose you're right," Angelica responded woefully. "Herrington *is* the better catch. But he looks at me as if I were a—a *thing* rather than a person. Mr. Stanton is different. He's cheerful, and he makes me laugh."

Lydia snorted. "Cheerful is nice, but *rich* is better. You can laugh when you're a duchess and everyone refers to you as Your

Grace. Come," she huffed, taking her friend by the arm. "If I don't drag you away now, you'll be standing at the altar with the wrong man."

A devilish plan began to form in Alessandro's mind. At least *one* of Mélisande's friends would be out of his way in short order.

Turning, he watched Mélisande glide through the final steps of the quadrille with Stamma. When the dance ended and she dipped into a deep curtsy, Alessandro knew it was his cue.

Stamma grinned at his approach. "Come to take the initiative, eh? Good luck trying to capture her, lad," he winked. "She's no dullard. You'll need all your wits to put her in checkmate." He chuckled at his own clever turn of words.

Alessandro clamped his jaw, wishing his friend would shut up and disappear. He glanced at Mélisande and watched a knowing smile curve one corner of her luscious mouth. Mesmerized, he stared in silence until Stamma cleared his throat a second time. Blinking back into awareness of his surroundings, Alessandro almost laughed aloud. He might have taken the initiative, but her counterattack was something to be reckoned with! A man would have to be made of stone to remain unmoved by the look in her eyes.

He held out his arm. "My lady," he murmured, sweeping a bow. The sudden intensity of her gaze as they joined hands and moved to first positions caught Alessandro off guard, and his breath stilled momentarily.

At last, blessedly, the musicians struck up the prelude. Throughout the entire dance, their gazes remained locked as they wove, circled, and dipped, fingers brushing, desire mounting. The very air between them seemed almost to crackle with tension.

As the music drew to a finish, Mélisande glanced to her left, lighting on the musicians' blind.

"You don't happen to know the waltz, do you?" she asked.

He found his tongue with some difficulty. "I learned it in Vienna before it became popular in France."

Without preamble, she grabbed him by the hand and quickly pulled him behind the blind. Startled, the musicians began to rise, but she motioned them back down, addressing them in an authoritative tone. *"Mes amies, préparez à jouer la valse maintenant!"*

Delighted, they immediately began shifting the pages of their set.

Lord Ludley, who happened to be standing nearby, bustled over. "Melly, it's too early!" he hissed. "What are you about? Where is Stanton?"

Mélisande turned to him with a careless laugh. "Change of plans, Luddy, darling. I've a new partner! Be a gem and announce it, won't you?"

"But—" His eyes fell on Gravina, and his panicked expression evaporated. Smiling, he scuttled back around the blind. "Ladies and gentlemen," he addressed the milling throng, "I've prepared for your entertainment tonight the special exhibition of a new dance..."

Behind the screen, Mélisande faced Alessandro. Giving him a siren's smile, she took his arm.

They walked out from behind the screen and moved to the center of the floor, ignoring the murmurs and gasps that followed.

Upon seeing them take positions, Ludley hastily wrapped up his speech and frantically motioned for the musicians to begin.

As the opening strains commenced, Alessandro tugged his partner's hand sharply and pulled her close, wrapping his other hand snugly about her waist, acutely aware of its lack of a corset.

The tempo increased and the pair began to move in unison. Beginning with small steps, they swayed back and forth; then the music swelled and the world disappeared.

Mélisande's long legs matched him step for step as they began to spin and glide in widening circles, never stumbling, never hesitating. He was sure and confident in his movements, a skilled dancer. Apparently pleased, she allowed a bit more give in her waist, encouraging him with her body. When he did not immediately respond, she eyed him askance, raising a brow as if to taunt, *Is this the best you can do?*

He answered her with a satyr's grin, pulling her closer on the next turn and pressing his hand hard against her pliant waist.

The pair took flight. Across the ballroom they soared in great, sweeping arcs that seemed impossible without the benefit of wings. Mélisande laughed aloud with unrestrained delight. Held securely in his embrace, she closed her eyes and tilted her head back.

When she looked back at him, her eyes blazed like living jewels full of joy and desire. In that moment, Alessandro knew he'd lost his soul.

"Outrageous!" Mélisande heard one old matron gasp as they passed by.

"That dance belongs between the sheets, as does that vixen!" another gentleman commented more appreciatively, earning a few chuckles of agreement from his cohorts.

"The impropriety!" trumpeted another woman. "I should disown her at once were she *my* daughter!"

"Shocking! No wonder Pelham wouldn't marry her—she's too brazen even for *him*!"

One after another, onlookers offered up their vicious observations.

As the pair continued to dance, however, the exclamations of disapproval were slowly overwhelmed (for the most part) by murmurs of admiration from among the younger set.

The waltz ended, and they glided to a halt, inches apart.

Mélisande was oblivious to all save the want consuming her. Her partner's hot, black gaze held her, telling her of his matching desire. So wrapped up in each other were they that the wild applause and excited babble of their audience didn't even register until they were completely surrounded.

Alessandro released his hold on her waist but kept hold of her hand, concealing the connection in the folds of his coat skirts as they stood close amid the press of bodies.

Ludley, appearing much relieved to see the majority of his guests congratulating the pair rather than running them out of his ballroom in disgrace, wriggled through, parting the waves of the crush like a charging walrus. "Magnificent!" he bellowed. "Melly, my dear, when you first suggested it, I'd my doubts, but you've certainly proven me wrong!" He frowned. "Of course it'll probably be banned; but nevertheless, I'm sure it'll be all the rage in a few years' time. Forbidden fruit and all that, you know."

Mélisande's blood hammered in her ears, pulsing through her awakened body, threatening to incinerate her. After an interminable few moments spent receiving compliments and automatically answering countless inquiries regarding her dancing instructor, she'd had enough.

"Oh dear, I'm afraid I feel a bit unwell," she said quite clearly, squeezing Alessandro's hand hard before letting go. Feigning weakness, she leaned on his arm as if in need of support and opened her fan to cool her glowing cheeks.

Taking her hint, Alessandro played along. "Come, my lady, and let us take the air outside. It'll be cooler." Pressing forward with polite apologies, he forged a path through their admirers. When they finally made it to the terrace doors, he flipped a coin to the attendant.

The young man caught it deftly and shut the door behind them, standing before it to prevent anyone else from immediately following.

It was only a brief delay, but it was all they needed. The second they were outside in the blessedly cool night, Mélisande dropped all pretense of weakness and grabbed his hand. Immediately, she yanked him hard to the right, forcing him to keep up as she broke into a run. Keeping close to the wall, she led him around the corner instead of toward the stairs.

The balcony here appeared to wrap around the building for a short distance and then simply end in a wall. Knowing better, Mélisande continued to lead him along to the end and then suddenly darted to the side—directly into the wall. For an instant, Alessandro resisted and tried to pull her away in the opposite direction, but then he, too, was pulled into the gap.

Hawthorne Manor had been built around an existing structure, and some of the old secrets still remained. The cleverly concealed opening revealed a passage that doubled back behind the original wall, leading to a steep, narrow flight of switchback stairs.

Mélisande paused, holding a finger to her lips to silence his questions. She removed her shoes, indicating he should do the same. Quiet as mice, they began to climb.

Occasional openings yawned to their left or right as they continued to ascend. She led him past these, knowing that none of them led to where she wanted to be. After what seemed an eternity spent groping for footing in the dark, she turned a sharp corner and a few steps later emerged into bright moonlight.

Smiling, she turned to Alessandro. "The original owner of this house was an astrologer. He had this place built so he could watch the sky. Come and see," she whispered, leading him across the flat expanse to the very edge.

Together, they peeked over the lip of the embrasure. Far below was the wide balcony from which they'd escaped. The massive gardens stretched out beyond, threaded by lamp-lit paths that twinkled faintly in the night. A small crowd had indeed followed them outside. Most were milling about on the balcony, but a few were determinedly headed to the garden bowers, presumably hoping to catch them in a tryst. No one seemed to be making for the secret stair.

Mélisande waited, nearly bursting with the excitement of their escape. After so long, *he* was here, in the flesh, the only man who'd ever made her feel completely alive.

Turning to face her, he bowed. "You, dear Countess, are a caution. Frightened the devil out of me, running into the wall like that. How on earth did you know it was there?"

"A servant showed it to me years ago when I summered here with my parents as a child," she laughed. "One day I grew bored and decided to explore it. I'm glad I remembered it, and extremely glad it wasn't sealed off."

"As am I." He sauntered over to where she stood. "I looked for you, you know. I searched for you for days, asked after you everywhere. You simply vanished. I wondered at times if I'd conjured you in a dream."

"I am quite real, I assure you."

"Are you?" He leaned closer. "I'm afraid I shall have to prove it to myself."

What began as a gentle kiss rapidly turned incendiary. Enfolding her in his arms, Alessandro claimed her mouth and branded it as his.

He was everything she remembered and more. His hands were sure, his skill at arousal undeniable, but the desire that awakened in her was more than the result of a confident touch. She'd been kissed before and it had been, for the most part, pleasant enough. But only Alessandro seemed able to incite this maddening *hunger*.

Mélisande melted into him, molding her every curve against his hardness.

Her skin tingled as his hands roamed across her back, his palms traveling slowly down until they cupped her bottom, pulling her hard against him. There was no mistaking the urgency of his desire. A rush of heat enveloped her, tightening the pit of her belly. With a throaty chuckle, she brushed the tip of her tongue against his bottom lip, tasting him.

Backing up against one of the crenellations that decorated the manor, he sat in the sill of one, pulling her onto his lap. Delicately, he caressed the line of her jaw and neck, running reverent fingers down to brush the tops of her breasts, slipping beneath to cup his palm around the side of one. His thumb grazed her nipple, sending tiny streaks of lightning pleasure straight to her core.

His hand left her breast to meander lower, fanning out over her belly to press against another sensitive mound. She whimpered with delight, arching upward to meet his touch.

Gathering her skirts, he slid one hand up her stockinged leg, burning a slow trail up to the secret place between her thighs. Gently, he nudged her legs apart, and Mélisande felt him slip between her slick folds, finding with unerring accuracy the little jewel nestled at the fore.

Mélisande cried out, rendered mindless, boneless—shameless. When he inserted a single digit into her dampness, her breath burst forth in a short gasp followed by a long, feral moan as he courted the gem of her womanhood with consummate skill, bringing her to the brink of ecstasy.

A new, delicious tension began to build. Time stretched into infinity as the tide ebbed and flowed within her, increasing in intensity with every passing moment. Warmth tingled throughout her whole body as the sensation mounted.

Though she craved the touch of his hand, it left her feeling somehow incomplete. She wanted more. Before she had time to process that primal thought, however, her body convulsed in a paroxysm of undiluted pleasure. Wave after wave of it washed over her, until she thought she might drown.

Alessandro's mouth swept down to muffle her outcry as she quaked and shivered in his arms.

A strange, warm languor gripped Mélisande as he slowly removed his hand and peered down at her, his eyes gleaming with triumph. Gazing back up at him, the irony of her situation struck her with something akin to hilarity. *I am my mother's daughter after all.* She looked to the source of her pleasure: handsome, intelligent, exciting—a cheerful seeker of pleasure. He pretended nothing to the contrary, openly enjoying his delinquent life.

The idea that had begun to form in her mind became more appealing with each passing moment. Maman had said that love and passion were two entirely separate things. Never would she be so foolish as to give this man her heart, but with him as her guide...he would be the perfect instructor, allowing her to enjoy learning the ways of pleasure without risking emotional entanglement. And once her thirst was quenched and their attraction had run its course, they would both be free to do as they pleased.

Could she? Ought she? She was so weary of playing it safe, and of suffering endless disappointment. After what had just happened, she knew she was *very* tired of being a virgin. Looking at Alessandro again, she made a decision. He would do quite nicely indeed.

"May I inquire as to your sudden smile?" Alessandro asked. "I would like to assume I am the cause of it, but something tells me otherwise."

"I'm simply amazed at how Fate has delivered to me *exactly* what I desired," she replied, nestling into him and tilting her head back to gaze up at the stars.

"How so?" he ventured, wrapping his arms more closely around her.

She smiled, enjoying how his embrace drove away the encroaching chill. "I once vowed I'd never act rashly out of passion, and yet here I am on the roof with a notorious rakehell and my skirts tossed up. And I feel no shame—not even the tiniest shred. What does that say about me?"

It was a rhetorical question born out of the surprise of self-discovery. *Is this tendency toward wickedness inherent in my blood? Am I truly tainted by my mother's sin?* It must be so, or she would be suffering an agony of conscience. Instead, she felt only desire and a sense of liberation.

"You've had your way with me, my lord, and I've thoroughly enjoyed it." Gathering her courage, she forged ahead. It was now or never. "In fact, I'd *very* much like to repeat it. I propose that we become lovers, you and I."

## Chapter Seven

### IN WHICH BARGAINS ARE MADE

ALESSANDRO WAS MORE THAN HAPPY TO OBLIGE, OF course, but the tone of her request was a trifle disturbing. He'd been propositioned countless times, but never in this odd fashion and *never* by a young, unmarried woman of respectable reputation.

It made him rather uneasy. Over the years, he'd met a number of ladies possessed of an angelic façade, only to discover they were the very devil once behind closed doors. Those experiences had been immensely enjoyable, but for some strange reason, he didn't take any pleasure in the idea that she might be of that ilk.

"Why?" he asked.

Mélisande sat up and wound her arms about his neck, looking him squarely in the face. "Because I *like* you," she stated, her eyes betraying just how very much she liked him indeed. "You don't pretend to be anything you're not. And because I've waited a very long time for someone to stir me again. Five years have passed since we met in Versailles, and until tonight, not a single man has managed to make me feel that way," she added, caressing his ear.

"And what makes you think I'll agree to this...arrangement?"

85

"Because you're a man who seeks pleasure," she continued in a wicked whisper. "And rest assured that what I propose is a friendship of sorts, *not* a romantic entanglement."

Alessandro raised a brow. *A friendship of sorts?*

"I see," he answered slowly. With a deep breath he took the bait. "Let us say I did agree to become your paramour; the pleasures we would explore naturally pose a certain…risk. Surely you don't wish to bear a child out of wedlock?"

"There are ways to prevent such things," she said dismissively. "I may be inexperienced, but I'm not entirely ignorant."

The roses blooming in her cheeks belied the cool answer. "And what of your future husband?" he asked. "Will he not care that you've sampled the delights of the bedchamber with another?"

"I'll worry about that—*should* I ever decide to take a husband," she said, raising a brow. "My wealth will no doubt persuade him to overlook my past." She inched closer, her sultry smile returning. "But before I settle for some boring country lord and the tedium of domesticity, I wish to first experience passion."

Alessandro was stunned by the sheer magnitude of her naïveté. Such a sensual creature would certainly never be content with a boring country lord.

"I have no unreasonable expectations, Your Grace," she continued, breaking his reverie. Her dark lashes veiled her eyes, casting deep shadows across her cheeks. "I observed you for quite some time in Versailles, and I listened to your past *amours* when they spoke of you," she confessed. "I am fully aware that you are uninterested in being bound to any woman. I can accept that."

"Can you?" he asked, watching the play of moonlight across her delicate features.

"I can. When you are ready to move on, I'll let you go—without any bitterness," she added, flicking him a cautious glance.

"In fact, I hope that, as with your former lovers, we may part as friends."

After a long moment, he nodded. Now it was all becoming clear. Her body was his for the taking, but not her heart. "I am quite pleased to accommodate your desire to be educated in the ways of passion, but how am I to do so without destroying your reputation? You realize you have very likely already ruined yourself by spiriting away with me," he warned.

"There is another way back," she told him. "It will put us out near the ballroom. From there we can simply join the crowd, and by the time we're noticed, no one will really know how long we've been gone. Does this mean you accept?"

He bowed with a flourish. "With great pleasure, my lady."

Her happy smile was like the sun breaking through on a rainy day. He longed to kiss it, but they had not the time.

"We had better go," she said. "The moon is already high."

When she eased off his lap, a groan very nearly escaped him. He wasn't going to be able to stand without embarrassment. Looking up, he saw her gaze resting directly on the source of his discomfort. When her eyes finally met his, the little imp wore a knowing smile. With a deliberately lecherous grin, he stood, fully revealing the strength of the desire straining against the confines of his breeches. "I'm afraid our conversation has rendered me unfit to rejoin the festivities just yet."

Mélisande boldly perused the evidence of his masculinity. Stepping up, she placed a hand on his chest and slid it down toward the bulge.

Despite his delight at her daring, Alessandro knew better than to give in to the rash invitation. He clasped her wrist and halted her hand's naughty descent, feeling it tremble in his grasp. She might play the wanton, but she was no light skirt, not really. He could tell the difference.

"I think it best to ease into our arrangement slowly," he murmured, thinking of her reputation. He kissed the wayward fingers, watching her quiver in response. It sent another pulse to his already aching groin. This was going to be a long night. "Your hair has become disheveled." He reached out to deftly smooth an errant curl back into place, and then focused his attention on her gown. "Turn," he commanded, taking her by the shoulder and gently spinning her about.

The midnight silk had become hopelessly rumpled in the back where she had sat upon it. He twitched the wrinkles out as best he could, wetting his fingers to dampen the worst of them here and there. The air would dry it quickly, hopefully allowing the creases to fall out of the material.

"Presentable," he proclaimed, looking her up and down with a critical eye. "No one would ever think you'd been shamelessly kissing me on a rooftop," he teased. In truth, no one who saw her would think anything *but* that she'd been well kissed. Probably more than kissed.

Her swollen lips now twitched with mirth. "I'm glad you find *my* appearance acceptable, Your Grace, but I'm afraid *you* look as if the very devil has been raking his pitchfork through your hair." When she was done taming his wayward locks, she again leaned in to kiss him on the mouth.

Alessandro fought to keep his hands at his sides as she smoothed her hands along the planes of his face, feeling the texture of his skin. He allowed her to explore his mouth at her leisure in a sweet kiss that left him longing for more.

"Thank you," Mélisande whispered.

When she pulled away, his pulse whirred in his ears. He knew she wasn't thanking him for fixing her gown.

"I never like to disappoint a lady," he said, making an effort to sound cavalier. Instead, the words came out in a shaken, gravelly rasp, completely ruining the effect.

Smiling, she turned away. "Come."

Alessandro took a deep, rather unsteady breath and followed. This was going to be extremely challenging. *You know this game; you are a master of it,* he told himself.

She led him to another stair cut into the wall opposite from where they had originally emerged. Before they entered, she paused. "I realize you and I know next to nothing of one another, really. I should like it very much if we could truly become friends."

"I am most happy to hear you say it," he agreed, smiling gently as she moved forward once more. "I look forward to knowing all aspects of you, not merely the physical." Indeed, he realized he wanted far more of her than just her delicious body in his bed.

Again Mélisande paused. "When we reenter, we must act as though we have been in conversation for some time. Do you happen to play chess?"

"I have played since I was a small child. Stamma tells me I have potential." He chuckled, amused at the sudden change in the direction of the conversation.

"Excellent! That will make it easy, then. Everyone knows I'm mad for chess." She grinned. "We'll simply act as if we've been engaged in a private match. No one would dare question me on my whereabouts, at least not directly."

After several minutes of navigating steep stairs and narrow, twisting tunnels, Alessandro heard the muffled murmuring of people.

Mélisande stopped, holding out a hand to prevent him bumping into her. When the coast was clear, she stepped forth, pushing aside a heavy tapestry concealing the opening. They emerged just behind a statue nestled in an alcove off the main hall.

*How appropriate*, Alessandro thought, patting Venus's beautifully sculpted backside with fondness.

Mélisande turned to him, eyes twinkling. He held out his arm, and together they sauntered out of the alcove and into the hall.

"Have you met Philidor?" she asked, quietly starting the conversation.

Intense dislike filled Alessandro. "Indeed," he grumbled. "He visited my father not long after he won his match against Stamma. All he did was talk of his victory and himself."

Few noticed their arrival, and those who did simply noted with raised brows that the couple had been visiting the goddess of love.

"I see you have as little fondness for the man as I," Mélisande murmured, smirking as they blended back into the crush. "He is a narcissistic ass. An excellent strategist when it comes to chess, but a complete waste, otherwise."

"Not that I disagree in the least with your assessment, but how did you come to dislike him so?" He'd heard her issue the challenge earlier that evening and wondered at such ire.

"You don't know?"

He shook his head. "I know only what I heard in the library while you were playing Stamma."

"He boasted of his win over Stamma, belittling his intelligence as well as mine, and then had the audacity to propose a match against me—with my virginity as the stakes. He insulted me in front of everyone, saying I might as well concede before even setting the board because the only games women were fit to play were those of the bedchamber. He was more than a little drunk, and his behavior was completely, inexcusably barbaric."

It sounded exactly like something Philidor might say. The man's opinion of the female sex in general was primitive, at best. Alessandro had to work hard to keep from laughing aloud, for any male who thought of this woman as a mindless bauble was due to have his perspective mightily adjusted; it was only a matter of time.

"And you slapped him?"

"So that my hand ached terribly for several hours afterward," she confirmed with bloodthirsty good cheer.

"An appropriate response," he responded. "I wish I'd been there to see it. And I certainly hope *I* shan't be the recipient of such treatment for my forward behavior," he added softly, stroking the back of her hand where it rested on his arm.

She remained silent, but her lips curled at one corner. Immediately upon entering the upper gallery of the ballroom, she stopped and turned to him. "I must speak with my friends. I'm afraid some of them can be a bit overprotective," she told him. "Naturally, they'll be concerned, but I shall see to it no one calls you out."

"Your thoughtful consideration is much appreciated, as I wish neither myself nor any of your friends to come to harm," he responded, reaching up to stroke a featherlight finger along the line of her jaw.

Her lashes lowered. When Alessandro lifted her chin to capture her gaze once more, the naked desire in her jewellike eyes struck him like a physical blow. He felt it in every fiber of his being, as though he were a great bell that had just been rung.

But in a blink, the moment was gone.

Turning, Mélisande descended the stair, drawing many a second glance from those she passed. It wasn't just her unusual attire that drew their eyes. She'd been awakened and it sang out in the languid movements of her body, a silent summons, as she meandered her way through the crowd.

Alessandro's hands fairly itched as he watched her. There was much to accomplish before he could indulge the impulse. Among other things, he must rent his own residence and move out of Luddy's house. Finding a place this late in the Season would be a real challenge, even outside the fashionable district, which was why he'd agreed to stay in London as Luddy's guest in the first place, but succeed he would.

He also needed to clear the way for their *affaire* to proceed unhindered by her associations. That, he could begin working on immediately. It was time to set the pieces in motion.

# Chapter Eight

## SMOKE AND MIRRORS

AFTER OBSERVING THE LAY OF THE LAND, ALESSANDRO worked his way through the crush to the other side of the gallery where one Lady Angelica Mallowby held court. Surrounded by a crowd of besotted gentlemen, the golden-haired debutante flirted with consummate skill, hiding her becomingly shy smile behind her fan while encouraging her admirers with her eyes.

But he knew her heart wasn't in it. Those cerulean eyes kept straying, searching for something. And Alessandro knew what— or rather *who*, that something was. It was time to use that knowledge to divest the lovely Mélisande of one of her guardians. If Stanton was happily occupied with Lady Angelica, he would be unlikely to interfere in anyone else's affairs.

Sweeping a gallant bow before the young lady, he gave her his most brilliant smile. "I had to see for myself if the rumors were true."

Angelica's eyes widened, but before she could utter so much as a single syllable, her redheaded companion—Lydia, he remembered—cut in. "And you are?" she asked with hauteur.

He stared at her until she blushed. The flood of color was most unbecoming for someone of her complexion. Turning his attention back to Angelica, he softened. "Alessandro Orsini, Duke of Gravina, Emissary of the Roman Curia and Prince of the Holy Roman Empire by order of Charles VI, at your service. I simply had to see for myself," he repeated.

Curiosity won out over good sense. "Of what do you speak, Your Grace?" Angelica asked.

"Why, that one of heaven's own angels had deigned to visit the earth. I was, of course, skeptical of the tale when I heard it, but I now believe it to be quite true. I shall have to inform my superiors." Such worn flattery from a man nearly twice her age ought to make her laugh. Such was his intent, for it was hard to maintain one's defenses when one was amused.

Sure enough, Angelica's lips twitched, her cheeks growing rosy as she fought off an answering smile. But Lydia bent and hissed at her ear again, causing her to start and cast her gaze earthward again.

His eyes narrowed. The copper-haired wench was a problem. Obviously, she was Angelica's most trusted counsel, and he could foresee no means of getting around her. He would have to influence her via one of her other friends.

A pair of enormous lavender-blue eyes set in an elfin face caught his attention. A young lady of good family and meager funds, he immediately surmised, observing her modest gown with its concealing fichu.

*Perfect.*

"May I be so bold as to beg an introduction?" he asked softly, focusing solely on little Miss Lavender Eyes.

The girl flushed, looking to Angelica with a helpless, somewhat horrified expression.

"Oh, of—of course, Your Grace," Angelica stammered, visibly flummoxed over the sudden shift in his attention. "This is my dear friend, Miss Olivia Doulton."

Alessandro suppressed a smile as he made an elegant leg before Miss Doulton, who extended a hand. Hovering just an instant longer than was considered proper, he gently brushed it with his lips.

It was a calculated move. If he was right, and he almost always was when it came to women, she'd never been the recipient of such a bold flirtation.

Indeed, her eyes flew wide at the intimate contact, her blush deepening.

"Miss Doulton, I would be most honored if you would grant me the next dance. That is, of course, provided you are not already spoken for?" he asked with just the right amount of concern in his tone.

Obviously terrified, yet inordinately pleased to suddenly find herself the center of attention, Miss Doulton nodded, rising to take the arm he offered. "I would be delighted, Your Grace."

As he led her past the stares of her dumbfounded friends to the grand staircase, he felt the tremor in her slight form as her heartbeat accelerated. He patted the hand on his arm. "Have no fear, Miss Doulton. I shan't eat you up. I'm not really the big bad wolf."

A smile crept across her features. "I didn't think you were, Your Grace," she replied, then immediately blushed. "Why did you ask me to dance?"

Such directness was unexpected from such a meek miss. "I *was* going to ask Lady Angelica," he said, watching her eyes grow dull (it *was* the answer she'd expected, after all), "but her fiery-haired friend seemed bent on sabotaging my efforts," he chuckled. "And now I fear I shall never be able to deliver Stanton's message. I'm afraid he will be most disappointed."

"You wouldn't happen to be referring to Mr. Reginald Stanton?"

He managed a look of mild surprise. "Why, yes, the very same. Are you acquainted?"

"We've been introduced," she answered. "If you've a message from Mr. Stanton for Lady Angelica, I should be delighted to convey it."

He hesitated, pausing their descent. "I would, but he wished me to tell her directly. It is a matter of utmost secrecy." He lowered his voice. "He would prefer that his interest remain a private matter, you understand."

"I promise to tell only Angelica," she vowed. "I shall wait until we are utterly alone to speak with her."

He gave the appearance of teetering on the brink of an agonizing decision. "I suppose that would suffice, but if he finds out I told anyone other than Lady Angelica, he will be wroth."

Miss Doulton's mouth formed an adorable O and she shook her head a little, denying even the possibility.

"Then you are willing to help me?"

She nodded, and just like that, he had his secret weapon. He resumed their progress down the stair. Leaning close, he whispered, "Reggie—that is, Mr. Stanton—holds Lady Angelica in high esteem. The *very* highest. Being only a viscount's son, he knows he's beneath her," he continued, letting just a little righteous indignation enter his voice, as though upset by the unfairness of it all. "But he simply cannot put aside his tender feelings for her. She has possessed his mind, heart, and soul, and he would do anything to obtain her favor."

He paused a moment before delivering the *coup de grâce*. "Reggie has vowed that if he should somehow win her heart and hand, he will spend every waking moment of the rest of his life ensuring her complete happiness. His affection is unwavering, his intentions most noble and honorable, I assure you."

Her eyes glistened with sudden emotion, and he visualized the jaws of the trap closing around his prey. The tale of Mr.

Stanton's unrequited love was the stuff of romantic dreams and passionate ballads, sure to make any young lady's heart ache.

"Your Grace," she said, her quiet voice all aquiver, "I shall be delighted to convey your message to my friend on Mr. Stanton's behalf."

Reginald Stanton III was as good as bagged! He observed his companion as she struggled for composure. She was a sweet little thing and not at all unpleasant to look at. It was a shame she was cast into shadow by Lady Angelica, really.

It was an ill he could easily remedy.

"You know, Miss Olivia, Lady Angelica may shine brightly, but you have your own beauty," he said quietly, taking the opportunity to use her given name. "Tell me, why do you hide it so?"

Her bottom lip began to tremble, and her eyes filled. "A candle cannot outshine the sun. It's not her fault she is so beautiful," she said sadly. "I have neither the face nor the form to attract such notice, or the means to buy it. Mama says I shall be fortunate indeed to attain any gentleman's regard, and that I must be grateful to Angelica for allowing me to be her companion. She hopes that one of her admirers will look to me as a second choice."

Alessandro reached out and raised her chin with a gentle finger, smoothing away a tear that had traced a path down her cheek.

"Allow me to help you," he said kindly. "I can, you know."

She blushed and again began to tremble.

"I can make them see you for what you really are: a beautiful young woman with much to offer," he tempted. "You would be surprised at how little effort it would take to open their eyes. I know what fascinates my own sex," he persisted in a teasing tone. "You believe your beauty pales beside Lady Angelica's, but I tell you: you are lovely and possess all you need to attract any gentleman's interest."

She stilled, a mouse hypnotized by a serpent's gaze. Her mouth worked soundlessly for a moment before she finally found her voice. "W-why would you wish to help me?"

"Because you are helping my friend find happiness." He meant it; with her assistance, Stanton would be one less thing to worry about during his pursuit of Mélisande. And helping this little girl would be practically effortless. It would be his good deed for the day.

Miss Doulton worked up her courage at last. "How?"

It was that easy. "Take out the fichu," he commanded, stepping in front of her to shield her from view. When she remained frozen in disbelief, he reached out and quick as lightning plucked the offending cloth from her bodice.

A gasp burst forth from Miss Doulton and her hands flew up to cover her exposed décolletage.

A décolletage that Alessandro now noted was not quite as unfortunate as he'd originally thought. He frowned as he looked her up and down. He could do nothing about the unfashionable cut of her gown, but..."Bite your lips," he whispered.

She gaped at him.

"Bite them, or I shall have to make them look kissed," he added, raising a suggestive brow. The threat caused immediate, saucer-eyed compliance, more from anxiety than obedience, he suspected. He nodded with satisfaction as her lips took on a fullness that was sure to arouse male interest.

"Now, we dance." Before she could protest, he propelled her through the crush. His partner proved to be quite graceful on the ballroom floor, even if he had to abbreviate his steps a bit to accommodate her shorter stride.

If her eyes were a little fevered and her cheeks a little flushed, Alessandro knew it was all to the good. Nothing was as enticing to a man as an impassioned woman, and this petite little pixie was fast showing all the signs of becoming quite stirred.

With practiced charm, he maintained eye contact with her the entire time. He knew he was encouraging an infatuation, but it didn't matter. She'd soon be swamped by fascinated men and forget all about him. It was his way of repaying her for helping to remove an obstacle between himself and Mélisande.

## Chapter Nine

### THE ART OF WAR

*M*ÉLISANDE SMILED BRIGHTLY AS SHE APPROACHED THE cluster of gentlemen. David did not smile back. In fact, he didn't even acknowledge her presence at all.

How rude.

Herrington was among those in the gathering. The man glared at her with chilly disdain, and Mélisande matched his cool appraisal, making it obvious she found him somehow lacking. She smiled in satisfaction when he finally excused himself and stalked away.

When the group broke, David offered his arm without a word and began leading her toward the outer hall.

His pace was leisurely, but Mélisande wasn't fooled. He was furious, probably over her partnering with Orsini—*Gravina*, she reminded herself—for the waltz. That was unfortunate, because she really needed his help. There was no way she could do this alone; she simply didn't have the knowledge.

But *he* did. And knowing David as she did, she also knew there was no point in trying to sweeten the reality. With him, the direct approach was always best. David ushered her to the nearest door, checking first to be sure the room was unoccupied before unceremoniously shoving her in.

His eyes when he turned to face her were two chips of ice. She'd seen the look before, although never directed at her. It was the look he wore when facing his father.

A tiny twinge of fear stabbed through her.

He stared her down, his lips thinning to a slash as he waited.

"I want him," she stated, her chin lifting in defiance. "I've wanted him since the day I met him. And I shall have him." She moved to a large gilt mirror on the wall and began adjusting her hair, glancing at him in its reflection.

He lifted a brow.

"It's pointless to argue," she continued, growing cross at his continued silence. "I've no desire for a husband, as you well know, and therefore have no need to preserve my virginity. To even imagine that I would remain pristine until I reach my grave is purely ridiculous." She let out an unladylike snort. "Let us be realistic. It has to happen someday, and now is as good a time as any."

"I will not allow it, Melly. I forbid it."

Mélisande straightened her spine and glared at him in the mirror. "Not *allow*? *Forbid*?" Her voice rang off the walls as she turned to face him. "You, sirrah, shall forbid me nothing! You are neither my guardian nor my keeper!"

David's dark brows collided.

"I never took you for a hypocrite, but now I begin to wonder," she threw at him, working her way up to a full rant. "That you of all people, a complete degenerate, would think to teach me morality is a bloody laugh. If I—"

"I don't propose to teach you anything!" he shot back at her. "That would be impossible, wouldn't it? And even if I did make the attempt, it would be a case of the blind leading the blind, and well I know it. I'm only trying to save you from yourself, damn you!"

"I don't want to be saved!" she hissed. "I know exactly what I do want, however, and it isn't a lecture from you! What I want is out there now, awaiting my return."

"Oh, yes." David nodded, his tone sarcastic. "I can well imagine. He waits for you like a fox waits for a trusting bird to fly into its open jaws! Do you really think you're a match for a seducer like him just because your mother was a courtesan? I can tell you right now, you're not. Choose someone else to practice on, *anyone* else, but not him."

"The decision has been made," she breezed, ignoring his upset. "I intend to take him to my bed tonight."

He strode over to stand only inches away from her, wrath evident in his every movement. But where many men would have backed away, Mélisande stood her ground.

"I'll kill him first."

His voice was chill, like something straight out of a grave. He meant it, she knew. But this was what she wanted, and she'd be damned if anyone, even her dearest friend, would stand in her way.

"Do so, and I shall never forgive you or speak to you again," she vowed just as coldly.

"You are impassioned, Melly. You don't know what—"

"And about bloody time, wouldn't you say? I've only waited five *years* for this to happen!"

"Your judgment is clouded by desire, your logic impaired," he said. "I beg you to rethink this."

She forced herself to respond in a calm, reasonable manner. "I'm thinking clearly for the first time in my life. I know what I want and I *will* have it. And not you, nor anyone or anything else is going to stop me. Now, you can either help me, or you can damn well get out of my way."

"You want me to help you have an *affaire* with Gravina?" he asked with an incredulous bark of laughter. "Surely you don't think I'll damn myself by doing such a thing?"

"You're the only person I know who can teach me how to go about it without getting caught," she calmly replied. "I'm *going* to do this, David, with or without your approval. You may as well give in now, because I'm not going to change my mind."

Silence stretched as they stared at one another.

"One condition," he said at last.

Mélisande raised a brow and mirrored his cross-armed stance, waiting.

"If you get yourself with child, we get married." His tone brooked no argument.

After getting over the initial shock of his offer, Mélisande began to laugh in earnest. "Your motives are admirable, but such gallantry is misplaced. I've long known how to avoid conceiving."

"Nevertheless, I'll have your word."

Rapping her fan on the back of a chair, Mélisande smiled. "I'm not a child anymore, David. I've never asked you or anyone else to fight my battles for me. I'm quite capable of taking care of myself."

David sighed and shook his head. "I understand you wish to retain your autonomy, but this is not just about you. You know what it's like to have the threat of bastardy hanging over your head. Surely you would not expose another innocent to such suffering, whether in secret or otherwise?"

Her stomach roiled. Damn him for knowing exactly how to gouge her conscience!

"If disaster strikes, you *must* come to me immediately," he continued. "No one would question it if we married, and my name would provide a safe haven for both you and the child. I want your word," he demanded again.

Mélisande gritted her teeth. Such a promise was pointless, since she would never need to follow through on it, but she would say the words if it made him cooperate. "Fine. If I find myself in an untenable situation, I'll marry you," she grumbled, fighting the urge to roll her eyes.

"Your promise."

"Yes, yes. Very well. I promise. Now, naturally, I wish to begin as soon as possible," she said, moving on to the more important topic, "but I've no idea how to go about such things. How *do* people conduct *affaires*?"

"You cannot simply jump into this, Melly. It will take careful planning. If you were to choose someone else," he tried again, "someone a bit less…noteworthy, perhaps, you could at least be discreet. But with Gravina, you have little chance of an *affaire* going unnoticed. Go ahead and take a lover. Take *ten*, if it pleases you, but not him!"

The venom in his tone took her by surprise. "You truly despise him, don't you? Why?" she asked, suspicious. "He's done you no wrong."

"You were barely out of nappies."

"I was nearly fifteen!" Mélisande retorted, exasperated. "My parents were already planning my *our*—wedding, for pity's sake. And why should it matter, anyway? You were only twelve when you tupped your bloody governess, and I happen to know she was more than ten years older than you! Besides, he didn't know how old I was. I was dressed in my mother's gown and I didn't exactly announce my age—David, he didn't know!" she insisted, seeing his jaw tighten in rejection of the facts. "I was just as much to blame for his conduct," she admitted. "I kissed him back, after all."

Pinching the bridge of his nose, David sighed. "Couldn't you choose someone *else* to initiate your fall from grace?"

"No," she replied firmly. Gravina was the only one who had ever made her feel *any*thing. She'd waited five years. It could be another ten before anyone else appeared, or it might never happen again. She could not simply let him walk away. If she did, she would regret it the rest of her life.

"He's not so awful, David—you'll see. He's a lot like you, or at least a lot like you *used* to be," she dug at him. "Truthfully, I think we're going to be great friends. He has his redeeming qualities like anyone else. Like you."

He blanched at the comparison. "I can see it's useless trying to convince you to take a safer course."

Her smile broadened. "You ought to know by now that the safer path has never been my lot." Ignoring his baleful glare, she continued. "Now. I believe location should be the first matter addressed."

A sullen mask of resignation settled over David's features, and she knew she'd won.

"The gentleman usually does the arranging," he told her. "In this case, however," he cut in before she could voice her protest, "I believe it would be to your advantage to retain control over the logistics. You'll need to rent a house. It should be modest, nondescript, and in an area unfrequented by those who move within our level of society."

Mélisande's mind leapt ahead. "It will need to be furnished and maintained. I'll have to make purchases, hire staff," she mused, "but I cannot suddenly begin making property inquiries and looking at furnishings, can I? Everyone would know within the day, and if they found out I was equipping a second town residence..."

"Indeed," David replied. "You'll need an agent to do it for you. I would avoid using anyone familiar. Maintaining anonymity is going to be of the utmost importance."

Even as he said it, she knew it was impossible. Her voice and features were unmistakable. If she wore a veil to obscure her face, there was still her height and bearing, and of course it would all be over the moment she spoke. The more she thought about it, the more dangerous it seemed. She was an unwed, wealthy countess. An unscrupulous agent would most certainly threaten her with blackmail.

She told him her thoughts. "But," she added, her enthusiasm returning, "*men* make such arrangements all the time with no difficulty at all. If *you* were to do it, your solicitor would think you were merely setting up another mistress." She waited anxiously, knowing that what she was asking was very nearly beyond the pale, even for David.

"Fine. I'll do it," he snapped, glaring. "But only to save your fool's hide from being lauded as a strumpet across the whole of England! Melly, you truly have *no* appreciation for the dangers involved in this insane decision! Even if you manage to avoid conceiving out of wedlock, there are other considerations. Society's appetite for scandal knows no bounds. If you are exposed, it will be their meat and bread for a year and a day."

"I'm quite used to being the subject of speculation." Mélisande laughed.

"Not the kind I speak of. There are certain aspects of your family's history that will not bear close examination. All it would take is a French seamstress or lady's maid with a vague memory of your mother's surname to trigger disaster. If someone were to uncover your mother's involvement with Louis, you could lose everything."

Not wanting him to back out, Mélisande proceeded carefully. "Even *if* someone questioned my legitimacy, what proof is there? I cannot be disinherited on the basis of supposition and rumor."

"Perhaps not. But even so, that rumor would haunt you and your children for the rest of your lives. People would always wonder."

"I have very great appreciation for the danger, David, and I understand what's at stake—truly I do—but even you must agree that after so long, the possibility of an inquiry pertaining to my legitimacy is remote, at best." She waited half a heartbeat before continuing. "I assure you I shall be the soul of discretion. And I am most grateful for your assistance. You are quite correct in that I have not the faintest idea how to arrange something of this nature. I would soon be lost without your guidance."

"Wonderful. You're thanking me for helping you become a harlot."

"David—"

He shook his head and sighed. "Never mind me. I'll learn to live with my choices, just the same as you. For good or ill."

"Then, you'll help?" She waited.

"You'll need to hire a coach and driver, as well as servants to maintain the residence," he said at last. "I know several trustworthy, reliable people, provided you are willing to pay well," he said pointedly. "Secrecy comes at a high price."

"Money is no object," she replied briskly, glad he was finally cooperating. "What else?" At his queer expression, she drew in a deep breath and rested her hands on her hips. "David, I *must* know how it's done. I can't expect you to manage things for me the entire time, and I don't imagine you wish to do so, either."

"You'll need to watch yourself on your arrivals and departures. Arrange to have the coachman drive around to the carriage house at least an hour before you intend to leave, as if you are having a visitor. Board there, and be sure the curtains are drawn before leaving. Disembark under cover at your destination, as well—not around front. And be sure to return before dawn, when there will be fewer people about on the streets to see an unmarked carriage arriving at your gate."

The need for secrecy was paramount. As a man, David could come and go as he pleased and never worry about his activities attracting undue interest. Mélisande knew she did not have that freedom.

"You'll need to arm your driver, as well," he added. "He should double as a bodyguard. It'll cost a goodly sum to secure such loyalty, but it'll be absolutely necessary if you're to be trotting about town in the wee hours. And you should also carry a pistol and be prepared to use it," he said with a hard stare. "Your carriage may be accosted by thieves. Terrible things can happen to women who travel alone at night, Melly."

"I shall carry two," she told him. "I've no compunction about killing a man should he enter my carriage uninvited." And she didn't. Anyone who dared attack her deserved to be shot. "Papa taught us how to shoot together, remember?"

"Indeed. You can always flee to the Colonies, if things don't go well," he said with heavy sarcasm. "God knows if anyone can survive in that beastly backwater, it's you. Now, you'll need new clothes," he continued, ticking off a finger. "They should be modest, but of good cut and material."

He ticked off another finger. "Carry very little money, only enough to secure the services of a runner and hire a coach."

A third finger. "Remain veiled while traveling and never under any circumstances become separated from your driver for any reason," he stressed. "And keep the curtains drawn at all times when meeting with your…" He stopped awkwardly.

"I understand," she told him, nodding. She'd put him in a terrible position with her request, but there was no alternative. "I must remain anonymous," she prompted.

"At *all* costs," he again adjured. "Flirt as outrageously as you please in public, only make certain no one catches you acting upon those flirtations beyond a certain point. Anything up to a modest kiss is acceptable without any real danger of reprisal. But if you get caught with your skirts up, God help you."

Mélisande raised a brow. "And what should I tell him?" she asked. "If the male usually does all the arranging, mightn't he be annoyed?"

"He should be bloody well delighted at having to bear neither the responsibility nor the cost!" David spat. "After all, you've made it easy for him, haven't you? All he has to do is show up!"

Mélisande arched a brow. "If you would rather I did this on my own...?" She might have to trust Gravina's skill and discretion, after all. The thought did not please her, but there was little other choice if David decided to renege.

"No," David replied, rubbing his head. "No. You'd be sure to commit some disastrous blunder, it being your first time. You need someone to show you how to conduct your *affaires* with some discretion."

"My first time? You speak as if I plan to make a habit of this," Mélisande laughed, uncomfortable with the insinuation.

"Don't you?" he asked, fixing her with an intent stare. "As you said, *let us be realistic*," he drawled. "Once one has enjoyed the delights of Eros, it is but a matter of time before one seeks those delights again. It's an addictive pleasure, Melly. And as you've no wish to marry the man, you *will* repeat your current course of action in the future."

Mélisande's cheeks heated under his mocking gaze. "I've no plans to become a courtesan, if that's what you're insinuating!"

"Perhaps not intentionally, but once you cross the line, things will look quite different from the other side, I assure you." His shoulders lifted in a gesture of surrender. "If, for whatever reason, you choose to follow in your mother's footsteps, I must take responsibility for my part in it and help you as I can to avoid the worst of the dangers involved."

Mélisande drew herself up to her full height, eyes flashing. "I am a countess, David. And a bloody wealthy one, at that! I've no need to sell my favors for money or advancement. And nor did my mother. She was of noble birth and *chose* to become mistress to a king! She certainly didn't sell herself to the highest bidder!"

David's smile was full of irony. "Not all courtesans are in it for gain, Melly. There are those who do it purely for pleasure. Look at Lady Sutterfield, for example."

"Lady Sutterfield? A libertine?" Mélisande laughed. That particular matron was a highly respected widow—and one of *her* most vocal critics.

"Oh, indeed." David's smile turned wolfish. "I know for a fact the lady maintains several lovers simultaneously and participates in all *sorts* of naughty indulgences. Yet she's respected by everyone because she maintains the appearance of strict propriety. It's a lie, and a damned good one." He chuckled with clear appreciation. "She plays the part of a proper, chaste lady in public and keeps her debauchery quiet. That I'm telling you this violates a promise I made her years ago, but I trust you'll hold your tongue."

The very idea of Lady Sutterfield engaging in anything even remotely resembling rampant debauchery was preposterous, but looking in his eyes, Mélisande knew he was telling the truth.

"She *never* flaunts her peccadilloes," David continued, "and the gentlemen she takes to her bed never reveal her secrets. She's exceedingly selective and unerringly discreet. You must cultivate the same qualities if you expect to remain socially acceptable." He paused. "So many people lead double lives, Melly. If you knew the secrets some people keep, you'd be unable to look them in the eye. And you rub shoulders with them practically every day, you go to their balls, their parties." He gave her a long look. "You even call some of them your friends."

*He means himself.*

She swallowed past the dryness in her throat. This was the David she'd heard talk of in dark whispers. This was his other life, the life he'd never allowed her to see. It was one thing to hear of his dissipation via the gossiping tongues of others; it was another entirely to hear *him* speak of it. It was disconcerting, to say the least.

"The truth remains hidden because they—*we*," he amended, "all follow the same unwritten law: do as you like behind closed doors, but never parade your indulgences publicly or you'll be ostracized by the very same people secretly committing the same, or worse, sins. That's the world in which we live, Melly. That's the world of which you will become part, if you do this."

Mélisande's mind whirled. Not only was her view of David rapidly changing, but her view of herself, as well. If this *affaire* was just a one-time occurrence, a mere fling before settling down, she could see it through to its natural end in relative safety. But if it wasn't, if her passionate nature was permanently awakened, then she must be prepared to accept the consequences. She must be prepared to don the mantle of deceit permanently, like Lady Sutterfield.

"No wonder you are so jaded," she muttered. "Do you know many? Courtesans, I mean?" He grinned. "Have you never wondered why my father has been so *very* furious with me all these years?"

"I've overheard him call you a bloody wastrel several times," she said with a laugh that made her sound far older than her years. "He told Papa you spent monstrous amounts of money while living the prodigal life here in London. Said you'd drive the family into bankruptcy with your penchant for gambling hells and other unsavory pursuits."

All traces of humor left David's face. "I haven't touched the family coffers since before we broke our engagement. He lies to cover the shame of having a son with an unseemly habit of playing the merchant—and what's worse, successfully. I think he could forgive me if I'd failed miserably in my ventures, but I'm afraid I've managed to make enough money to sustain myself in comfort and completely annoy him. And I intend to make a great deal more. As for my other 'unsavory pursuits,' " he added, "I've kept several mistresses over the years, openly supporting each in what some have called obscene luxury."

His smile returned, but it was a vicious expression. "My father's henchmen keep him well informed, and I delight in giving them interesting news. Nothing pleases me better than to give them a good, rousing show. The overt presentation of some lavish bauble or a new coach and four to my current mistress, for instance. I usually receive a howling missive from him within a month or so of such an act. I quite enjoy reading them over breakfast; I find it aids the digestion."

Mélisande couldn't help laughing, in spite of her shock. "I knew you'd led a rather wayward life, David, but I never imagined. Truly, I thought you'd gained your reputation mostly through overblown gossip."

"Whatever rumors you've heard are probably watered down."

"And yet you'd help me enter into such a life?" she asked with some doubt.

"Melly"—he sighed, crossing his arms—"as your friend, of course I would prefer you take a different path. But as you so quickly pointed out, I really have no say in the matter, do I? And, as your friend, it would be unthinkable of me to allow you to ruin yourself out of ignorance if I can prevent it. Thus, my knowledge is at your disposal, even if it pains me to give it. Believe me when I say that never in my most demented dreams did I ever imagine tutoring *you* in the art of clandestine immorality."

Her eyes were sharp and clear as she spoke. "I thank you for your sacrifice, David. You are a true friend, and it means a great deal to have your support."

"I admit, I'd hoped to change your mind with the brutal truths," he said, "but so be it."

"I had not realized it would be so very complicated," she mused, chewing her lip. "I cannot take him to my bed tonight. It shall have to wait until the proper arrangements can be made. But," she said, giving him a knowing look, "do not think that I shall wait too long."

"I'll contact my solicitor in the morning. One more thing, Melly," he added. "If Gravina should decide not to be discreet, you *will* have a problem, one that will most likely require a duel to resolve. Naturally, I shall be the one to challenge him. If that happens, everyone will expect us to marry. Am I clear?" he asked, raising a brow.

"Only if there is a child to consider," she answered. "That was the bargain. If there is no child, there will be no marriage."

"You would rather be branded a harlot than marry me?" he asked, unbelieving. "Am I so very repugnant, then?"

"One would almost think you *wanted* to marry me," she said, crossing her arms and fixing him with a frank stare.

A scathing snort burst from his lips. "I have no desire for you, Melly," he answered. "I'll not deny that you are one of the most beautiful women in England, but I might as well be a eunuch where you are concerned. You are, however, my closest friend, and I have no wish to see you miserable. As I pointed out years ago, if we married, we could lead entirely separate lives. You could do as you liked and I would care not. Many marriages are so arranged. Most, in fact."

"And what of heirs?"

"I've no desire for children of my own, as you well know. The blood in my veins is far more tainted than yours could ever be, for all my legitimacy," he said bitterly. "As odd as it may sound, I'd welcome a cuckoo and treat him or her as my own. I'd be a good father to your children and a good husband to you, if in name only." He grinned suddenly, mirth returning to his features. "It'd be a nasty knock to my father, although the old bastard would never know it. That alone might make it worth it."

Mélisande released the breath she'd been holding. "You're not your father, you know," she blurted, knowing she was treading on delicate ground. "You're nothing like him. Just because he's—"

"I may not be like him, but we share the same blood. I will not risk history repeating itself through me."

"And what if you met a woman you could truly love? Would you not resent being bound to me?"

A grim smile twisted his lips. "It'll never happen, Melly. I simply haven't the heart for romance. You of all people know that."

"I guess we're both too pragmatic for sentimentality," she replied softly, thinking of her own parents' imperfect marriage. The clock on the mantelpiece caught her eye. "It's getting late. We'd best return."

"Indeed. Before we, too, provide grist for the gossip mill. I'll see to the arrangements we discussed. And I'll draw from my own accounts to pay for it," he added. "The less of a trail you leave behind you the better. You can pay me back later."

He turned to leave, but before he could open the door, Mélisande interrupted.

"David?"

"What now?"

She paused awkwardly. "We've been friends for as long as I can remember, and I want you to know I'm very glad for it. Thank you. For everything."

He smiled, a genuine smile with no hint of mockery or cynicism lurking beneath it. "Again, what I'm doing shouldn't in any way warrant your gratitude, Melly. If I wasn't already marked for hell's flames, I soon will be, for I'm as good as handing you straight to the devil. All the same, I'm glad for your friendship, as well. We're a terrible pair, aren't we?"

# *Chapter Ten*

## OH, WHAT A TANGLED WEB

"MELLY!" ALESSANDRO EXCLAIMED, STEPPING FORWARD to greet her. As anticipated, everyone in earshot turned. Naturally, they would expect such familiarity from her contemporaries, but not from a newcomer like him.

Disengaging herself from her escort, Mélisande's gaze slid over to the young woman whose side he'd just left. "You've acquired another admirer, I see," she murmured as he kissed her hand.

Though her tone was amused, he knew better than to leave any room for doubt. "A new ally in a good cause," he whispered for her ears alone, giving her fingers a reassuring squeeze before releasing her. "Ah, Pelham, I was wondering if you might be interested in a round of primero tonight? I'm told you're an excellent player."

"I'd be delighted, but I'm afraid I have other obligations this evening. Perhaps later this week?" answered Pelham.

*That* certainly raised a few eyebrows, Alessandro noted. "I shall look forward to it," he replied.

"Perhaps Melly might like to join us," Pelham added, turning to her. "It's been a while since we played. We can invite Stanton and Charlotte, too."

"What a wonderful idea," Mélisande exclaimed. "I'm having a little party this Thursday evening, and I'm certain we can manage to squeeze in a round or two beforehand if you come early. It's been far too long since I gave you a good drubbing."

"I shall prepare my last will and testament," muttered Pelham.

"I'm not *that* good!" laughed Mélisande.

Pelham snorted. "Woe to the man who believes it. He'll soon find himself destitute."

"Let us hope she at least lets us depart with our dignity intact, if not our purses," Alessandro chimed in, shooting her a teasing glance.

A small sound at his elbow told him that Miss Doulton had at last gathered her courage. "Ah, but I am remiss in my manners!" he said, turning. "My friends, allow me to introduce Miss Olivia Doulton, an acquaintance of our own Mr. Stanton. Miss Doulton, this is Lady Wilmington and Lord Pelham."

Looking to Mélisande, he waited. Familiarity with a woman of Mélisande's rank would be a high mark in Miss Doulton's favor and greatly increase her chances of finding a moneyed husband. A girl of her means was unlikely to get another opportunity like this, and gratitude, he'd found, was a highly useful tool.

"I'm very pleased to make your acquaintance, my lady," Miss Doulton said, curtsying.

"Please—call me Melly."

"Miss Doulton was just asking me about the waltz," Alessandro continued. "She is quite interested in learning it. I told her you might be willing to share the name of your instructor."

"Indeed yes," Mélisande answered, seeming to catch on. "Perhaps you'd like to come to tea Thursday and we can discuss it?"

The girl beamed. "Why, thank you. I accept your gracious invitation."

"I look forward to it," Mélisande told her with a smile. "I'm also having a party that evening and several of my friends are coming early for a few rounds of chess and cards. Do you play?"

Alessandro had to refrain from chuckling aloud at the audible sighs of envy that issued forth from the fringe of onlookers. He was most pleased indeed.

"I do, my la—I mean Melly," Miss Doulton corrected herself, continuing only after receiving a slight nod of approval from her new acquaintance. "I play whist and have recently begun to learn chess. Unlike your ladyship, I'm afraid I'm not very good yet," she admitted.

"Well, practice makes perfect, after all," Mélisande replied, her manner indulgent. "The only way to improve is to play. I'll play a round or two with you myself and then match you with an appropriate partner, if you like," she offered. The smile she received in answer could have lit the whole of Kensington Palace. "Come at two, then. And I expect *you* to be there early, as well," she told Pelham.

"I shall arrive at dawn, armed and ready," came the man's droll response.

Ignoring his sarcasm, Mélisande cocked her head. "I believe they just announced the next dance, a *sarabande*. One of your favorites, is it not?" she asked Pelham too brightly, her eyes conveying an indisputable command as they flicked over to Miss Doulton.

Pelham's eyes sparkled with humor. "Actually, I thought y—"

"I'm already obligated somewhere else or I'd claim you myself," Mélisande interrupted him, "but I'm *sure* there are other ladies in need of a partner." Her smile broadened, her eyes narrowing.

Watching the interplay, Alessandro got the distinct impression that Pelham would pay through the nose if he refused. Apparently, Pelham interpreted her look the same way, as well, for he turned to the lady in question with a smile.

"Miss Doulton, I would be honored if you would grant me this next dance," Pelham murmured, darting a black look at Mélisande just before Miss Doulton looked up at him in surprise.

"I would be delighted, Lord Pelham," the girl replied a little breathlessly.

Alessandro smiled at Mélisande's handling of the situation. She'd quite neatly transferred the burden of Miss Doulton's affection from him to Pelham, who would undoubtedly shift it to some more deserving soul later that evening.

Mélisande now turned to him with a look that heated the blood in his veins. "Shall we retire to the library for that rematch?" she suggested.

"Indeed, I should like a chance to reclaim my dignity."

Her smile was feline. "I admit our last game wasn't really fair, seeing that the conditions under which we played were to my distinct advantage. Perhaps this time I should give you the first move."

Alessandro grinned at her double entendre. "I thank you for the generous offer, but I require no handicap to take you, my lady."

Before she could respond with more than a low chuckle, they were interrupted by the arrival of Stanton and his sister. Alessandro greeted them, praying Miss Doulton had the good grace to hold her tongue, for Stanton would not look kindly on him for meddling in his private affairs.

As he watched, he noted another interesting interaction taking place: Stanton's sister, Miss Charlotte, appeared rather put out at the sight of Miss Doulton hanging at Pelham's elbow. Indeed, her gaze could have frozen the Thames. Casting a surreptitious glance at Pelham, he noted the man's eyes were fastened on her.

The instant Charlotte looked at him, however, Pelham affected a look of supreme indifference.

*Most interesting indeed.*

The new arrivals inspired the group to continue making small talk for several minutes, until Pelham excused himself and Miss Doulton from the conversation in order to dance.

Alessandro seized the opportunity. "Our game, my lady?"

"Indeed, yes," Mélisande responded with enthusiasm.

"You shall not defeat me this time, dear Countess," he said for everyone's benefit. "Fortune has surely forgiven me by now and returned to favor me."

"Oh? Perhaps a small wager is in order," she taunted.

"And what would you wager?"

They were out of earshot now, and her smile turned naughty. "A forfeit. One to be determined at the time and place of the winner's choosing."

"A dangerous bet, my lady. You know not what concession I might claim."

Her lips curved upward, the motion slow and provocative. "The prize might be dangerous indeed—for you."

Heads turned as he laughed aloud, but he paid them no mind. Their progress through the throng was avidly watched. Some faces were friendly and admiring, but many were tight with disapproval. He noted that Mélisande met every stare with a pleasant smile, forcing an embarrassed dropping of eyes from those inclined to be disagreeable.

Admiration filled him. Many, if not most, women would have quailed beneath some of those withering looks, yet she remained unruffled. It spoke volumes about her backbone. Along with everything else he'd discovered about her, he found her courage attractive.

At last they left the crowded ballroom for quieter halls. Instead of stopping at the door to the library, however, he led

Mélisande past it and around the corner where he turned, pulling her into his arms.

Alessandro savored the feel of her as she melted against him, her lips parting. His tongue teased and taunted, dipping into the warm well of her mouth, emulating a more primal rhythm that incited them both. The hunger that possessed him would never be sated with a mere kiss, no matter how passionate, but it was a beginning.

With every shared breath, his desire grew. His cock was swelling, again straining against confinement. He *must* stop. If he didn't, he'd pick her up and carry her to his chamber, and then there would be no salvaging the situation. With regret, he pulled back, feeling her tremble with the uneven pace of her breath. "We must find a way to be together soon, *amora*."

Cautiously, Mélisande poked her head back around the corner, making certain no one was there to overhear before whispering, "I shall have an address for our liaisons within the week."

She reached up to smooth back his hair where she'd mussed it, and her touch sent a tremor through Alessandro. He wanted nothing more than to fling her to the floor right there in the hall. Then her words sank in, and surprise jerked him back from the brink. "You wish to make the arrangements?"

"Was I not the one who proposed this *affaire*?" she asked, lifting a brow. "Once I have procured a suitable place, we may begin our…association."

Reaching across the gap between them, he traced her gown's neckline. "Let us hope the arrangements do not take very long." If it took more than a fortnight, a very important bit of his anatomy would suffer permanent petrifaction. *Dio*, how he ached!

For a long moment, the air between them fairly shimmered with heat. But before it could go any further, a noise from around the corner snapped them both back into awareness.

Alessandro moved them around the corner as if they'd been taking an innocent stroll to look at the art decorating the length of the hall. "I find this one somewhat disturbing," he said, stopping to stare at a depiction of a woman being beheaded. Despite the fact that the headsman's axe was poised to strike the death-blow, the lady's expression was one of eerie serenity. It was titled *The Thornless Rose.*

"Why on earth would anyone choose to display such a horrid thing?" Mélisande exclaimed with quiet revulsion.

Their audience was a pair of young ladies. Even at a distance, Alessandro immediately recognized one of them. There could be no mistaking the pile of fiery red curls that bobbed as Lady Lydia Hampton bent to whisper in her companion's ear.

A soft, high-pitched titter echoed back down the hall.

Ignoring it, the couple ducked into the library to join the others in games until the last dance. They'd be safe from prying eyes there.

The moment the door closed behind them, Mélisande seemed to relax. The sight of Stamma hunched over a chessboard by the fire brought a smile to her lips.

He looked up as they entered, his face brightening.

"No, don't get up," Mélisande called, waving him back down.

The chair opposite was empty. In fact, there were very few people in the room. A trio of gentlemen played cards at another table and a footman stood nearby. Otherwise, the place was deserted. Taking the seat across from her friend, she observed the board.

Alessandro noted that he'd laid out the pieces to replicate his game with Philidor.

"I see you're still ruminating over that old game," Mélisande grumbled, wriggling deep into the thickly padded chair. Her shoes dropped to the floor one by one as she tucked her feet beneath her skirts, relaxing against the back of the chair with a long, contented sigh.

Alessandro smiled inwardly, finding her blatant disregard for convention endearing. Apparently, Stamma was used to her contrary behavior as well, for the man didn't even bat an eyelash. Flashing his opponent a brief smile, the master reached out to move the white king's side bishop.

Mélisande took over for black and made her move, a deliberate variation from the game Philidor had played.

For a long while, the only sounds were those of the pieces clicking across the board, the fire crackling in the hearth, and the low murmurs of the men playing cards in the corner. They played twice more. By checkmate of their third game, several more people had trickled silently into the room to watch.

Throughout, Mélisande made no move to adjust her dress or posture. She appeared completely at ease, curled into her chair with her toes peeping out from beneath the edge of her gown, a faint smile playing about her mouth as she pitted her wits against those of her renowned opponent.

The fact that she was able to comfortably ignore her observers and concentrate well enough to win the last game spoke to the sharpness and self-discipline of her mind. Alessandro was again impressed.

Stamma broke the long silence. "That was a new strategy, Melly. I wasn't aware you'd been studying other styles of play."

She smiled sweetly, giving him an impish wink. "It is always good to study the paths one's enemy tends to take, the better to catch him in an ambush."

The men in the room chuckled, including Stamma. Just then a footman entered and announced the last dance of the evening would be played in one quarter of an hour.

Mélisande uncoiled, reaching down for her shoes, but Alessandro got to them first. Quick as lightning he snatched them away, eyes twinkling as he knelt at her feet.

"May I?"

"Am I Cendrillon, then?" she laughed. "And are you my prince?"

"I am indeed, but I need no crystal slipper to lead me to my heart's desire," Alessandro whispered, grinning as he grasped one of her slim ankles. Gently, he slid the shoe onto her slender foot with a bold caress.

Eyes afire, Mélisande lifted her other foot.

Stamma chattered on about chess and some of the personages he'd met on his travels throughout Europe, ignorant of the fact that neither of his companions were listening to a word he said.

Back in the ballroom, they found Pelham, Stanton, and Miss Charlotte chatting with Lady Angelica and Miss Doulton. The mischief Alessandro had set into motion was already coming to fruition, for Angelica gazed at Reggie with calf eyes, while her little lavender-eyed friend looked at Pelham as if she'd like to eat him with a spoon. When her would-be rival grew distracted by their approach, he noted how Charlotte took the opportunity to station herself at Pelham's side. By the time Miss Doulton took note, her stealthy takeover was *fait accompli*.

Mélisande nudged Alessandro gently.

"But what of you?" he whispered, a sharp stab of disappointment piercing him at the thought of having to give up even a single moment with her.

Her lips firmed in denial, condemning him to the sacrifice. At the last minute, however, he was saved by an eager young man who boldly broached their circle to beg the privilege of Miss Doulton's last dance.

With one last regretful glance at Pelham, the girl accepted.

Alessandro floated Mélisande through the steps of the quadrille, the music swirling around them, the colors and sounds of the ball blending as in a dream until all they could see was each other. The last note sang out on the violin strings, and while everyone else called praises to the host and hostess, the pair slipped out onto the terrace.

The air was cool and crisp, a welcome relief from the swelter and closeness of the ballroom. Together they breathed in the fresh air, listening to the haunting cries of the peacocks calling from the lawn, watching the footmen put out the lanterns lining the garden paths. One by one, the lights winked out like stars fleeing the dawn, leaving only darkness behind.

"I would like to call on you tomorrow."

"People will think you're courting me if you call so soon after tonight's display," she teased, her lips curving.

"Would that be so bad?" The words had slipped out before he'd had a chance to think them through. What had possessed him to say such a thing? He barely knew her, and what he did know made his question seem very foolish indeed. She'd made it clear she didn't *want* a husband. "It would most certainly save us a great deal of trouble, should we ever be caught in a compromising situation," he added, attempting to justify himself. "And when you tire of my company, you may publicly toss me out on my ear."

"We will not *be* caught," she assured him. "If you wish to call at my residence, you may, but I think it better for you to do so as a friend, like David or Monsieur Stamma. If people thought I'd accepted you as a suitor, I would have every unmarried man in England knocking on my door all over again," she grumbled. "We must be discreet. I'll begin making arrangements immediately."

"I look forward to the day," Alessandro murmured. "However"—he moved in behind her—"should you find yourself unwilling to wait until that time arrives, simply send word and I shall call at your window."

"First I was Cendrillon, now I am to be Juliet? Alas, my dear Romeo, I believe climbing the trellis an unnecessary risk to both your neck and my reputation. A suitable location will be ready within the week, a place where we may take our time in comfort and privacy."

Alessandro knew when to concede. The message was clear: she wanted to be in control. He smiled softly into the darkness. "Until tomorrow, then, Countess," he said, taking her hand from the railing to place a soft kiss on its palm before laying it over his arm and leading her back inside to find her companions.

Every time his eyes met Mélisande's as they awaited the carriage, he felt a silent calling between them. It sang in his blood and hummed in his bones.

Finally it was time. She smiled back at him as he handed her up into the carriage, her eyes twin glimmers of torchlight reflected back at him from the darkness. The footman shut the door, and in a clatter of hooves and creaking of wheels, she was gone.

Another pair of eyes followed Mélisande's departure: eyes filled with cold fury. Jaw clenched, Herrington turned before Gravina could catch him staring.

She deliberately taunted him, luring other men into her nets while snubbing only him.

Slowly, breath by breath, serenity reinstated itself. Let the temptress shake her feathers with her ridiculous Italian plaything, for now. Once his suspicions were proven to be truth, her little game would be over. Then the witch'd have to play according to *his* rules.

He had only to wait for word from Whitehurst. The ship should reach France by the end of the week. Once his man reached Versailles, it was only a matter of time.

## Chapter Eleven

### PLANS WITHIN PLANS

ÉLISANDE COUNTED THE SECONDS AS THEY ROLLED away from Ludley's house. Any moment now...

"Melly, I was thinking perhaps Charlie might stay with Reggie and me for the remainder of the Season," David said, his tone casual. "Your offer to oversee her debut was a generous one, and I know you enjoy each other's company, but it may be better for her to remain under her brother's care, considering recent developments."

"Allow me to reassure you that Charlotte's interests remain paramount in my considerations," Mélisande replied. She knew exactly why David was making such an offer, and it nettled. Though she might be putting her *own* future at risk, she had no intention of risking Charlotte's.

Perhaps it might not be so bad if people thought Alessandro a legitimate suitor after all. As long as he behaved himself appropriately, no one would be the wiser. Her own reputation might suffer a bit from the appearance of blind stupidity, but she would be excused for having had a temporary lapse of judgment over a handsome face. It was a perfectly acceptable price to pay to preserve Charlotte's good name.

And when it was time, she'd do exactly as he'd suggested and toss him to the dogs in front of God and all of creation.

Her mind worked, piecing the plan together. As long as their public interactions were conducted with all due propriety, it would work. If he ever grossly misbehaved, however, she'd have no choice but to end all visible association. A chaperone who allowed a man to take liberties with her person might signify a possible lack of chastity in her charge, and that was something she could not allow. The stain of such a scandal would never be fully washed off.

"Should the circumstances warrant it, I swear to you that I will *ask* that Charlotte be removed from my house," Mélisande countered. "I will request her relocation before I allow my actions to endanger her good name. You have my word. I have no desire to be the cause of her ruination."

"Ruination?" asked Charlotte. "Reggie, David—what on earth is she talking about?"

In the pitch black of the carriage's interior, Mélisande touched the tip of her slipper to David's foot in warning. "His Grace has asked permission to court me, Charlotte. And I have given it. His reputation is the source of David's concern."

"But, but—you hardly know the man!" Charlotte gasped. "You've only just met! How can you even consider accepting?"

"Actually, I met him years ago, in Versailles." Mélisande patted the concerned little hand that had found its way onto her arm. "Upon meeting again tonight, we discovered our feelings for one another remain unchanged."

Charlotte's mouth hung open. "You never mentioned an unrequited love to me."

Mélisande winced at her assumption of love, but let it go. "My parents had commanded me to stay away from him, Charlotte. I was terrified that he would speak of me to his friends and reveal my disobedience, so I gave him a false surname. Then I couldn't figure out how to tell him the truth. We left Versailles so quickly that I never had a chance to do so. I dared not tell Maman and Papa about him. I held my tongue out of cowardice."

"How awful," whispered Charlotte.

"He told me tonight that once he realized I was gone, he searched for me, but to the few people in Versailles who knew of my existence, I was Mademoiselle Compton, not d'Orleans." Mélisande patted Charlotte's hand again, laughing a little. "I can only guess that heaven must intend for us to be together, for Providence has reunited us against all odds. I could not accept his proposal immediately, of course, but I have given him permission to court me."

"And how do you intend to avoid Charlotte's becoming caught up in your scandalous romance?" David interrupted, spoiling the moment. "The man's reputation is well-known."

"Really, David, you worry overmuch," Mélisande answered, wanting to throttle the sarcasm right out of him. "As long as he behaves properly, there is no danger. I shall speak with him and explain the situation. He is a gentleman, and I'm certain he shall conduct himself appropriately."

David's disbelieving chuckle sounded across the blackness. "It isn't his *behavior* that concerns me, Melly. He's predictable, at best. However, your actions tonight, specifically your little disappearing act, bespoke an extreme lack of good judgment," he admonished. "You'll be lucky if you aren't painted a strumpet in tomorrow's papers."

"Word of his suit should remedy any untoward presumptions," Mélisande countered. "As for my conduct, I shall be a paragon of proper behavior, I assure you."

David's soft, derisive laughter floated back to her from the shadows. "Yes, I can well imagine. But you'd best be careful when *not* in public, as well. If you get caught—"

"Then *I* shall deal with the consequences!" Mélisande aimed a swift kick at his shin with the pointed toe of her jewel-encrusted shoe. His responding grunt of pain was most satisfying.

"What do you mean 'get caught'?" asked Charlotte.

Much to everyone's surprise, Reggie answered her. "They intend to become lovers, Charlotte. *Before* the wedding takes place."

"Reggie," began Mélisande, "I don't think it quite—"

At the same time, David growled, "That *isn't* precisely how I'd have p—"

"What difference does it make?" Charlotte's irritated voice rose above the hubbub. "They are to be married, after all."

"What difference?" exclaimed her brother, sounding much put out. "Clearly, our mother left *several* gaps in your education. Important ones!"

"Winifred's sister told her that it's quite common for couples to indulge in certain intimacies before the vows are spoken," Charlotte said in an urbane manner, dismissing his concerns.

"Winifred's sister is a complete—"

"Why should Melly be held to a different standard than half the people we know, including our own parents?" she continued, ignoring him. "I *can* count, you know. A few years ago, I realized your birthday came a good deal earlier than it ought. By some two months, I believe. I'm no fool to believe you were simply 'eager for this world,' as mother put it when I asked."

"Charlotte." His voice had taken a definite edge.

"I know you think me a sheltered ninny, Reggie, but the truth is that I'm not nearly as ignorant as you think. I've grown up with you and David, after all," she laughed, sounding far older than her years.

"I'm not entirely sure what you mean, Charlotte, but if you imply that I have been anything less than a shining example of gentlemanly behavior in your presence, I shall take great offense,"

Reggie huffed. "And if you imply that Pelham has behaved inappropriately, I shall be forced to call him out, so think carefully before you speak."

"I imply nothing of the sort," Charlotte admonished. "Reggie, I've been hearing of David's adventures since I was ten. Our parents whispered about his behavior when they thought I wasn't listening, my friends have relayed all manner of interesting tales, and if that isn't enough, his mistresses were the talk of the powder room at tonight's ball! At least until the waltz," she added peevishly.

She struck the final blow before he could counter. "You ought to know your *own* conduct of late hasn't been viewed favorably, either. Winifred told me tonight that your reputation is almost as bad as David's now."

"*Me?*" Reggie sputtered. "What have I ever done that could possibly even *begin* to measure with Pelham's level of degeneracy? If you're going to make comparisons, choose someone other than the devil himself for my rival!"

"Have a care," said David.

"You bloody well know it's true!" Reggie retorted.

"How either of you can dare criticize Melly for falling in love is beyond reason!" Charlotte shouted over the men. "Hypocrites, the both of you! And don't give me any nonsense about it being different for men!"

Stunned silence followed her outburst.

"Now then, gentlemen, if you please," Charlotte continued, having once more gained everyone's attention. "We are all adults here. If Melly wishes to discreetly sample the pleasures of marriage before the vows are spoken, that is her choice. Once her engagement is announced, it won't matter in any case."

"Charlie, I'm afraid it isn't quite as simple as you think," David said as Reggie let out an indignant croak.

"I'm afraid it most certainly is," she shot back. "And you needn't take that patronizing tone with me. Why just last Season,

Lady Willoughby was caught in a terribly compromising situation with Lord Willoughby, but once they announced their engagement, everyone was falling over themselves to have her at their parties. She was in no way ruined. Why should Melly be any different?"

Mélisande choked. While alarmingly humorous, Charlotte's innocent misunderstanding *could* prove useful. If anyone did dare comment, she would jump to squash any ugly rumors.

"Charlie, you're absolutely right," said David, sounding contrite. "I've been terribly unfair in all this. After all, Melly certainly deserves to be given the same leniency as everyone else. I suppose we need not worry as long as you and Gravina are discreet, right, Melly? After all, you *will* be man and wife as soon as decency allows."

"Indeed, and as such, there is absolutely no need for any further upset," cut in Charlotte. "I should remain with Melly until the wedding as a show of support."

"You'll make a lovely maid of honor, Charlie," David drawled.

"Indeed, I would have no one else." Mélisande forced herself to sound cheery as she prepared to launch another swift kick at David if he so much as breathed. If he thought there was any place where he was safe, he'd soon think differently! "And I do appreciate your support. All of you. I'm afraid I did lose my head a bit tonight. I shall endeavor to be more cautious in the future."

"One can hope," grumbled David.

Mélisande drew back her foot.

"As for that business matter we discussed earlier this evening," he added, "I shall begin gathering information immediately."

"Thank you," Mélisande replied, mollified. The carriage finally arrived at her residence, and she and Charlotte bade the gentlemen farewell. Now she only needed to escape to her chamber without being interrogated. As soon as they stepped inside, she held a hand to her brow and sighed, immediately drawing a concerned look from her companion.

"Are you quite well?" inquired Charlotte.

"Just a headache," Mélisande told her. "I was unprepared for such emotional turmoil—I truly never expected to see him again. I thought he'd forgotten me long ago." That part was true, at least.

"Poor dear! You should go and rest," Charlotte said with an encouraging smile. "We can discuss it all tomorrow. And I'll help you with the plans as much as I am able."

Feeling like a complete heel, Mélisande played along. "Thank you, Charlotte. I appreciate your support, truly I do. I believe I will retire now." She let out a long yawn. "Good night, and thank you again. You really are a true friend!"

Making good her escape, she ascended the steps without looking back. Charlotte wouldn't be getting any details tonight.

Mélisande had only just sat down to breakfast when David was shown in, waving a flag of truce in the form of a sheaf of papers.

"Steinberg was certainly surprised to see me this morning," he announced, tossing the bundle down in front of her. "I thought the poor man was going to faint when I walked in."

Eagerly, she snatched up the stack and tore at the twine.

"This morning's visit was the first time I've ever actually stepped foot in his offices. Hopefully the last, as well." He shuddered. "Ghastly place. One would think that with as much as I pay the man, he could afford to maintain a decent office in which to receive his clients."

"Mmm-hmm," she replied absently.

"I hope you appreciate my efforts. I was up practically all night writing letters, taking care of your 'business.' And my visit to Steinberg required me to be up at an ungodly hour. I barely slept at all," he added, a little louder. Leaning over, he tipped down the top edge of the papers with a finger. "It appears you've had even less sleep than I. You look the very devil. Did you not find rest last night?"

"That is none of your concern." She shot him a withering stare. "And I shall thank you to keep a civil tongue." Jerking the papers back into position, she proceeded to continue ignoring him.

He chuckled and dropped unceremoniously into the chair next to her, helping himself to several items from the serving dishes.

Mélisande signaled a servant to bring coffee and another place setting.

"Where's Charlie?" David bit off a piece of toast. "Shouldn't she be up by now?"

"After all the excitement last night? Still asleep, no doubt— as I'd like to be myself." She sighed, snatching back the piece of bacon he'd purloined from her plate and giving him another glare.

He took a piece of unguarded toast instead. "Good. I doubt you'd wish her privy to this discussion anyway," he muttered.

Mélisande dismissed the servants after they'd completed their task. Her staff knew to keep silent about David's frequent, unscheduled visits, but she wasn't willing to take unnecessary risks where they could be avoided. The subject they were about to discuss was extremely delicate, and the fewer ears that heard it, the better.

She continued to sift through the documents while her guest ate. A frown began to crease her brow. After digesting several more pages, she looked at him in wonderment. "How on earth did you manage to come up with this so quickly? I thought it would take at least a day or two."

Grinning smugly, he took a bite of bacon. "If you must know, I made inquiries for my own purposes over a week ago."

She slapped the papers down on the table. "Oh, David! Not *another* mistress? And you're willing to give your love nest up for me? How very altruistic. Who *is* your new ladybird, if I may ask?" she inquired, raising a brow and sampling her poached egg.

David's smile broadened, but he remained silent.

Mélisande rolled her eyes. "I'm sure the papers will get wind of it soon enough. I'll just wait and see from whose window you tumble," she said, poking fun at one of his more embarrassing past faux pas.

"There will be no climbing out of windows for me, nor any hardship suffered," he responded. "I simply told my solicitor that I required *two* new residences instead of one."

"David! What *must* the man think?"

"What people think of me is their concern, not mine. I believe this one"—he plucked a heavy vellum sheet out of the stack, checked it, and placed it on top—"will serve your purposes nicely."

Quickly, she perused the information. It was unfurnished, which was fine, as she preferred to decorate according to her own tastes. The location was decent, too. Not too close, but not an unreasonable distance away. And most importantly, it was available immediately. She didn't even blink at the exorbitant asking price.

"If you approve, then I shall bow to your wisdom," she said, handing him back the document. "What about furnishings and the other items we discussed?"

"I've already sent my man to seek appropriate staff. If needs must, I can see if a few of those already in my employ might be willing to split their services. I'm already acquainted with them well enough to know they're trustworthy, and the location is conveniently close, which is why I'm not so loath to give up the place as you might think."

Her brow furrowed. She must have misheard him. "Are you implying that you already currently support a mistress in that part of town?"

Eyes alight with humor, David sat back and folded his arms. "And yet you've been looking for a place to house another?"

His lips began to twitch.

"Ye gods!" she whispered, aghast. "So now your solicitor thinks you have not two but *three* mistresses?"

"Again, it matters not what he thinks. I'm unconcerned with his opinion of my character so long as he obeys my orders. I don't pay him to worry about my moral rectitude. Now, as for the interior, can I assume you prefer a similar décor to this?" David asked, gesturing vaguely at the feminine surroundings.

"No," she replied without hesitation. "I wish it to be more like Papa's rooms back home. Not a hunter's lodge, you understand— I don't want gloom, but I don't want it to look like Lady Whitby's powder room, either."

"In other words, a place where a man can be comfortable?"

"No, a place where *I* can be comfortable," she said with a fond smile. "I used to love spending time in Papa's rooms better than any other place in the house. In fact, I may redecorate this house as well," she mused, eyeing the delicate pink-striped wainscoting, lacy curtains, and floral paintings. "Maman adored pink, but I find it a bit much, myself. How long do you think before it'll be ready?"

"Not more than a few days, I expect. Eager to traipse down the primrose path, are we?" he jibed. "Patience is a virtue, but virtues aren't something you're overly concerned with these days, it seems."

"Ah, the pot calls the kettle black." Ignoring his sniping tone, she smiled sweetly as she bit into another piece of bacon.

"Yes, but this pot has been black for some time and knows it." He chuckled. "The fact that the shiny copper kettle has suddenly decided to blacken *herself* comes as a bit of a surprise."

"Ahem," Mélisande cleared her throat, glancing to the doorway as a yawning Charlotte appeared.

The girl brightened upon seeing David, and Mélisande sighed. *I'm going to have to discourage that...* She looked over at him: he was shoveling food into his mouth and had barely paused to greet the new arrival. Even then, it was only a curt nod and a grunt. For a so-called authority when it came to women, he was certainly oblivious.

It didn't seem to matter to Charlotte, however. "What brings you here so early?" she asked, leaning over his shoulder to see what he was reading.

David flipped the paper over. "None of your business, poppet," he responded absently, moving the papers to the other side and continuing to read.

Mélisande winced as a flicker of pained irritation crossed Charlotte's face. Should she tell David he was the object of such ardent juvenile affection? If he should laugh and poke fun at Charlotte, she would be devastated.

Meanwhile, Charlotte moved to the other side, still trying to read over his shoulder.

"I'm assisting Melly with some business, if you must know," David told her a bit sharply, again moving the papers out of view. "Tedious stuff, but necessary. You certainly shan't ever have to worry about such things, little one," he added with a patronizing smile. "By the end of the Season, you'll have a husband to manage such pesky details for you."

At the word *husband*, Mélisande observed Charlotte look at him as one might a particularly delectable confection. Thankfully, David was intent on his breakfast and didn't notice her predatory expression.

*We definitely must have that talk sooner rather than later.*

She was distracted from all such thoughts when the butler appeared to announce a guest. The Duke of Gravina had come to call. A quick glance at the clock on the mantel told her it was not yet even midmorning.

"*Merde!*" she swore under her breath. Rising, she excused herself, not bothering to have the servant show her guest into the parlor to await her leisure. Thank God she had other company present, although it certainly wouldn't stop her giving him a piece of her mind. She swept into the entry hall like an avenging Fury.

"You should have waited until this afternoon to call," she snapped as she entered. "I'm sure anyone who saw your arrival will be wondering at such an early visit."

"I could not help myself," he confessed, having the good grace to look contrite. "I shall take my leave immediately and return this afternoon, if you like."

All recriminations died on her lips at the look in his eyes. They shone with some unnamed emotion, the violet shadows beneath them telling her he'd not slept well, either.

"No," she said. "Your premature arrival may actually work to our advantage, as it provides an opportunity to discuss a matter of some importance in private. Follow me," she commanded.

As they exited the foyer, she signaled a footman. "Have tea sent to the blue parlor at once," she ordered without pausing, lest her trembling become visible. They entered the parlor and she closed the door, not caring what the servants might think. With any luck, it was about to be moot.

The moment the door shut, the few feet separating them vanished.

Alessandro kissed her in an echo of the pent-up desire that had been building from the moment she'd left him the night before. "I had to see you. I had to know you were real," he rasped hoarsely, lips moving from her mouth to her jaw, trailing little kisses from there to the tender place just below her ear.

A thrill shot through Mélisande, spreading warmth to every part of her aching body. "I assure you I am quite real," she whispered, brushing her lips against his neck. A pang of longing took her for a split second as she tasted his skin, but she fought it and pulled back. It was not the time or place for such things, no matter how much she wished otherwise.

"There is something we need to discuss," she said, gathering her wits. Purposefully avoiding the settee, she took a seat in one of the chairs. She needed to think, which was impossible to do with him too near. "I have in my care Reggie's sister, Charlotte, whom you met last night. Her parents are unable to travel to London due to infirmity, so I offered to bring her out in their stead. She's living here with me through the Season, and preserving her reputation is my first responsibility."

Alessandro's immediate nod made it clear he understood. "I shall act with the utmost propriety during my visits here," he promised. "I have no desire to ruin you or your friend."

"It still might not be enough to prevent harmful rumors. Alessandro, we must be extremely careful," she warned.

"If I must stay away, then I shall do so, but I hope it won't be necessary." His eyes pleaded with her.

She hesitated, clasping her hands. There really was no other choice. "You said last night that it might be better if people thought you a suitor. I have thought about it, and I am willing to do it, if you are. Not for my sake, but for Charlotte's," she added quickly, "and with the assurance that when we are ready to part ways, we shall devise a suitable means of mutual public release from any perceived obligation."

Mélisande waited, praying he had not reconsidered.

"I agree to the ruse," Alessandro finally told her. "But we will still need to use caution in conducting our liaisons."

"Of course. I've already sent several messages this morning regarding a location for our rendezvous," she lied. "Everything should be ready in a matter of days." She hoped.

Before he could comment, a timid knock sounded at the door.

"Enter," Mélisande called, thinking it was the servants bringing tea.

Charlotte's head appeared around the door. "David asked me to inform you he will be leaving shortly," she announced.

Mélisande looked askance at Alessandro. At his almost imperceptible nod, she turned back to Charlotte. "Please ask him to stay a moment longer and join us here, and you may join us as well, Charlotte."

She was calmly pouring tea with the aid of a servant when they entered.

"Well?" said David, lifting a brow as he came to stand in front of her, his gaze flicking over to Gravina, who stood by the windows looking out over the gardens.

Mélisande offered him a cup, telling him with her eyes to stop being rude.

He declined with a curt shake of his head.

She put the cup down and folded her hands in her lap. "We have some news to share," she began, turning to signal Alessandro.

On cue, he moved forward to stand beside her chair. Placing a warm hand on her shoulder, he announced in a clear voice, "Lady Wilmington has agreed to become my wife."

The delicate sound of china shattering on parquet startled them all as a carafe of cream slipped from the serving girl's fingers. Liquid ran in translucent rivulets across the polished floor as everyone drew in an astonished breath.

Quickly, Mélisande forced her lips to form a placid smile. She had intended to announce that they were officially courting, not that they were engaged to be *married*! Perhaps he hadn't quite understood what it was she'd wanted him to do?

It didn't matter. Now that Charlotte and a servant had borne witness to his announcement, there was no way to rectify the situation without an unacceptable amount of embarrassment.

# Chapter Twelve

## DAMAGE CONTROL

ERHAPS IT WAS A RASH IMPULSE, BUT IT DIDN'T FEEL like a mistake. Alessandro waited, his stomach as tight as the head of a drum. He hadn't planned for things to unfold in quite this manner, but when the opportunity had presented itself, he hadn't hesitated.

For five long years, Mélisande had lived in his thoughts and dreams. Though they'd met only once, he'd never forgotten her. And he knew that for those same five years, she'd searched fruitlessly for another man to reignite the flame *he'd* set. If, as she'd said, Fate had delivered to her exactly what she desired, then it had done the same for him.

He'd originally planned to make her his mistress, but he'd grown tired of shallow things that didn't last. He wanted more than just an *affaire*.

Pelham finally broke the awkward silence. "Leave us," he commanded the stunned servant. "Now." Though he'd spoken softly, the girl dropped her cloth and ran from the room as though chased by the devil. Shutting the door behind her, Pelham walked over to Mélisande, carefully avoiding the half-mopped pool of cream on the floor. He flicked the sheets in his hand into her lap. "I'm certainly glad to hear of His Grace's honorable intentions, considering what the papers had to say this morning."

Alessandro watched as she spread them flat and began to read. Over her shoulder, he saw amid the social columns a grossly exaggerated caricature. He was depicted wearing the leering face and fangs of a slavering wolf, and she was garbed in nothing more than an artfully draped banner that read *"Folie Jolie."*

"Don't be ridiculous." She sighed, dismissing it with a wave. "We knew when we planned the waltz that it would likely result in just this sort of rubbish." She wadded up the paper and pitched it into the hearth, where it was quickly consumed in the crackling flames.

"Yes, but that was *before* you unexpectedly switched dance partners!" Pelham snapped, going to the window.

"Let us remain calm," she replied with cool dignity. "Once all the fuss has died down, we'll simply—" She paused as her eye fell upon Charlotte, who was hanging on her every word. "...begin making the arrangements," she finished, looking rather pale.

Alessandro knew she'd been about to say *call it off and make the appropriate excuses.*

"Well then, allow me to be the first to congratulate you," said Pelham. He made a short bow before them. "When will you make the official announcement?"

Mélisande's pale cheeks now reddened. "Not for some time, obviously. People know he only just arrived here. We'll need to let the uproar die down a bit, lest people think the wrong thing. Perhaps a party next month?"

"Ahh, but they *already* think the wrong thing," Pelham countered. "And the papers have already condemned you. You know as well as I that news of your engagement will get out no matter how you threaten or bribe the servants. The entire household knows by now, if not the street entire. You really should make an announcement sooner rather than later, if only for Charlie's sake."

"I will post an announcement in the papers at the end of the week."

"And when will the happy day be?" Pelham prodded, ignoring her venomous glare. He was obviously enjoying her discomfiture.

Alessandro smiled and answered for her. "Why not early autumn?"

Mélisande wondered if he had lost his mind, but he appeared quite serious. In fact, he seemed almost merry. Just then, he caught her eye and winked at her, as if to say, *I've got everything under control.*

Charlotte piped up at last, clearly unable to contain herself any longer. "Shall we not at least have a small party to celebrate?" she suggested.

Mélisande wanted to crawl beneath a rock. A large one with a deep hole beneath it. It was terrible to deceive Charlotte in this manner, but there was no other choice. She couldn't tell her innocent young friend the truth. "I suppose we could," she replied. "I'm already having a gathering this Thursday. Why not announce it then?"

Charlotte let out a tiny, rapturous squeal of joy, and David's smile spread—a smirk that Mélisande's hand itched to slap off. By contrast, Alessandro's grin of delight seemed strangely genuine. Stepping up to the mark, she plastered a smile on her own face. Turning to her newly affianced, she placed her hand in his. "My friends will be so pleased to hear the news."

Word of their "secret" engagement spread across town with a swiftness that would have been astonishing had it not been expected. From house to house it ran like wildfire, first among the servants, then among their mistresses, and lastly among the menfolk. By the next morning, the rumor was in all the London papers.

Wednesday morning, David finally brought her to see the house she'd purchased and to meet her new staff.

Jim Mackie was a giant of a man, quite formidable at over six feet four inches, with flaming hair, a barrel chest, and ham shanks for arms. He would serve as her new coachman and double as a personal guard. He bobbed a respectful bow to his new mistress.

"I thank ye fer the job, m'lady. I'll guard ye as if ye was the Queen 'erself," Mackie promised in an accent so thick Mélisande could barely understand him. "An me son'll do right by ye as well, yer ladyship," he added, nudging the child beside him. Jamie, who was ten, bobbed as well. He'd been hired along with his father to work as a serving boy with the promise of training as an under-butler. He would also serve as her runner when she wanted to have Jim pick her up or when she wanted to communicate with Alessandro.

Then there was Mrs. Wells, the housekeeper; Kate, her lady's maid; a butler; a cook; and two footmen besides. Mélisande toured the house and found everything in order, with the exception of some missing furnishings that were to be delivered the following morning.

A little thrill of excitement ran through her. And fear. By Friday morning, she would be a virgin no more.

Thursday finally arrived—and dragged. To Mélisande, each hour seemed to last forever. Finally, at half past one, Alessandro arrived.

She watched from the parlor window as he stepped from his carriage, anticipation tightening her middle. It had been several days since she had seen him. He was still the same man she'd met in Versailles, but now she noticed a subtle difference. His walk was less of a swagger now and more of a stride, his manner less impertinent and more dignified.

As he entered the room, she noticed that he'd exchanged his somber black and grey for a rust-colored jacket trimmed with gold buttons and lace. The warm shade suited him very well, she thought. And more appropriate than black, considering they were about to celebrate a "joyous occasion."

Without preamble, Alessandro reached into his pocket and withdrew a small wooden box.

Even though she knew this was a sham, the sight of that box in his hand made Mélisande tremble from top to toe-tip. Their clever ruse suddenly seemed fraught with pitfalls—the biggest one having to do with the nervous fluttering in her gut.

He opened the case to reveal a large emerald nestled in an ornate setting of heavy gold and bright diamonds. "Will you do me the honor?" he asked, presenting her with his offering.

He looked and sounded so perfectly grave that any other woman would have thought him quite serious. She knew better. Nonetheless, her foolish heart beat a little faster. "I will," she responded, extending her left hand. The ring slid onto her finger as though it had been made for her.

He took her face between his hands and brushed his lips against her mouth.

The warmth of that gentle kiss sank all the way down into her bones. She drew a shaky breath, wondering why she suddenly felt like crying. There was no time to ponder it, however, for at that moment, her butler chose to appear in the doorway and announce that Miss Charlotte and Miss Winifred awaited her in the drawing room and that her other guests were beginning to arrive.

Reggie was the first, followed shortly by Stamma, Kesselman, and an eager Miss Doulton. After a quick round of chess to test Miss Doulton's skill, Mélisande introduced her to Kesselman. When she glanced their way half an hour later, the two were completely absorbed with one another, the chessboard forgotten.

Another hour went by, and still David had not appeared. By the time Charlotte had asked her where he was for the tenth time, Mélisande was wroth. And when he finally showed up, she let him know it. "It's nearly five o' clock," she scolded, drawing him aside so the others wouldn't hear. "Where the devil have you been?"

"Anxious, are we?" A knowing brow lifted.

She glared. "You should have been here hours ago."

"I had a bit of trouble on the way here." His gaze dropped to the ring on her hand. "I see you've acquired an appropriate prop for the charade. I hope it wasn't too costly. You've a mob of creditors to pay off—which, incidentally, is why I am late. One of them accosted me as I was leaving White's to demand immediate payment for some furnishings I purchased for the house."

"What? But that's ridiculous." She laughed. "You've never had money problems."

"Yes, well, someone has been spreading rumors to the contrary. The man told me he'd heard that one of my major investments had taken a turn for the worse and that I was soon to be penniless. Actually threatened me with debtors' prison if I didn't pay him on the spot, if you can believe it. *Me.* If I ever discover who started such a lie, I shall ruin him and run him out of London."

"Did you pay him?"

"Of course not." He snorted. "Firstly, I don't react well to threats. Secondly, I don't typically carry hundreds of pounds on my person. I told him he'll have to wait like all the others until I settle accounts at the end of the month. Fortunately for him, that's only a few days away. I suspect he's put a watch on my house to make certain I don't take ship." He laughed.

"Hopefully once he is paid, he'll help discount the malicious rumor."

"I'm not willing to wait for his beneficence," said David. "I've already begun my campaign against it. I went to see the man who'd told him the falsehood, and then two more after him. None of them knew where the news had originated. I shall resume my search tomorrow."

"My apologies for being sharp with you," she said. "And thank you for seeing to everything. I'm sorry it has caused you trouble."

"Again, don't mention it," he said wryly. "You'd best see to your guests," he added, nodding at the door, where stood Lady Angelica Mallowby and her mother.

Mélisande's palms began to sweat just a little. If Lady Mallowby, who'd openly disapproved of her on several occasions, had deigned to attend her party, then the whole of London must be waiting to hear her report. Nothing but the heaviest pressure from her most influential friends could have convinced that woman to enter the "lion's den," as she'd once dubbed Mélisande's house. That she'd brought her daughter was even more surprising.

Leaving David behind, she went to welcome them. The next hour was spent making introductions and ushering people to tables.

When everyone had at last arrived, she gave Alessandro the signal.

An expectant hush fell as he joined her at the front of the room. Mélisande nearly laughed aloud as she watched several people actually lean in. Any moment now, they'd begin slavering and licking their chops.

"Dear friends," she began, scanning the eager faces, "I am so pleased to see each and every one of you. I invited you here to join me in celebrating the return of my good friend Mr. Stamma"—she gestured toward him with a smile—"but I am pleased to announce that this gathering now has another, very special purpose."

She looked to Alessandro, giving him the floor.

His eyes were luminous as he ensnared her left hand, lifting it to his lips and showing off the jewel that now graced it. "I am delighted to announce that Lady Wilmington has agreed to become my duchess. The wedding will take place this autumn, and you are all invited!" he proclaimed.

Even though she knew it was all a pretense, happiness filled Mélisande as she watched her friends react to the news. Stamma grinned and boasted that he'd known they were a perfect match all along. Charlotte sniffled and dabbed at her eyes, sneaking a glance at David from beneath her lashes. David, she noted with satisfaction, had lost his mocking sneer.

Mélisande meandered about, accepting congratulations and answering inquiries about the anticipated nuptials. Though polite to a fault, her guests' amazement at her hasty engagement was clear. By the time the party ended, she'd had enough of their speculative stares and hurriedly hushed conversations. Their doubts would be silenced in a few months' time when she *didn't* swell with child.

She glanced at the clock on the mantlepiece, and the fluttering in her midsection, which had begun to subside, now returned. It was almost time.

# Chapter Thirteen

## DOWN THE PRIMROSE PATH

*A*LESSANDRO'S CARRIAGE TRUNDLED THROUGH INCREAS ingly quiet streets, at last pulling up before a smart little house in a quiet part of London. Disembarking, he stood for a moment in the warm glow of the gate lamps.

Her instructions had been for him to arrive at midnight, and he was a bit early. An hour was considered "a bit" by some, he told himself. He hadn't been this anxious to see a woman since he was a young buck. What was it about this one that made him feel so different?

His hand hesitated on the knocker. Perhaps he ought to come back at the appointed time. After all, it wouldn't do to appear overly eager.

*Oh, for pity's sake, one would think I'd never bedded a woman before!* He knocked.

The butler showed him into a small, well-appointed parlor and went to inform his mistress of her guest's arrival. He returned shortly to say that Madam was currently indisposed, but would be down within the hour.

Alessandro politely declined the drink he was offered and sat watching the clock on the mantel, cooling his heels for approximately three whole minutes before heading upstairs. Much to his delight, he discovered "Madam" still in her bath. Her back was to the door, and she was giving her attendant instructions for her dress. She did not hear him enter.

He stood, hand frozen to the knob as he watched the girl rinsing the soap from her mistress's shoulders. Mélisande's dark hair had been pinned atop her head, and a few wet tendrils clung to her long, graceful neck.

The servant girl saw him out of the corner of her eye and made to announce him, but he stopped her, placing a quick finger across his lips.

An impudent grin was her only response. She puttered about the room a moment longer before making her exit, brushing past with an appreciative glance.

Alessandro closed the door and padded over until he was directly behind Mélisande. Leaning down, he placed a soft kiss on one gleaming shoulder, flicking his tongue across her bare skin to catch a glittering droplet.

Water sloshed over the sides of the heavy wooden tub as she turned, squealing in alarm.

Laughing, he jumped back. "I know you told me midnight, but I simply couldn't wait a moment longer." He pulled off his now sodden jacket and tossed it over the back of a nearby chair. Reaching out, he pushed a rope of damp hair off her shoulder, watching, fascinated, as gooseflesh prickled across her skin.

Still chuckling, Alessandro cupped some of her warm bath-water in his hands, pouring it over her chilled skin.

She suddenly remembered her nakedness. Crossing her arms over herself with another squeak of dismay, Mélisande sank beneath the surface of the water, again sending much of it onto the rug below.

Having spied a drying sheet warming by the fire, Alessandro went over to fetch it. He brought it back and held it out for her to step into.

She looked up at him as if he were mad.

"For a woman prepared to make love on a rooftop beneath the stars, you are far more timid than I expected," he said with a grin. "You realize that, as your lover, I *will* see all of you."

"Of course," Mélisande snipped. "I am not ignorant of the details of intimacy. I—you simply surprised me, that's all."

Quirking a brow, Alessandro shook the cloth meaningfully, waiting.

She hesitated only a moment before setting her jaw and rising.

His mouth went dry. Before him stood a naked goddess. Sparkling rivulets of water trickled down her lithe body. She reminded him of a statue he'd seen in Rome: Diana the Huntress. Tall and strong, yet graced with luscious feminine curves, she could have been the deity herself rising from a river bath.

His body's instant reaction rivaled that of another statue he'd once seen in a Venetian garden. Slowly, his unblinking gaze journeyed over her, taking in every inch of smooth, creamy skin. It took all his willpower to speak past the knot in his throat, and when he did, his voice twanged like that of an untried youth. "You possess the most beautiful female form I have ever seen."

At his hoarse admission, Mélisande's shy smile transformed into one of womanly triumph, and she stood a little taller.

The motion, though subtle, sent a shower of droplets into the pool at her thighs. Extending his arms wide, he wrapped her in the sheet, guiding her as she stepped from the tub.

The feel of her warm body through the thin, wet cloth nearly unseated his reason. Releasing her, he stepped back, struggling for self-control as she gave him her back and began drying herself.

He could not stop himself from reaching out. As each swath of pearly skin was gradually exposed, he ran worshipping hands across it, feeling the softness and warmth of her against his palms, the firm muscle and the gentle roundness of her curves.

He traced the swanlike column of her neck, down her shoulder and across her back, following the bend of her waist as it flowed into a slim hip and thigh.

Mélisande stood, quivering, as she allowed him to stroke her. She blushed fiercely when his palms slid down to cup her bottom, resting there for a moment before moving back up and around to caress the tender sides of her breasts.

Looking over her shoulder, she gazed at him, her chosen lover, for a long moment. Something in her eyes slowly changed. Turning fully, she faced him, the damp sheet slipping to the floor.

Alessandro breathed a silent prayer for self-discipline as his gaze drifted down to rest upon perfect, rose-tipped breasts. As it dropped lower, past the shallow dip of her navel, he had to close his eyes and wait through the violent tremor that wracked his body.

"Mélisande…"

In answer to his hoarse plea, she moved closer, wrapping her arms about his neck.

Alessandro enfolded her in his arms, smoothing the curve of her spine, pressing her close. He shuddered as she leaned into him, his arms tightening as he gave in to desire. Crushing her close, his mouth slanted across hers, his tongue gently demanding entrance. Her lips parted obediently and he played in the velvet darkness between them, drinking deeply.

After a moment, he broke away and swooped down, knocking her long legs out from under her and catching her up in his strong arms. He carried her over to the bed and set her gently on its edge.

Mélisande watched with avid curiosity as he disrobed.

He had no reason to be ashamed. Though he was neither broad nor heavily muscled, many women had found his form quite pleasing, for he had a swordsman's physique: lean, with long, rippling muscles hardened to whipcord strength. There was hardly an ounce of fat anywhere to be found on him, unlike most English lords, who proudly boasted of their beef-fed bellies. Crisp hair lightly peppered his chest, and dueling scars twisted across his skin here and there, the older ones faded to a pale pinkish white, the newer ones still dark and angry.

Her eyes dropped, fascinated, to the trail of dark hair disappearing into his breeches. When he reached down to unbutton them, she blushed and quickly looked away.

Smiling to himself, Alessandro waited. When she finally gathered the courage to look at him again, he bent and pulled them off quickly, his rod springing back to stand proudly erect as he straightened.

Mélisande gasped, scrambling toward the middle of the huge bed.

Laughing, Alessandro grabbed her ankle and pulled her back, barely avoiding a nasty blow in a very tender place. After a brief struggle, he managed to capture a flailing wrist and haul her up into a sitting position beside him.

She was shaking all over. Compassion filled him, as well as a little fear, fear she would change her mind about their arrangement. "Mélisande, my love," he said raggedly, "do not tell me you are afraid? Is this not what you want?"

"I didn't think it would be so…" She trailed off, her gaze sliding down to the source of her apprehension. Her wide eyes were filled with fear.

"Your concerns are needless," he assured her. "I know how to make you ready so that our fit will be perfection," he promised, his voice turning warm and gravelly as he began to nuzzle her neck.

Mélisande had trouble believing him, but the kisses he was trailing down her neck felt so delicious she was willing to allow him to continue. She softened, breathing deeply as he continued downward to the little beauty mark above her heart. When his tongue flicked across her nipple, she gasped.

Gently he stroked its erect tip again. A moment later, his warm mouth closed over it, and he began to tease, alternating between flicking and gentle suction.

The low, animal sound that followed shocked Mélisande when she realized it had come from her own throat. His every touch seemed to cause a corresponding ache at the juncture of her thighs. When she felt she could take no more, she grabbed him roughly by the hair and brought his mouth up to meet hers.

He kissed her long and deeply, giving in to her demands for the moment. But before Mélisande could regain her wits, he slipped from her grasp and dipped again to grace the other breast with the same attentions he had given its mate.

Mélisande drowned in the sensation, desire unfurling within her like the petals of a flower opening to the sun. Never before had she felt such desperate, consuming hunger!

Releasing her, Alessandro eased off the bed, sinking to his knees. Reaching beneath her, he cupped her rump and scooted her to the edge. Still muzzy and dazed with pleasure, she looked down at him with bewildered curiosity. Grinning devilishly, he ran his hands down from her thighs to her knees and with gentle pressure made to part them.

Thrown into a state of absolute shock, Mélisande resisted.

"I want to see *all* of you," Alessandro whispered harshly, his dark eyes ravenous. "Every. Last. Inch." He leaned down and kissed her knees, then the inside of a creamy thigh. "There will be no limit to the intimacies we will share this night and for many nights to come. Are you going to let modesty or fear get in the way of your pleasure?"

*He's right.* There was no room for reticence between them, no room and no time. Besides, he was an experienced lover, she reasoned. There was probably nothing she could do that was capable of shocking or embarrassing him, so why should it embarrass her? Still, she trembled a little as his warm hands smoothed over her flesh, heating it in spite of the chill air and her damp skin.

Desire quickly overtook modesty and she acquiesced, until at last her legs were spread wide and she lay exposed before him.

Quickly, he shifted forward. Running his hands along the sensitive flesh of her silky inner thighs, he grazed her core with his thumb. The breath exploded from her lungs as he dipped into her dewy center and rubbed the tip of her hood with that slickness.

"Let me show you the meaning of pleasure, my Mélisande," Alessandro murmured, his eyes meeting hers in a scorching stare. Slowly, he began stroking the moist outer region in a gentle massage.

"I—I've been told to expect pain the first time," she whispered shakily through the haze. "I am ready." It would have to hurt only this once, and then afterward she could concentrate on the more pleasant aspects of lovemaking.

Smiling tenderly, Alessandro shook his head. "Not quite yet, my love. But soon. And I will make it so that it is but a momentary sting quickly forgotten," he promised, continuing to massage and stroke her until she relaxed again.

With the lightest of touches, he caressed the inner folds of her blossom, parting her with gentle fingers, revealing the engorged bud hidden within the recesses.

The initial shock at feeling his hot breath on the core of her femininity translated instantly into pure pleasure as Alessandro's mouth closed over her and drew gently upon her swollen flesh. His tongue slipped between her folds to tease, and Mélisande's hands, which had thrust forward to push him away, now stilled and twined into his thick hair, pulling him closer.

Alessandro flicked the bud of her womanhood much as he had her nipples, and she moaned, unable to bear it in silence. Arching back in surrender, she lay down, exposing more of her delicate flesh to this new, delightful torment.

He took full advantage.

Writhing and gasping with each tender stroke of his tongue, the tension built within Mélisande until she felt she would die of it. A hot, tingling sensation pulsated within, threatening to overwhelm her, and she pulled at Alessandro's hair, wanting more. He laughed softly, and with a wild thrill, she felt the low rumbling of it resonate through her womanly flesh.

Rising up, he again grasped her bottom, sliding her toward him to seat her snugly against himself. His turgid manhood stood between them, hot, thick, and hard against the gentle curve of her belly.

Mélisande tasted herself as he claimed her mouth. It was inconceivably shocking, and the most erotic thing she could possibly imagine. She gave herself up to that dark kiss, her hands skimming over his hard shoulders, tracing his collarbone as his tongue teased her bottom lip. His skin was warm velvet stretched over unyielding rock, and she could not resist the overwhelming compulsion to touch him.

He stood and leaned over her, maneuvering them both fully onto the bed, pressing her full length against his body. He began to again tease her breasts while he gently stroked her petals, sliding the tip of one finger in and out, grazing the delicate, swollen bud hidden within.

When her breathing grew erratic and her hips began to move rhythmically of their own volition, he shifted and settled himself between her knees, again dipping to taste her. Her hips bucked as his tongue tormented her, her hands clutching at his hair.

At last, Alessandro rose and guided himself to her moist entrance.

As the blunt, dewed tip of his manhood pushed aside her folds, Mélisande's eyes flew wide with fear. He hesitated only an instant before plunging into her tight passage, muffling her outcry with his mouth as he claimed her utterly.

She felt her maiden's barrier give way with only momentary resistance, the sharp stab of fiery pain immediately followed by a hot, throbbing fullness that seeped into her very bones as her body accommodated his length and girth. He remained motionless inside her, holding steady, his arms trembling with the effort. Soon, the discomfort faded into a new sensation.

*They were one being.*

His every movement was felt deep within her core. After a few moments, a new tension began to build there as the fire of his initial penetration was replaced by a deep, pleasurable ache that caused her to wriggle her hips to seat him more firmly. She squeezed her buttocks together to shift upward and felt the length of him harden anew. His answering groan seemed torn from somewhere deep inside.

Alessandro began to move then, retreating a little and then coming back slowly into her slickness, again and again, until he was withdrawing nearly the full length of himself before easing back in.

Mélisande shuddered and closed her eyes, her head thrown back, little moans escaping her throat. Her legs cradled his torso and her hips rose to meet him, welcoming, encouraging. There was only pleasure now, intense pleasure. It mounted with each long stroke until she began to again feel the sweet, tingling tension at the place where their bodies were joined. Slowly, it radiated out to the rest of her, continuing to build, until at last she dug her nails into his flesh.

Her ragged voice cried out his name, just once, as the tension finally broke, shattering Mélisande's world into countless fragments of ecstasy. Liquid, molten heat welled from the deeps, suffusing her from the inside out as she and Alessandro moved together to that most ancient of rhythms. With each pulse, she became more deeply immersed in the pleasurable sensations running riot through her body.

Her mind had only one coherent thought: *this is what I was made for.*

Alessandro slowly withdrew nearly all the way to hover at her entrance. She clutched him impatiently until, with a groan, he sank back into her. Her body embracing him wholly, he shouted in exultation as his own pleasure at last burst forth. Clasping her tightly, he shuddered, burying his head in the curve of her neck.

Mélisande held him thus, listening to his breath rasp in her ear.

In the stillness that followed, the lovers lay together heart to heart, breaths slowing, limbs entwined, souls forever bound.

# Chapter Fourteen

## A RAKE'S TALE

REMEMBERING THAT SHE WAS BUT NEWLY OPENED, Alessandro raised himself up from where he lay. "Are you all right?" he asked, steeling himself.

Despite all his skill at lovemaking, he knew that for women, pain was an inevitable part of surrendering one's virginity. He'd been a callow youth with no real knowledge of how to pleasure a female the first time he'd deflowered a virgin, and his memory of the experience was one of guilt at the pain he'd caused.

But when he looked into Mélisande's eyes, Alessandro saw only the tranquil, sated expression of a woman well loved.

A shy smile curved her beautiful lips. "I'm wonderful," she whispered. "You were right; there was hardly any pain at all." Her eyes dropped in embarrassment and a rosy blush stained her cheeks.

He smiled back at her, feeling a surge of tenderness as he traced the outer edge of a delicate ear. "We need to separate, and you should probably bathe again. The warm water will help ease the pain," he said, kissing the corner of her mouth. Her effect on him was truly incredible. Already he could feel a renewing of desire. Lest he risk hurting her, he needed to withdraw before he became fully hard again.

He began to move, but stopped in terror when she gasped. To his astonishment, instead of crying out or pushing him away, her legs wrapped around his waist and drew him back in.

His manhood rallied to the challenge as her motions compelled him to move with her. In amazement, he watched as she came to crisis again. The pleasure of seeing her beautiful face in the throes of ecstasy was well worth the effort. When it was over, he kissed her deeply, withdrawing at last to lie at her side.

He wanted to laugh aloud but had no air left in his lungs with which to do so. They had done nothing unconventional, yet he felt more fulfilled than ever before. He'd bedded many women, some of them famed courtesans, but none of them compared to this woman.

After resting a moment, he propped himself up on one elbow. He could not stop staring at her. "Mélisande," he murmured, his heart aching as he stroked her cheek and followed the touch with a feathery kiss.

Turning, she met his lips in a lingering kiss that spoke of longings fulfilled. Then, before he could react, she broke away, stood, and walked to the tub. Without so much as a backward glance, she climbed in and began to wash in the now-tepid water.

Confused, Alessandro stared after her for a moment and then scrambled off the bed to follow. She did not look up at his approach, nor even acknowledge him as he stood waiting.

"Mélisande, look at me." He reached out and tipped her chin up with a gentle hand. A riot of turbulent emotions warred in her forest eyes, fear and confusion among the most prominent. "You have nothing to fear from me," he reassured.

She chuckled, and the broken sound cut at his heart like a thousand shards of glass.

Having completed her ministrations, she stood. "I don't fear you."

Grabbing a drying sheet, he offered it to her. "Then what is it, *amora*?" He struggled to maintain composure. The distance between them was growing with every second that passed. He could see it in her eyes as the walls of her fortress went up, stone by stone, layer upon layer, shutting him out.

She bowed her head. "I *was* very afraid," she admitted. "Afraid you would not want me once you saw me, afraid of disappointing you as a lover, and afraid of the pain."

"And how do you feel now?"

"I never imagined it would be like that," she said, her surprise evident. "I expected pain and hoped for at least some small amount of pleasure, but I certainly didn't expect what just happened. That was…"

No fool, Alessandro realized he'd been subtly redirected. The beginnings of her tender emotions for him had been snuffed out like the flame of a candle as she chose to focus on the physical aspect of what they'd done, rather than the heart. There was nothing to do now but play at her pace and try to rekindle it. It would take time to cultivate a fire that could not be extinguished, but time was a luxury he possessed.

"I am glad I was able to give you pleasure." He stroked her soft skin with a reverent hand. "I hope to bring you joy many, many times over. It truly only improves with practice. I shall enjoy showing you just how delightful it can be."

She peered at him sidelong. "You are not at all what I expected. You place a great deal of importance on giving pleasure as opposed to receiving it. Most men are not so minded. They know only how to take."

"If I was interested only in my own release, I would simply amuse myself and have done," he replied, "but I have learned that pleasure experienced alone is a mere shadow of that which is shared." Leaning over, he caressed a still-damp shoulder. "And pleasure should never be *taken*, but always *given* in equal measure."

"Is it always like this?" she asked, moving back to the bed. "Because if it is, I can't help wondering why anyone would ever want to leave the bedchamber," she said with a sinful smile, climbing in.

Joining her, Alessandro kissed that smile. "I share your opinion, *amora*, and I certainly hope to bring you such pleasure each and every time. But we should not make love again tonight," he warned. "Already I fear you will be indisposed tomorrow. We should wait a few days."

Mélisande nodded, but he could tell she didn't like it. The feeling was mutual, for he would gladly make love to her all night, were it possible.

"That does not mean we cannot see each other, of course," he amended rather hastily. "As you said, we should become friends." *Good friends...*

"Of course," she answered, toying with a corner of the sheet. "I should like that very much, truly. I've been curious about you since the day I first saw you," she admitted. "I know next to nothing of you, really, other than what I observed in Versailles and what I know of you now."

His heart sank, for he could well imagine the impression he must have made. "Our attraction to one another has rather taken precedence, hasn't it? What would you know? You may ask me anything," he bade her, relaxing against the pillows and preparing to be interrogated.

Mélisande grinned and settled into the crook of his arm. "What made you become such a shameless *roué*? Or were you simply born with an obsession for the opposite sex?"

He laughed at her directness. "Indeed not; I was raised in an exceedingly prudish household," he said with disdain. "My father served as Prince Assistant to the Papal Throne, and as such, we—my brother and I—were bound by the strictest code of conduct. Any form of enjoyment was practically synonymous with committing a mortal sin." He rolled his eyes, making her giggle. "Naturally, I rebelled."

"How you must have frustrated him!"

"Indeed, such was my chief pursuit," he agreed, laughing with her. "By the time I was eighteen, I was such an embarrassment to the family that to get me out of sight, my father had me made an emissary of the Roman Curia—a servant of the Holy Church, if you can imagine—and sent out of the country to trouble foreign courts. It was a benevolent form of banishment. One I was happy to suffer."

"Mmm, the prodigal son," she murmured, running her hand across his chest. The sprinkling of hair over the muscle there seemed to fascinate her. He understood, for her rounded smoothness held the same attraction for him.

"Indeed. I returned every few years to visit my mother—and endure my father's criticism, of course," he added. "I tried to keep tales of my exploits from reaching his ears, but he always seemed to know everything. I found out later that he had his spies reporting back to him on my activities. When he died last year, he said I was his greatest disappointment."

"What an awful thing to say to one's child!"

Alessandro smiled and patted her hand, loving her for springing to his defense, even though her sympathy was misplaced. It suddenly occurred to him that this was the first time in many years that a woman had asked to hear his story. Many, *many* years. Usually, it was he who listened while they talked.

"He was laughing as he said it," he reassured her. "I'll never be the pious stick he was, nor was I anything like my brother. Pietro was the ducal heir until three years ago. Unfortunately for me, he died without an heir." He sighed, feeling the sadness return for the first time in a long while. "Father was never the same. All his joy, what little he ever had, died with his firstborn. I now bear the burden of his titles: Duke of Gravina, Emissary of the Curia, Prince of the Holy Roman Empire, et cetera, et cetera," he said. "A lot of titular nonsense, but it sounds awfully impressive when one is formally introduced."

Mélisande lifted a brow and traced his jawline with a fingertip. "And how is it that such an important personage is here in England engaging in, shall we say, 'pleasurable recreation' rather than back home tending to the business associated with all those burdensome titles?"

"My father rather frequently complained to his peers regarding my shameful proclivities. Thus, when I inherited his titles, the Curia found a way to prevent my contaminating their holiness with my wicked ways." He grinned. "Knowing my love of vagrancy, and yet respecting my not inconsiderable diplomatic skills, they sent me here to advance their political position with the English king."

"And your mother? What is she like?"

Alessandro's gaze softened. "You would like her a great deal, I think," he told her, fully believing it. "She has courage and spirit. She was a trial to my father at times, but they loved each other."

"And does she share your father's opinion of your lifestyle?"

"She tolerates my wayward behavior with much grumbling and a great deal of unsolicited advice." He chuckled. "She wishes me to settle down and take my place as the head of our family. And I shall, one day," he added, forcing himself not to look at her. God forbid that she look him in the eyes and see the hope burning in his heart. "One day, I will continue our esteemed line and make her happy again."

"I, too, was a disappointment to my parents," she told him. "Now they are both gone, and I am certainly not living up to their high expectations of me."

"Do we not all fall short of both divine and human expectations?"

"I suppose you're right," she replied, smiling again. "But enough of gloom and doom. Tell me more about the man behind the wicked reputation."

"What else would you like to know?"

Her eyes lit. "Everything," she said eagerly. "I already know you enjoy chess and dancing, but what of life's other enjoyments? Besides the one we've just explored, that is; although"—her gaze dropped to his stiring member—"I can certainly understand why you're so keen on it." Grinning naughtily, she reached down to grasp him. "I myself am finding it quite entertaining."

He burst out laughing at her bawdiness, and then again at her blush. For a virgin, she said and did the most unexpected things! "I find you"—he paused, distracted by her hand's slow movement up and down his swelling length—"delightfully surprising." His laughter quickly turned into desire. "I know you to be a gently born virgin—at least until recently," he said, raising a brow, "yet you have all the boldness of a seasoned courtesan."

Mélisande colored, and her hand stopped momentarily. "Actually, my mother *was* a courtesan. Isabelle Jeannette d'Orleans. It was her surname I gave you when we first met."

On hearing the name of Louis's first and most beloved mistress, Alessandro stilled. *It is as I suspected, then...* Isabelle d'Orleans was a legend in Versailles, her name still occasionally mentioned at court by the older set.

A log popped in the hearth, briefly bathing the room in a warm glow. His gaze dropped to the tiny mole on Mélisande's left breast, the one shared by King Louis and Louis's mother. Moving down, his gaze rested on the oddly shaped birthmark on her right hip. He'd had the honor of attending the French monarch in his morning dress once, and he'd noticed that same, singular mark in the exact same place. Mélisande's eyes, too, were her paternal grandmother's.

"My father fell in love with her when he first visited Versailles, and they were married before he left," Mélisande continued. "My mother taught me many things. She once said that passion makes us bold, frees us from inhibition."

*Her mother must have married to prevent a scandal.*

"Alessandro?"

"Apologies, *amora*. I must be getting tired." He wondered if she knew her true parentage. No wonder she was so passionate! Her mother was famed for her torrid *affaire* with the French king, who was himself a lusty man.

"I'm a little tired, as well," Mélisande admitted. She looked to the cold tub with distaste. Rising, she yanked the bellpull, then threw on a wrap and stood by the hearth to warm up.

A knock sounded on the door, and at Mélisande's call to enter, young Kate peeked in. "My lady?"

Alessandro grinned as he flung the coverlet over himself just before her curious gaze landed on him. The servants would get no report on the size of his shaft this night.

Mélisande's thoughts had apparently just jumped to the same conclusion, for her cheeks reddened. She looked as though she wanted to dive beneath the bedcovers and hide. "I'd like hot water brought up as quickly as possible, enough to wash with," she requested, her tone brisk.

"Right away, my lady," the girl answered, her gaze dropping to the floor respectfully. "Is that all, ma'am?"

"I'm a bit starved," Alessandro added, marking the rumbling of his stomach. He'd worked up quite an appetite.

"Some food, as well, then," Mélisande ordered. "Tell cook to send whatever is available."

With a quick bob, Kate departed.

Mélisande sank back onto the bed with a groan of mortification.

Laughing, Alessandro pulled her against him, and together they waited, enjoying the crackling of the fire and the warmth of each other's companionship.

When the maid returned, she was followed by an army of servants. Two footmen began to remove the now cold water from the first tub and pitch it out of a nearby window. When it was empty, they refilled it from buckets of steaming water passed hand to hand up the stairs.

As soon as the door closed behind them, Mélisande emerged from beneath the coverlet, stripped, and stepped into the water.

She washed far too quickly, in Alessandro's opinion. Some women looked better gowned and bejeweled, but Mélisande needed no such ornamentation. After admiring her nakedness for a moment, he brought her a drying sheet and then washed himself as well. By the time they were both dry and wrapped in robes, another knock sounded.

Young Kate was back with food. Mountains of it. When her mistress remarked upon the speed of service, she laughed. "We began heating water as soon as his lordship arrived, ma'am, and cook started preparing the food this afternoon."

Together, they feasted on the roast capon with herbed potatoes, freshly baked bread, and a chocolate trifle. When they were done, footmen came and removed the dishes.

The clock on the mantelpiece chimed, drawing Alessandro's attention. It was already past three. "You should prepare for your journey home," he advised.

Mélisande tried not to show her disappointment. "I should like it very much if you called tomorrow."

"Unfortunately, I have an audience with your king tomorrow morning," he answered with a frown.

"I understand," she said with deliberate insouciance. *Of course I can't expect to see him every day. It's not as if we're really engaged, after all.* "I shall probably want to rest anyway." She began brushing her hair.

"I imagine you will," he replied with a naughty smile.

Unable to help herself, she grinned.

"If there is time, I will call afterward," he told her, "but I know not how long it will take to accomplish my task." He rose and retrieved his jacket from beside the hearth and frowned at the water-stained cuffs. When he was done dressing himself, he helped her with swift, sure hands.

*He's done this a thousand times*, Mélisande thought as he finished tying the last ribbon.

"Your carriage must leave first. I will then follow at a safe distance," Alessandro said as they neared the bottom of the stair.

"You needn't worry for my safety," Mélisande assured him, pleased at his concern. "My driver is armed, and I've a pair of loaded pistols with me in the event he is unable to deter an attack. I shall be quite safe. It would be more suspicious if our conveyances were seen traveling the same road at this hour."

"Very well, but I shall at least remain here until your driver returns," he persisted. "If he is not back within the hour, I shall follow his route and come looking for you myself." His tone brooked no argument. "You may count yourself fortunate that I don't insist upon escorting you home. I know the dangers associated with being seen together, but the dangers of London at night are far greater."

Nodding assent, she moved to the door, but he caught her arm and spun her about before she could exit. Despite the warmth that uncurled in her belly at his touch, a flash of irritation struck at his handling her so in front of the servants.

But instead of the kiss she anticipated, he merely caressed her cheek once before twitching her veil down over her face. His eyes twinkled at her even through the lace. The devil *knew* she'd expected him to kiss her!

"You must be more careful, *amora*," said Alessandro, laughter in his voice. "We wouldn't want anyone discovering our nocturnal activities."

Mélisande swallowed her disappointment. "Until our next meeting, then," she said, inclining her head. She turned and stepped into the night without a backward glance, leaving behind the cocoon of warmth and light. When the carriage door closed, she ventured a peep through the curtains. Alessandro still stood there, a dark silhouette in the doorway. His hand lifted in farewell, though it was impossible for him to have known she was looking. She smiled in the darkness and watched until the carriage turned the corner.

Regarding herself in the mirror, Mélisande knew her body looked as it ever had. There were no outward signs of their lovemaking, save the deep shadows beneath her eyes. A faint smile curled her lips. Grabbing her nightgown, she turned from her image with a nod of satisfaction, unaware that even if her body showed no visible change, her eyes certainly did.

As she reached to douse the lamp at her bedside, her gaze lit upon the ring on her finger, drawn to the jewel as the light illuminated something strange in its depths. She'd not taken it off since Alessandro had put it on her hand. Removing it now, she examined it carefully.

To her surprise, there was a design carved in relief on the back of the stone. It was a crest—and it matched the one painted on the door of Alessandro's carriage. She brought it closer to the light to read an inscription engraved on the inside of the band: *Per amare ed onorare*—to love and to honor.

Her heart began to pound unevenly. This was no paste plaything, nor even an expensive bauble. Like the ruby Louis had given her, this was a family heirloom, a treasure passed from generation to generation.

*Why would he give something so precious to me?* She had to assume he meant for her to give it back when they parted ways, but why give it to her at all? Jamming the ring back onto her finger, she blew out the lamp and tried to dismiss the words from her mind. But "to love and to honor" kept popping back into her thoughts as she sought sleep.

*Enough is enough!* she chastised herself. *He's a brief distraction, a pleasurable dalliance, nothing more!*

But though she tried not to dwell upon it, she could not help wondering what it would be like if things were different between them.

# Chapter Fifteen

## PRINCE CHARMING AND THE KING

FROM ACROSS THE CHESSBOARD, GEORGE EYED THE Italian duke with amusement. An entertaining fellow, to be sure. Boisterous and ribald, even by English standards. A lively addition to his court, if a temporary one.

"I am a fortunate man, Your Majesty," said his opponent, moving another piece.

"The board says otherwise." George chuckled, castling to put his rook in a position to take Gravina's king. "Check. How so?"

Gravina moved his king out of danger. "The woman I asked about before—the one I met in Versailles—I found her."

The announcement caused George to pause in confusion. When he'd first arrived at court, Gravina had inquired after a woman by the surname d'Orleans. At the time, he'd thought it strange that an Italian would ask after Isabelle. The man had been disappointed to learn that she had died more than a year prior. "You mean you found her grave?" he asked, resuming play.

Gravina laughed and moved his knight to block him. "No, Your Majesty. The lady is quite alive. We discovered each other again at Lord Ludley's ball and have since renewed our acquaintance. When we first met, she told me her surname was d'Orleans, but it was really Compton."

George carefully concealed his surprise. Isabelle had mentioned something in her letters about Melly being different after their visit to Versailles. She'd suspected something had happened there to cause her to break her betrothal. Perhaps the reason was sitting across from him even now. "Mélisande Compton?" he asked, taking Gravina's knight.

Gravina smiled. "The same." He scooted his queen to a white square.

"Exactly how did you become acquainted in Versailles?"

Gravina gave him a devilish grin. "She wandered into the garden where I happened to be seeking a moment of solitude. We talked for a little, and then I suppose she let curiosity get the better of her. I was delighted to oblige, of course."

"I see," murmured George. He was beginning to see all too clearly. Yesterday he'd heard about the infamous waltz. Until this moment, he'd thought it just another one of Melly's harmless escapades. She'd proven herself capable of avoiding any real trouble so far, and the idea of watching her cause a stir with Gravina had actually been somewhat entertaining— but now… "And?" he prompted, sliding his bishop into place. "Check."

Gravina again moved his king. "She vanished."

"You searched for her?" George asked, repositioning his knight. "Checkmate in three moves."

Gravina frowned for a moment at the board as if startled to find himself beaten. "I asked everyone about her," he finally answered, tipping his king, "but no one knew anything. She'd been seen by others the day we met, but never before and never again after." He frowned again and began reordering the pieces for another game. "I even went to speak with the d'Orleans family, but they disavowed any knowledge of her. It was the strangest thing."

"And now you believe you have solved the mystery?"

Gravina nodded. "I have. Her father was visiting the French king on an important errand for Your Majesty, something to do with discouraging French support for the Jacobites. They departed Versailles the morning after our encounter."

George knew why Wilmington had been sent to France. What he didn't understand was why Melly had assumed her mother's surname while there. "I see. And what is your interest in her now? Surely after so many years, your feelings cannot have remained intact."

"I beg to differ, Your Majesty," said Gravina. "If anything, they have grown in strength. I have searched for her from Spain to Russia, everywhere my travels have taken me, and I have had neither peace nor contentment until now. I wish to marry her—and the feeling is mutual."

"You are certain of this?"

"It may be considered a bit hasty, Your Majesty," Gravina admitted, "but she has already accepted my suit. I have given her my ring in troth before witnesses. The engagement is to be announced publicly today."

George felt his blood begin to heat. *A bit hasty?* Melly damn well knew she needed his approval before there could be any sort of wedding! He maintained a calm exterior in spite of his vexation. "I don't mind telling you that Lady Wilmington has become a matter of increasing concern," he told him. "On several recent occasions, her behavior has come dangerously close to eliciting my intervention. I've been a hairbreadth from commanding her to marry Newcastle's heir, despite her objections."

Gravina's face whitened.

*So, he really does have feelings for her,* thought George. "However, if a happier alternative exists, I shall not be displeased."

"You will allow it?" Gravina asked. "Given her entitlement, I was concerned you might not grant your blessing, as I am not English."

George waved his words away. "I've already decreed that whomever she marries shall have no claim to the earldom. Her firstborn son shall inherit all. Which brings me to the subject of children," he added, watching the other man carefully. "She is the sole heir to the earldom. Until her birth, Lord Wilmington was the last of his line. I understand you are a duke in your own country; however, in this, I must put England's interests first. Lady Wilmington must remain in England and bear a son to inherit the Wilmington title. Upon his birth, I will make him a ward of the Crown, entrusted to his mother's care, of course— but he will not be allowed to leave these shores. One can assume that Lady Wilmington will want to remain here with her child. I have no wish to rob you of a son, but you must understand that Wilmington was my friend. If at all possible, I must see that his lands are inherited by someone of his line."

Clearly, the king knew nothing of Mélisande's true heritage— and Alessandro was certain she would rather it remain so. He would not expose her for his own gain, either. To do so would earn him only her enmity. *There must be another way. I simply need time to find it.*

For now he had no choice but to accept the terms if he wanted to continue to court her. "I would prefer to take her back to Italy, naturally, but if needs must, then for her sake I will remain in England," Alessandro finally replied.

George frowned. "You would abandon your responsibilities in your own country?"

*He didn't think I would be willing to make such a sacrifice.* "I can manage things from afar. A yearly visit should suffice, as long as my mother is able to oversee the daily running of the estate. She has done so most admirably for the last twenty years. My father's duties to the Holy Roman Empire required his absence for extended periods of time. She is quite capable."

"Understand, Lady Wilmington's firstborn son *will* be the next Earl of Wilmington," warned George. "There will be no reversal of my decision."

"I shall declare my second son to be the ducal heir," Alessandro answered. "He will be trained to bear the responsibility alongside my firstborn until he is old enough to assume my title."

"You are certain?" asked George. "If she bears only one male child, he shall belong to England."

"According to our laws, a daughter may inherit if there are no male heirs." His father would have suffered an attack to hear him say such a thing.

The king's gaze rested on him for a long moment, and then the monarch smiled. It was not a smile that inspired relief.

"Very well, then," George said. "You have my blessing. Melly will make a fine wife, if you can tame her. My goddaughter is a bit strong willed, but a man couldn't hope for better."

The hair rose on Alessandro's neck. *Daughter of the French king, godchild of the English.* What capricious star had shone upon Mélisande's birth?

"She has no idea you've come to me with this, does she?" the king suddenly asked, his bright blue eyes gleeful.

"She does not, Your Majesty," Alessandro answered. "Our engagement has been announced informally among friends, but I felt it best to speak with Your Majesty before any public announcement was made."

"Very wise," said the king, arching a brow. "I wish you luck in your wooing. Now, let us discuss the matter of James Stuart," he continued, clearly ready to move on to other matters.

Alessandro breathed a sigh of relief. The matter of marrying Mélisande was of far more importance to him than his "mission of peace," truth be told. His presence here was a token gesture only, a demonstration of Rome's willingness to listen to the Hanoverian's argument—a willingness that did not actually exist. Rome wholeheartedly supported the Catholic Stuart's claim, and that wasn't going to change.

His mother would be livid, but he refused to return to Italy without Mélisande, if indeed he could even convince her to have him.

Though he was anxious to leave the royal presence, Alessandro spent the remainder of the morning playing chess and discussing political matters. Upon at last being dismissed, he barely restrained himself from running to the stables to saddle his own horse. Instead, he waited, as was proper, for his mount to be brought around.

Alessandro practically flew down Rotten Row, riding as fast as possible without actually galloping. It was the fashionable hour, and he was having to circumvent an increasingly annoying amount of traffic clogging the thoroughfare.

He nodded politely at several acquaintances, though he trotted past, avoiding conversations. By the time he managed to reach Mélisande's house, it was just teatime.

"Your business with His Majesty?" she asked, waiting until the servants had left and the door was closed.

"Completed, and most satisfactorily," he told her. In his rush he'd become disheveled and windblown, his cravat loose and his hair on end. He ran a hand through it to try and tame the unruly curls, succeeding only in making it worse.

She reached out to smooth it down, and he stilled at her touch. Unbidden, an image formed in his mind's eye: Mélisande touching the hair of a child, his child, while wearing the same tender smile she wore now. Even as that happy fantasy flicked through his thoughts, his blood ignited with the need to make love to her, to again claim her and reaffirm that she was his and his alone.

Mélisande was close enough to see the darker motes within his cinnamon eyes. His hand rose to cover hers, holding her palm to his cheek for a moment before turning to kiss it. Heat shimmered through her.

"I've thought of nothing but you the entire day," he confessed, pulling her into his arms.

She melted into him as he held her close and nuzzled her neck to taste her skin at the sensitive place just below her ear. Pressing her mouth hungrily against his, she clung to him as his tongue swirled and teased. A moist heat began to build at the juncture of her thighs as he slid a hand beneath the edge of her neckline to ease a still-swollen breast out of her bodice.

Already knowing the pleasure his touch would bring, her flesh anticipated it, craved it.

When she reached down to feel the hard length of him through his breeches, Alessandro groaned. Encouraged, Mélisande began to unbutton his flap. As soon as he was free, she grasped him firmly, chuckling wickedly at his grunt of pleasure as she ran her hand up and down his smooth cock.

He again claimed her lips, freeing his hands to quickly gather up the skirts of her gown. Backing up until he bumped against the edge of the settee, he then sat, pulling her down to straddle him. Reaching between them, he stroked and played until the flesh was dewed. Then, at his silent urging, she lifted so that he could guide himself to her slick entrance.

Eagerly, she sank down, uttering a low moan into his mouth at the pleasant ache and sudden tightness as his thick, hot shaft filled her.

Shifting his hands to her waist, Alessandro slowly raised her up.

When she slid back down, the sweetness of it was incomparable. Bracing her hands on his shoulders, Mélisande rode him slowly, feeling the bowstring grow taut within her. Tighter and tighter it wound, until it snapped in an explosion of bliss.

He swallowed her outcry as she peaked. A few more thrusts of her hips, and she felt his release shudder through him. Falling back against the cushions, he pulled her down with him to rest against his shoulder.

It was only a moment before the reality of the situation flooded Mélisande's awareness.

The servant might return to see if they needed more tea.

Charlotte sometimes forgot to knock.

That door could open at any moment.

"Alessandro, we cannot be seen!" she hissed, jerking upright.

Separating hurriedly, they worked to right their appearances and ensure there was no visible evidence of their lovemaking.

Mélisande's hands shook as she straightened her skirts. It was impossible for her to look at this man and not desire him. Her lack of self-discipline was frightening. Even now, knowing the risk, she wanted to be back in his arms. It dawned on her as she marked his steady hands and relaxed manner that this little interlude was nothing more to him than a mere reenactment of something he'd done countless times. What's more, he had nothing to lose.

*Whereas I...*

If they were caught, she knew he would simply return to Italy. But she would be publicly disgraced. Should she ever decide she *wanted* to marry, it would be almost impossible to do so after such a scandal, even with her fortune. Certainly, no respectable gentleman would ever consider it.

She could not simply defy convention and take a series of lovers, either. Men, though they claimed otherwise, were just as bad as her fellow sex when it came to gossip, boasting of their conquests among their peers. She'd overheard plenty of ribald jests and references made to the betting book at White's.

Women with a reputation were a curiosity, too. People loved to speculate about them and ferret out the juicy details of their lives. There were plenty of those, if one knew where to look. Everyone knew her mother was French, and her *affaire* with Louis was no secret in Versailles.

Isabelle Compton's life prior to her marriage was not a topic Mélisande wished discussed.

She should end this now and tell him that tonight would be their last night together. But even as she thought the words, she knew she could not speak them.

*I need an excuse, something to help me distance myself. Anything, any—*

A light knock sounded at the door, and they both started.

A pair of curious grey-blue eyes peeked through the opening. "I thought I heard voices in the hall earlier," said Charlotte with a sunny smile. "David mentioned yesterday that he might come for tea this afternoon." The excitement faded from her eyes as she realized he was not in the room.

Mélisande noted she was rather artfully *en deshabillé*. Earlier that morning, she'd been dressed impeccably; now, however, several errant curls strayed about her face, her lips were very red—likely from the stain of some berry, and the bosom of her bodice had been laced far too tightly, pushing her breasts up high for display.

Clearly, it was time for a chat.

Taking a seat, Charlotte helped herself to tea and began talking about the nuptial plans.

After a few moments, Mélisande ceased to pay attention, her thoughts instead slipping back in time. Blushing, she glanced at Alessandro, only to discover him staring back at her. One corner of his mouth lifted a fraction, and she knew he must be thinking the same thing.

"Melly?"

Her attention shifted back to Charlotte. Embarrassed to be caught without a response to whatever it was she'd been asked, she stammered an apology. "I'm afraid I must have been wool-gathering. What was it you wanted to know?"

Charlotte's blue eyes sparkled with merriment. "I asked your opinion regarding the use of autumn leaves and berries for decorations. Winifred suggested it when I told her about your wedding plans."

"Ah. Well," replied Mélisande, her chest constricting at the thought of this ceremony that would never happen. "I suppose it would be easy enough to gather leaves and such, and I'm sure it would look quite charming. It'll be a simple affair, in any case."

Alessandro rose abruptly, tugging at his cuffs and straightening his jacket. "Dear ladies, I'm afraid I've lingered far too long in your delightful company."

*Charlotte's nattering on about wedding preparations must have put him on edge*, thought Mélisande.

"The hour grows late," he added, softening his voice and looking directly at her, "and there are matters to which I must attend."

With a slight nod, she promised him she would be there.

# Chapter Sixteen

## LOVE IS A HORRIBLY COMPLICATED THING

MÉLISANDE POURED HERSELF A GLASS OF WINE AND brought it back to the bed. "We must be more careful," she told Alessandro as she eased under the coverlet. "In private is one thing, but outside these walls is another."

"I understand," said Alessandro. "I am sorry to have caused you distress. I promise you it will not happen again."

Part of her wished she hadn't said anything. The traitorous part. He looked so disappointed in himself, so contrite, so sincere. As if he truly regretted his actions that afternoon.

"I am as much to blame as you," she added, softening. "I ought to have had better sense than to let myself be carried away by the moment. I cannot afford to take such risks."

"You take a risk now, in coming here to meet with me. A far greater risk than that of being caught with your fiancé."

She chose not to point out the obvious: that he wasn't really her fiancé. "Indeed," she said wryly. "But this way, I have a much better chance of keeping the true nature of our relationship a secret. Plausible deniability is everything. Unless someone can provide incontrovertible proof that you are meeting *me*, I can claim otherwise. And I assure you that I have covered my tracks extremely well with regards to this place."

"A man would have to be a fool to underestimate your abilities," he said, shaking his head and smiling. "Of all the people I have known, you are the only one besides the empress of Russia who has been called 'formidable' by her friends."

"Oh? Who, if I may ask, referred to me in such unflattering terms?"

"Ludley." He laughed.

"Well, he would certainly know. After all, he's lost more wagers to me than he likes to admit. I've tried telling him it's no use betting against me, but he never listens."

"I've heard about your wagers," he said, laughing. "The one where you offered to personally reenact Lady Godiva's ride through the streets of London on your horse if he lost was particularly interesting."

Mélisande flushed. "That was several years ago, and I said it in a fit of pique. Fortunately, my horse was indeed the better of the two."

"Would you have made good on your bet if he hadn't been?"

"We'll never know, will we?" she said, giving him a saucy grin. His laughter made her want to kiss him, so she did.

"For a woman who values discretion, you certainly have a way of attracting notice."

Mélisande swirled the liquid in her glass, watching the way the golden liquid caught the firelight. "Mmm. I cannot seem to keep out of trouble. Had I been born a man, I would no doubt rival even you in the realm of sheer recklessness."

"As you were not, thanks be to the Almighty, I don't suppose we'll ever know, will we?" he teased.

Curiosity took hold of her. "How exactly did you come to be so well-known? Everyone from the youngest debutant to the oldest matron seems to have at least some passing knowledge of your exploits."

"Not by design, I assure you," he said. "It was certainly not my intention to acquire such notoriety."

"Some men deliberately seek the kind of reputation you seem to have obtained purely by accident," she told him, thinking again of the infamous book at White's.

"Ah, but their chief pleasure is derived from hearing other men's opinions of their conquests. I earned *my* infamy honestly, and care not what others think. My reputation is merely a result of indulging my obsession. A beautiful woman presents an irresistible mystery."

She snorted. "Most of the men I've met seem interested only in exploring the depth of my purse. As for beauty, even the most unfortunate-looking female can catch a husband, provided her dowry is large enough. I've heard men say one woman is as good as another in the dark."

"They are fools," said Alessandro, pushing aside her robe and dropping a kiss on her bare shoulder. "Women are as varied and unique as one flower is from another. Is not a rose vastly different from a daisy? And there are differences even between two of the same kind of flower."

"Some men don't know the difference between a rose and a dandelion," she scoffed. "I'm afraid your view is not a common one. Females are considered ornaments or playthings, meant only to bear children and see to a man's comfort, or to provide him with wealth. It never fails to amaze me how any man with a wife who manages his entire household can think she lacks intelligence."

Alessandro smiled. "My mother taught me at a very young age never to overlook a woman's mind, no matter how frivolous she might appear on the surface. She is an incredible woman, and my father would never have achieved the success he did if not for her, though he never acknowledged it. But not all men behave so." He laughed, his good humor returning. "Some of us are less pigheaded than others."

"Certainly," she replied with aplomb. "I know several very worthy gentlemen; however, even the best sometimes err.

Whenever one makes a pigheaded comment in my presence, I simply remind him of his place." She grinned and took another sip of wine.

He ran a fingertip down her arm. "I have always admired intelligent, daring women."

"So you've said. But tell me, how many have you loved?"

"I remember every single one," he said, "but I have never kept count. To do so would cheapen the memory, whether good or ill."

"But none could hold you." It was not a question.

"There was one," he said. "But because of my past, she did not believe me capable of love."

Mélisande's heart twinged first with sympathy—and then with guilt. She'd passed precisely the same judgment on him. Was it so unreasonable to think him capable of loving honestly? "Who was she?"

He looked away. "Do not ask me to speak of her, I beg you."

"Forgive me, I just thought that..." Feeling awkward, she looked up to find him staring at her expectantly. "I just thought that for a man like you, the world must be an endless buffet of pleasures. I never considered that it might become tiresome."

"Running from bed to bed is great sport when a man is young and his breeches are bursting into flames," he said with a faint smile. "But the older I get, the less it seems to appeal. The body can easily be sated, but the soul, it longs for something more. My brother, Pietro, once told me that it doesn't take a great lover to bed a different woman every night; it takes a great lover to bed the same woman night after night and leave her wanting more. At the time, I did not really believe him. But now, I begin to see the truth of his words."

Mélisande blinked in surprise. "Then you regret your past?"

"Not at all," he told her. "I've quite enjoyed my adventures. To say I regret my life would be to say it has been a waste, which it has not. But that does not mean I wish to be the man I was at the age of twenty for the remainder of it. That would be foolishness. No. I fully intend to one day marry, have children, and settle into the life of an ordinary, boring, plump country lord. Perhaps I shall even learn to like fishing." He smirked.

*This man will never be ordinary or boring*, thought Mélisande. Plump seemed a rather unlikely prospect as well. "Do you look to that day?"

"More and more, truthfully. Though you may find it hard to believe, I lead a very solitary life. I surround myself with people in order to stave off loneliness, but a man can find himself in the midst of a crowd and still be very isolated."

"I know what you mean," she agreed. "No matter how many friends I make, no matter how busy I am, it is the same for me. I constantly find myself alone in a roomful of people, and I grow weary of it in my heart."

"I would never have expected a woman so lovely and charming to be lonely."

A soft laugh escaped her. "I'm an unmarried, rich, *titled* woman, Alessandro. Since my parents' deaths, I have endured constant attention from men interested only in what they can gain from an alliance. They don't care about me. You would not believe the depths to which some have stooped in order to convince me of their 'undying love.' It sickens me. I trust few people, and of those rare few, there are but two in whom I confide."

"And what of a man who has no need of your wealth or title?"

"If that was the only prerequisite, I would have married David for convenience and simply had *affaires*, as he once suggested. But I want more. Perhaps I'm a foolish female after all, but I want love."

Her own words surprised her, but the more she thought about it, the more right it seemed. "I want happiness and contentment. I want passion! And it doesn't matter if the man is as poor as a church mouse. If he can bring me those things, I will gladly share all I have." She shook her head angrily. "I've been disappointed so many times by men I thought to be good and true, only to discover lying blackguards who cared nothing for me. Even *if* an honest man claimed to love me, I wouldn't believe it!"

Realizing she had just confessed her deepest thoughts and desires, Mélisande grew silent. Feeling horribly vulnerable, she regarded Alessandro cautiously to see his reaction, but he merely continued to stare into the hearth and rub her arm absently.

"You know," he responded haltingly, "in the beginning I was, like every other man, the pursuer. Then, as my reputation as a lover grew and eventually began to precede me, women pursued me rather than I them. It made me arrogant and vain." He turned to her, his smile sheepish. "What man would not become a peacock under such conditions?"

She laughed. "You *were* a bit conceited when I first met you."

A wicked gleam stole into his eyes. "Perhaps, but at least some small portion of my pride was well deserved, madam. Would you not agree?"

She felt her cheeks heat.

"I enjoyed myself immensely for a while," he continued. "But it soon became clear that most of my pursuers were less motivated by desire for me and more interested in what my reputation could do for them. I cannot tell you how many times I have been used to provoke the jealousy of another man. Thankfully, I have always managed to escape with my life. Proficiency with both blade and pistol is an unfortunate necessity when one lives as I have lived."

Mélisande had seen the scars on his body but hadn't really considered what they represented. "How many duels have you fought?"

"I'm afraid I have lost count. I stopped accepting challenges three years ago, after a woman I thought in love with me thanked me for ridding her of her husband, a man I later learned had committed no crime against her beyond having a brother she favored more. They had planned the entire thing."

A soft, bitter laugh escaped him. "I was no longer simply sought as a lover, but as a weapon. Wisdom comes with age, or so our priest always told me. Too late, I realized that my reputation had become a terrible millstone around my neck."

Disturbed by his grim tone, Mélisande tried to lighten the conversation. "It is never too late. And you speak as though you are an old man, but you are still young and handsome."

"I sometimes feel like an old man, though am just this year turned thirty-one," he said. "The things I have seen and done have aged my soul, and I have become hardened to the world in some respects. Like you, I know my wealth and title will guarantee a marriage, but I have no hope of marrying for love. What woman would risk her heart on a man with my past?"

His look was penetrating, and shame swept through her. "Alessandro…" She swallowed past the awkward lump in her throat. "I—I admit I chose to have an *affaire* with you because I knew—"

"Our situation is different," he interrupted. "You are no jade, despite your unflattering opinion of yourself."

"But I am!" she insisted. "I am incapable of love."

"No, you have difficulty with trust," he gently replied. "There is an enormous difference."

"The result is the same," she countered. "You cannot have love without trust."

"I agree," he conceded. "Therefore, I will tell you what you can trust with regards to me. I agreed to this *affaire* for my own very selfish reasons, and none of them had to do with material or social gain. I am a duke in my own country and have more than enough wealth of my own."

*Which is partly why I feel so comfortable with him,* Mélisande realized. There was nothing she possessed that he wanted besides the pleasure of her company. Something inside her relaxed. Although she'd known it all along, hearing him say it somehow made it more of a reality.

"And I know you did not choose me merely because of my reputation," he continued. "There is something else between us, something we both felt and recognized long ago."

Her mouth went dry as she watched his eyes darken.

*He means the undeniable attraction between us, of course. Doesn't he?*

She'd said she wanted them to become friends, but in retrospect perhaps that had been a bad idea. In truth, she hadn't expected to like him as much as she did.

The problem lay in that the real man didn't match up to the image she'd built in her mind, an image based on the bits and pieces she'd seen and heard in Versailles. She'd come into this arrangement expecting a callous reprobate who would gladly have his way with her and then leave without a backward glance. Now, she knew better.

It wasn't that he was perfect, by any means—but he wasn't anywhere near as reprehensible as he ought to be for a seasoned libertine, either. Whereas many men made her feel less than human without ever having laid a finger on her, he made her feel like a queen. He never questioned her intellect or her right to an opinion about anything. He listened to her. And he was as willing to share his thoughts with her as he was to hear what she had to say.

As though he felt she was his equal.

As though he truly cared about what she thought.

As though he cared about *her.*

# Chapter Seventeen

## FOOLS RUSH IN

*Three weeks later*

MÉLISANDE EYED THE CARD ON HER DESK WITH AMBIVA-lence. It was an invitation to a ball next month—hosted by none other than her *bête noire*, Herrington. She could refuse and just have Reggie take Charlotte without her, of course. But then Herrington would think her a coward, and she'd rather be damned than allow him to think such a…

*Charlotte!*

The girl had become quite troublesome of late with regards to her behavior—more specifically, her attempts to attract David's notice. While he appeared oblivious, others had begun to notice and comment. She'd tried to speak with her about it earlier this week, but to no avail.

It occurred to her that Charlotte had only *heard* about David's more unsavory side from others. But what if she actually witnessed him in action?

She looked at the card again, this time with a smile. David's uncle was the prime minister, which guaranteed he would receive an invitation to the event no matter how much Herrington loathed him. And because David never passed up a chance to irritate his enemy, he would accept.

And he would be on his absolute worst behavior.

She penned her gracious acceptance. If all went well, Charlotte would get a good look at the man she *thought* she wanted for a husband. Hopefully, she would then have the good sense to run the other way.

Sealing her response, Mélisande put it on the outgoing tray and went to prepare for Lady Skelton's picnic.

"I am the envy of all men today," Alessandro said to Charlotte in a loud whisper, eliciting a giggle. "I have the world's two most beautiful women at my side." He believed it, too, for one after another, heads turned as they walked across the green.

"It's a perfect day for a *fête champêtre*," said Mélisande, smiling. "Last year was a disaster. It began raining, and we all had to move indoors. Nothing like a lot of wet, miserable people crammed into a small space to enliven things."

They passed the garden pavillion, where the musicians played softly, and followed the path around the green, where fellow guests played at bowls. There, beneath the trees, Lady Skelton had arranged carpets for her guests to recline upon and enjoy the outdoors. Seeing one of these that was unoccupied, the trio claimed it. Almost immediately, servants appeared with delicious-looking hors d'oeuvres and cool drinks.

"Lady Skelton has outdone herself," said Mélisande as she arranged her pink-and-cream-striped skirts about her.

"Hadn't we better find my brother?" said Charlotte, leaning against a gnarled, old tree.

"There is no need," Alessandro replied, nodding toward Stanton, who was making his way over to them.

Her face fell.

"Well and well!" said Stanton as he approached. "Here you are at last."

"Where is David?" asked Charlotte.

"Occupied," said Stanton, sitting. "He'll be along in a bit."

"Sit down, Charlotte," commanded Mélisande, fixing her with a stern eye.

With a loud sigh the girl did as she was told, trained her eyes upon the field, and began humming softly to herself.

"I saw Lady Berkeley at Mrs. Montagu's salon yesterday," Mélisande said. "She is planning a wedding. The Earl of Carlisle has offered for her youngest daughter your friend Winifred."

Still humming, Charlotte continued staring out at the field as if she hadn't heard her.

"A most advantageous match for Lord Berkeley," Mélisande continued. "And Winifred certainly seems delighted. You visited her just last week, did you not?" She waited. "Did she say anything about anticipating such a momentous event?"

The humming stopped, and Alessandro saw Charlotte flick a nervous glance at her.

"She did not," the girl answered at last.

He hid a smile as she began picking at the lace on her sleeve. It seemed Mélisande had finally found a way to get her attention. Stanton seemed content to remain quiet and ignore the conversation entirely.

"Apparently, Miss Berkeley suffered a sprained ankle during a scavenger hunt this last Saturday and was rescued by Lord Carlisle," persisted Mélisande. "Lady Berkeley told me—in strictest confidence, of course—that during the time they were alone together, he compromised her."

Silence.

"She also confided that the gentleman had to be *persuaded* to come to scratch," continued Mélisande. "He claimed Winifred was not telling the truth, and that she merely sought to entrap him."

The look she gave Charlotte was long and piercing, and Alessandro saw the girl redden.

"Eventually, he was convinced by Winifred's father to do as honor demanded. Poor girl. I should never wish to be married to someone who did not wish to marry *me*."

"He will come to love Winnie in time."

Mélisande lifted a raven brow. "I cannot help but think she would be much happier with a husband who *already* loves her and *wants* to be with her."

"Yes, well, not all women are as fortunate as you, are they?" Charlotte snapped, putting her nose in the air. As she returned her gaze to the field, her face suddenly lit with a smile—a smile that evaporated just as quickly as it had appeared.

Turning, Alessandro saw that Pelham had arrived—and that he was not alone. At his side was Miss Olivia Doulton. Rising, he went to greet them.

"Lord Gravina, how nice to see you again," said Miss Doulton. "And of course Mr. Stanton, Miss Stanton, Melly." She nodded to each.

"Have you already joined a group?" asked Mélisande.

"I have not."

"Then you must join us," Alessandro offered.

Miss Doulton and Pelham accepted the invitation. The discussion was much livelier, now. But Alessandro soon marked that, like Charlotte, Miss Doulton kept close watch on the green. Her vigilance was explained when Lady Angelica Mallowby appeared.

At Miss Doulton's subtle gesture, Alessandro stood, leaving his seat—next to Stanton—open. Introductions were made, Lady Angelica sat beside Stanton, and the pair immediately began reacquainting themselves.

Cupid's messenger, it seemed, had performed her appointed task. Looking at Miss Doulton, he raised his glass slightly in salute.

"Lord Pelham was telling me about his horses," the girl told him, starting off the conversation. "Some of the best runners in the country, or so I've been informed." She turned to Pelham with a smile. "I believe you said Pegasus himself couldn't outfly them? Though I've heard Melly speak of them in somwhat less flattering terms."

"She would," he said, laughing. "We've been at odds with each other over who has the fastest horse since we were old enough to ride."

"Perhaps we should have a race this summer and settle the matter once and for all?" said Mélisande.

"Why not?" Pelham answered. "And you can act as judge," he told Miss Doulton.

Charlotte abruptly stood. "I should like to play a game of bowls. Miss Doulton, won't you join me?"

Startled, Miss Doulton arose. "I would be delighted."

Mélisande quickly got up, motioning for him to come as well. "Lord Gravina and I should also like to play."

Turning to Angelica, Miss Doulton apologized, "I do hope you'll excuse my abandoning you?"

"Of course," said Angelica, her gaze lingering on Stanton. "I shall be happy to keep Mr. Stanton company."

"David?" Charlotte prompted.

"You already have four players," he replied without looking at her.

"Oh, but I really think we ought to be evenly matched with two ladies and two gentlemen, don't you? Melly, why don't you sit this round out?" she said, turning away before either of them could answer.

"I can see you'll give no one any peace until you have your way," Pelham said, rising.

"Excellent," she clipped. "You can be on my team."

"I shall come along and keep score," said Mélisande, earning herself a glare from Charlotte.

On their way to the bowling green, a fellow guest stopped them on the path. Alessandro immediately noticed the way Mélisande stiffened.

"Countess, how delightful to see you," the man said, bowing.

"Likewise, Lord Herrington," she replied, her manner formal.

"Congratulations on your engagement, Lord Gravina," Herrington said, turning to address him. His smile did not reach his eyes. "I do hope you'll be very happy together."

"Thank you, I'm sure we will," Alessandro answered, not liking the fellow's cold, amber gaze. A memory from his boyhood flashed: his nurse making the *corna*, the sign against *malocchio*, the evil eye.

"Lord Herrington," interrupted Charlotte, "we were just about to play at bowls, if you would like to join us. Then we can all play. You can be on my team," she added, ignoring the look she received from Pelham.

Alessandro could see that this suggestion was most disagreeable to Mélisande. For some reason, she did not like this man. In fact, the only person who appeared fond of him at all was Charlotte, who, having been rather sullen and recalcitrant until now, was suddenly charming and animated.

"I would very much enjoy that, Miss Charlotte." Herrington offered her his arm. "Shall we?" The pair led the way, leaving the rest of the company no choice but to follow.

The entire time they played, Charlotte was cheerful and talkative—with Herrington. Everyone else might not have even been present, especially Pelham, whom she proceeded to ignore with a vengeance.

The moment an opportunity presented itself, Pelham made his excuses. "Miss Doulton, I beg your pardon, but I just saw my uncle pass by and must speak with him regarding a matter of some urgency." He bowed and then made as if to turn, but then hesitated. "If you would like to join me and are willing to forgive me in advance for boring you with matters of business for a few moments, I should be glad of your company."

Miss Doulton accepted his offer at once, her relief evident.

The moment they were out of sight, the atmosphere changed. Though she remained polite to Herrington, Charlotte no longer played the simpering coquette.

"What is the matter with Miss Charlotte today?" Alessandro whispered to Mélisande while Charlotte and Herrington took their turn. "Did she and Pelham have a disagreement?"

"No, there is something else afoot here," she answered, her face full of worry. Then she could say no more, for it was their turn to play.

Upon completing the last end and claiming the win for his team, Herrington parted company. "It was an honor to share in your game, my lady," he said to Charlotte, bowing over her hand. "I shall look forward to seeing you again."

"Thank goodness that bit of strangeness is over," Mélisande muttered as they left him behind. "I'll explain later," she added, nodding at Charlotte's back.

They rejoined Stanton and Lady Angelica, as well as Miss Doulton, who'd also returned. The three appeared to be in a celebratory mood. Alessandro noted that Pelham was not present.

Miss Doulton immediately moved to sit beside Mélisande. "It isn't official yet, but I wanted you to be among the first to know that I am now engaged to be married."

"Olivia, how exciting!" exclaimed Mélisande.

Looking to Charlotte, Alessandro marked her sudden pallor. She looked as though she was about to be violently ill.

"Mr. Kesselman asked me to marry him not half an hour ago, and I accepted," Miss Doulton continued, eyes sparkling.

Charlotte blinked in confusion. "Mr. Kesselman?"

"Yes, Charlotte," said Mélisande, openly amused. "You remember the young man from Germany you met at our engagement party?" She didn't wait for her to answer, but turned back to Miss Doulton. "But where is he now?"

The young woman blushed happily and ducked her head. "He has gone with Lord Pelham to find my grandfather. He's such a wonderful gentleman, Melly. So patient and kind-spirited. I cannot thank you enough for introducing us."

Herrington watched the little celebration from beneath the deep shade across the green, his gaze resting not on Mélisande but on her friend, Miss Stanton.

Whitehurst had not communicated with him in over a month now. The last he'd heard, the man was having difficulty gaining entry into the French king's inner court. He needed another plan.

By trying to incite Pelham to jealousy, Miss Stanton had unknowingly handed him the key to bending Mélisande to his will. She cared for the girl and would wish to protect her.

Archimedes said, "Give me a lever long enough and a fulcrum on which to place it, and I shall move the world." Jealousy was such a useful tool. With it, emotions could be manipulated, friends turned into enemies, and enemies subdued.

# Chapter Eighteen

## THE BEST-LAID PLANS

MÉLISANDE HAD BEEN RELUCTANT TO ASK ALESSANDRO for help, but given the disastrous afternoon at Lady Skelton's, it seemed wise. "I want to ask for your assistance in handling a rather delicate matter," she said, scooting closer. "Charlotte has developed a *tendre* for someone she oughtn't, and I'd like your help correcting the situation."

"You mean Pelham, of course." He chuckled. "It is a harmless infatuation, nothing more."

"It is far from harmless," Mélisande replied, feeling beleaguered. "She has an unrealistic, romantic view of him. As long as she maintains it, she'll refuse to consider anyone else. It is my hope that once she's stripped of it, she'll accept the suit of a decent young man."

His smile faded. "Ah, I see."

"It's not because he's a rake," she said, realizing now how it had sounded. "Alessandro, I know him as she does not. Even if she somehow managed to force him to marry her, she would not be happy as his wife."

"You cannot know that."

"I can and I do," she insisted.

"You once told me he was a brother to you. You cannot know what he would be like with someone else. He might be very different as a husband."

But Mélisande knew better. He could not know how David had suffered as a child, the things he'd witnessed in his father's house. But she did. She'd witnessed some of them with him. "I cannot reveal the reasons why, Alessandro, but you must trust me when I tell you that he will *never* let anyone into his heart," she said, looking him straight in the eye. "And Charlotte deserves someone who can love her back." She continued to stare at him. "Will you help?"

A long moment passed before he answered. "I will."

A tension she hadn't known was even present suddenly eased. "Thank you."

"Do not thank me yet, *amora*," he said, lying back against the pillows. "My help comes at a price."

In response to his teasing tone, Mélisande came to stand before him. Loosening the ties of her wrapper, she let it fall. "Oh? Does it? Name your price, then."

"You asked me to teach you the ways of love, did you not?"

"I did indeed."

Pulling aside the sheet, he grinned. "In return for my assistance, you will show me what you've learned thus far."

With curious hands, she explored his male form. His rapid intake of breath as she touched one of his nipples brought another smile to her lips. She circled it with the tip of a finger, watching as his eyes closed and the pulse at his throat jumped.

Her gaze dropped. Boldly, she ran her hand down the trail of dark, springy hair that led to the seat of his masculinity. Thick and heavy, it lay in wait. His breath caught again as she traced the sensitive flesh of the rim, his cock leaping at her light touch.

A strangled chuckle issued from her lover, and her gaze snapped to his face. He was smiling, but it was a pained expression that clearly said she was tormenting him.

Grinning, she mercilessly continued her unhurried exploration of his person, venturing down to feel the corded strength of his legs, molding well-shaped thighs and calves before traveling slowly back up again. Gathering her courage, she firmly grasped his manhood.

He moaned faintly in response, his buttocks clenching as he strained upward.

Her heart began to pound. *He* was now at *her* mercy. She felt positively uncivilized as a rush of lust filled her. Touching him boldly now, she noted the strangely soft skin and the hot pulsing of his shaft. A single drop of dew appeared at its tip, glistening in the firelight.

He groaned again and a shocking idea entered Mélisande's mind.

Alessandro's unbelieving gasp and widening eyes registered just before she took him into her mouth. His whole body jerked and trembled as she ran her tongue around his smooth glans, tasting the faint saltiness of the gem that had formed there.

A prolonged groan of ecstasy tore from his lungs as she experimented with light suction, flicking her tongue across his sensitive flesh. Mélisande felt his hips rise yet higher. It was all she could do not to crow in triumph. He was just as susceptible to his own tricks! She chuckled in satisfaction as he came up off the bed, the lack of grace in the movement betraying his loss of control.

Grabbing her, he pulled her up, laughing breathlessly as he plunked her down atop his lap. "Ye *gods*, woman, stop!" he gasped.

Flushing, she looked away, unable to bear meeting his eyes. "I'm sorry. I've heard men discussing such things with what seemed like great relish, and I thought you would like it. Did I do it wrong?"

"Not at all!" he answered unsteadily. "It is only that most women are quite reluctant to pleasure a man in that particular manner. That you have done so with such enthusiasm simply astonishes me."

"I was only returning the favor in kind," she said, still embarrassed. "I enjoyed it so much when you…" She halted, blushing.

"I can assure you I most certainly enjoyed it." He laughed. "But you must remember that a man is not like a woman. I can endure most love play for quite some time, but not that. That will bring me to crisis far too soon, and I would not wish to leave you wanting."

Mélisande looked down between them to where his manhood pressed against her. "I will not *let* you leave me wanting," she said, stroking him.

Arching a brow, Alessandro surrendered himself to her will. Rising up onto her knees, she straddled him, and with agonizing slowness, lowered, impaling herself.

It was an entirely different sensation, being atop him this way. The fullness she experienced was *complete*. Each and every tiny pulse and throb of his member was felt intensely. The pressure swelled within her like an enormous wave when he lifted his hips and ground up into her, touching her very core.

Moaning, she shifted forward, savoring the delicious friction between their bodies as he slid nearly all the way out of her passage. With a sigh of satisfaction, she pushed back and felt him fill her again.

Alessandro's hands skimmed down to graze the flesh just above the place where their bodies joined. She cried aloud at the intense sensation, bracing her hands against his chest. He lifted his hips again, and she rose with him, riding him.

When she began to tire, he pulled her up just enough to take the rosy tip of one breast into his mouth. Sucking hard, he flicked the swollen, aching bud with the tip of his tongue. Mélisande could only thrust her chest out for more. When he did the same to the other breast, she wailed her pleasure.

Her coming was like the tide, slow and inexorable. Gasping with each ecstatic pulse, she sank beneath the depths as crest after crest washed over her. Alessandro rocked with her, licking the sweat from her shoulder and nipping the flesh at the juncture of her neck. Before her peak could completely subside, he flipped her over and thrust deep, a guttural cry ripping from his throat.

Mélisande shook and strained with each powerful stroke, her muscles clenching tightly as the tide broke over her yet again.

At last, with a low groan, Alessandro poured his long, hot release into her.

Together they collapsed, muscles trembling from exhaustion. He held her tightly for a moment before rolling to the side, taking her with him.

Contentment filled her. Inexplicable peace. Being cradled in his arms felt...*right*.

The thought crystallized.

Somehow, against all logic and despite her vowing not to let it happen, she'd begun to love him. The thought frightened her to no end.

The morning of Herrington's ball, Mélisande sent a message to David and Reggie telling them Charlotte was indisposed and that she and Alessandro would meet them at the ball instead of traveling together as a group.

Upon seeing Charlotte that evening, Mélisande almost changed her mind about her plan.

The aqua silk mantua she'd had commissioned for Charlotte last month had been quite significantly altered. The lace at the neckline had been removed and the amount of décolletage now exposed was shocking. It would have been so on a married lady, Mélisande mused.

If Charlotte thought David would come running after her the minute he laid eyes on her, she was probably right. He would—to give her a stern talking to and then to lend her his kerchief to cover herself. That is, of course, if her brother did not see her first and take her over his knee. She hoped neither of them spotted the girl before her plan could come to fruition, but if she had to choose, she'd rather it be David. With him at least, there was a chance that Charlotte's embarrassment over his reaction might deter further pursuit.

"You look lovely, Charlotte," she said, keeping such thoughts to herself. "You'll certainly captivate the young men tonight. I just hope it's for the right reason," she added, unable to help herself.

"Regardless of the reason, captivating them is the whole purpose of my going to these balls, is it not?" said Charlotte. "I'm to catch a husband, and that's what I intend to do—by hook or crook." Her eyes shone with determination as she turned toward Alessandro. "What think you, my lord? Shall I bewitch my admirers?"

"You look enchanting, Miss Stanton," said Alessandro. He looked to Mélisande as the girl turned away, his expression worried.

Shaking her head slightly, she signaled him to remain silent. Her stomach tightened unpleasantly. Ironic that she, who'd spent the past several years courting scandal, would now be unsettled by the sight of her young friend's risqué gown. Though certainly no prude, perhaps she was a bit more conservative than she'd thought. "Come. The carriage awaits, and we don't want to be at the end of the line."

By the time they arrived, Mélisande had managed to settle her nerves. Their host's greeting was on the chilly side, which suited her just fine. Herrington's obvious annoyance at having not only her but her infamous fiancé at his ball further lightened her mood. If he didn't want her there, he should not have invited her.

She raised a brow. "I thank you for your kind invitation, Your Grace. I cannot imagine a more pleasurable means of entertainment on such a lovely evening."

Herrington's blush left little doubt that he'd immediately conjured several images of the "pleasurable entertainments" implied by her tone.

Tearing his gaze away from her to greet Charlotte, he blushed deeper, all the way to the roots of his hair.

Mélisande almost wished he would say something to Charlotte. In her present mood, she'd probably tell him to go straight to the devil—loudly. The thought made her smile.

When he saw her amusement, Herrington's expression shifted back to one of thinly veiled hostility.

With a smirk, Mélisande turned to leave with Alessandro. She could feel Herrington's gaze burning into her back. She hoped he enjoyed the view, because from this point on, that was all he would see of her.

Charlotte went with the now engaged Winifred, leaving the couple to their own devices. Mélisande didn't particularly care for Winifred's influence of late, but she felt it was the lesser of two evils. Better to allow Charlotte her companionship than to have her mooning about at David's elbow.

Together, she and Alessandro circulated throughout the room. When they failed to find David among the general assembly, they went to the gaming room, where they discovered him playing primero. He nodded a cordial greeting and continued to play.

"Elizabeth!" Mélisande exclaimed happily, seeing Mrs. Montagu sitting by the fire. "It's been far too long since we last saw each other. May I join you?" Surely Charlotte couldn't possibly get herself into trouble *this* early in the evening.

"Of course! Come. Sit. Both of you," Elizabeth replied, signaling a footman to bring another chair.

Mélisande was conscious of the fact that eyebrows rose over her invitation including Alessandro. They rose higher still when Elizabeth asked him to attend an exclusive reading by Henry Fielding of his new novel at her salon the week following. While part of her was pleased that he was being accepted, another part felt it would only make things more difficult in the end.

They bantered in friendly fashion until David excused himself. A few moments after he left, Alessandro did the same, leaving the two women to continue their game.

Elizabeth's eyes followed him. "And just what are our handsome friends up to, I wonder?"

For once, Mélisande sincerely hoped David was up to no good. She decided to tell Elizabeth about her plan.

"What say we keep an eye on them?" suggested Elizabeth, her eyes twinkling.

Mélisande agreed, and the two of them went in search of the men. She looked for Charlotte as well, but she was nowhere in sight. They found David deep in discussion with a group of gentlemen. Alessandro was there too. At her questioning look, he shrugged and shook his head. Eventually, he gave up and rejoined them.

She and Alessandro paired for both the first and second dances—scandalous, even for an engaged couple. She didn't care. Fervently hoping Herrington would cluck at her over it, she made her movements as provocative as possible.

Alessandro's cinnamon eyes darkened as they danced, his smile growing sensuous. Her pulse hammered wildly and her skin began to tingle in anticipation. That he still looked at her that way after nearly three months amazed her.

Reggie joined their group, looking for Charlotte, who he'd been told had decided to attend in spite of her headache. Mélisande suddenly realized she hadn't actually seen the girl for nearly an hour. She looked to where David stood, still in conversation with the same men. How ironic that the one night she actually needed him to misbehave, he'd chosen to do the opposite.

Charlotte was nowhere to be found.

Without it being announced, the musicians struck up the next piece, which was, to everyone's delight, a waltz. All eyes turned to the ballroom floor to see a couple moving through the steps with fluid grace.

Mélisande caught herself gaping in surprise. Herrington, the disapproving prig who'd lectured her about impropriety, was engaged in what had recently been dubbed "the most scandalous dance ever performed outside a gypsy camp." That he happened to be dancing with *Charlotte* only made the reality that much more bizarre—and alarming.

Just as they made the turn, Herrington caught her stare. The malicious triumph in his eyes froze the blood in her veins.

David strode up, rage written in his stiff motions. "Little fool!" he said. "Someone ought to give her a good thrashing."

Mélisande had never seen him so angry. "David, I—"

"Why did you lie to me and tell me she was ill at home? What have you done?"

"You think *I* did this? I had nothing to do with *that*, I can assure you," she said, pointing at the couple. "I was only trying to help her—"

"Ruin herself?" he cut in.

"This is nothing more than a childish prank on her part, David. She cannot be seriously considering—"

"She looks bloody serious to me," he interrupted again. "Herrington is only sniffing around her because of *you*," he went on, stabbing an accusing finger at her. "Except Charlie doesn't know it. Once she figures it out, it'll break her heart."

*I was wrong. He does care for her.*

"Now," he said, taking a deep breath, "I'm going to find Reggie and get her out of here—before I beat Herrington to death on his own ballroom floor."

Alessandro arrived just as he departed. "What has happened? Where is Pelham off to in such a rush?"

"I've made a terrible mistake," Mélisande answered. Gritting her teeth, she began telling him about her conflict with their host.

# Chapter Nineteen

## STEP INTO MY PARLOR

$\mathcal{A}$MID THUNDEROUS APPLAUSE, THE WALTZ ENDED. FOR the past hour, Herrington had been everything a young lady could hope for in a gallant gentleman—kind, attentive, and sympathetic—for Miss Charlotte Stanton was the key to his plan.

He watched as she again glanced in Pelham's direction. He was leaving. Her eyes began to fill. Quickly, he shepherded her out of the ballroom before she could cause a scene.

The moment the parlor door closed, she burst into hot, angry tears.

Herrington enfolded her in his arms, letting her weep and curse her rage against his chest. When she'd finally spent herself, he sat her down beside him and handed her his kerchief.

"Your Grace, I don't know what came over me, I must apol—"

"Look at me," he commanded. When she would not obey, he took her chin in his hand and tipped her face up to gaze into clear, blue-grey eyes brimming with bright tears. The tip of her upturned nose was charmingly pink from crying, as were her cheeks and mouth. The girl was actually quite pretty, he thought, even when weeping. It was something that could not be said of most women.

A strange sort of tenderness filled him, and he felt a twinge of sorrow for what he was about to do. He spoke, barely above a whisper. "I know what it is to love someone, and to be spurned by them. I, too, have loved someone who cares nothing for me. One who detests me, even."

As he'd intended, his words had an almost hypnotic effect on her.

"Who?"

"Your friend Mélisande," he answered with a brittle smile.

"Melly?" she blurted. "But you hate her!"

"Hate is a very strong word, Miss Charlotte. I am merely embittered by her disregard."

"But—I don't understand. How…?"

"Three years ago, I saw her and fancied her. I more than fancied her, in truth," he confessed. "I worshipped her from afar, too timid to approach such a glorious creature. Finally, one night after several glasses of champagne, I worked up enough courage to speak to her. I opened with a jest, thinking to impress her with my wit, and she mistook it for an insult. She has disliked me ever since."

And she had shamed him in front of everyone with her harpy's tongue! Herrington could not control the tremor of impotent rage that ran through him at the memory.

"It was unwise of me, perhaps, to speak to her with such familiarity before she'd been given an opportunity to know me better and see that I meant no offense," he continued. "I had no idea she would react so to my attempt at friendly banter. It was a simple misunderstanding. One I have never been allowed to correct."

Indeed. It was a wound that had festered for three years, rotting in the darkest recesses of his soul. The bitch had scorned him, subjected him to public humiliation, and all he had done was make a simple witticism to try and gain her attention.

She'd then proceeded to make him a complete laughingstock. Practically every female he'd met since that day had given him the cold shoulder or giggled at his approach.

The witch taunted him at every opportunity, as well, and he could not help but rise to the bait. She was a poison in his veins; even though he hated her, he still desired her. Every time he laid eyes on her he was stricken by almost debilitating lust. He would have her, and she would pay for his torment!

Charlotte placed a gentle hand upon his. "I can only imagine how truly awful it must be to know that she is now engaged to someone else."

Herrington turned her hand palm-up and kissed it. *She*, at least, was genuine. "I thank you for your compassion, Miss Charlotte. It is a testament to your sweet nature that you can be so kind after having been the victim of such similarly cruel indifference."

"In—indifference?"

"I've seen the way you look at Pelham." He watched her cheeks redden. "And I've witnessed his careless disregard. He is most undeserving of your devotion."

Charlotte stiffened and tried to pull back her hand, but he held it fast.

"It's no use wasting your love on a man like him, Miss Charlotte," he pressed gently. "He will never return it in kind. He is incapable of tenderness, being a shallow, heartless cad who would tear out your heart and tread on it with no remorse. I've seen him do so countless times with countless women."

The fire in her eyes contradicted him even before her words. "He would *never* do that to *me*," she said with all the confidence of a trusting child.

"Hasn't he already?" he asked, giving her a penetrating look. "How many times has he ignored you? Passed you by without a second glance no matter how you've tried to gain his attention?"

"He can't show his true feelings for me," she justified. "Reggie would kill him if he was anything less than a perfect gentleman toward me."

He pushed the knife a bit deeper into the wound. "If he loved you, he would be unable to hide it and would not care if the entire world saw it in his face. That you are Stanton's sister has nothing to do with it. If he wanted you, he would have made it known."

"He—he's afraid his reputation will ruin me!"

Herrington laughed. "God forgive me, but I cannot allow you to continue in such ignorance!" Releasing her hand, he grasped her by the shoulders and twisted the blade. "Pelham ignores you not to protect you or to hide his unrequited love for you, Miss Charlotte. He ignores you because he finds your innocence boring."

It was a deliberate goad, for any female dressed as she was tonight was out for blood. She would despise being referred to as even remotely childlike.

Just as he expected, Charlotte broke free of his hold and moved away. "I'm a woman grown, and he will one day see it."

"For your sake I hope he doesn't, Miss Charlotte," Herrington said softly, folding his now empty hands in his lap. "The day he does, you will regret tempting him, for he will break your heart even more than it is breaking now. You must be told the truth, for your own good. He will ruin you for his pleasure and toss you aside. You think you know him, but I assure you—"

"I know all about David's 'adventures,' if that's what you're referring to," Charlotte cut in crisply. "I'm not as ignorant as you might think. And I know he would *never* treat me so! You're wrong about him. I *do* know him, I've known him ever since I was born, and I know what I'm doing!"

"Do you really?" he asked. "Do you know what passion is? Have you ever felt it firsthand? Tasted it?" He folded his arms, sitting back. "Have you ever even been kissed?"

Charlotte squirmed. "What if I haven't?" she threw at him. "Once I am his wife, he will teach me all I need to know."

Herrington smiled at her naïveté. "You honestly believe that as his wife, you will fulfill the role of lover as well?"

"Why not?" she asked with unabashed hostility.

Striving to sound as patronizing as possible, he answered. "Unlike me, Miss Charlotte, most men believe a wife is merely a means to an heir. They don't view the marriage bed as a place of passion, but merely as a place for fulfilling one's duty to the line. A wife is expected to embody modesty, chastity, and motherhood, not lust and depravity! If you think Pelham will teach the future mother of his children to perform in the manner of his mistresses, I can assure you he will not."

He leaned forward again, pinning her with his stare, hardening his voice. "Yes, Miss Charlotte. *Mistresses.* Pelham currently keeps not one, but three. I know this for fact. Do you think a man like that will deny himself the pleasures to which he is accustomed for the sake of a few vows spoken in a church? How can an innocent like yourself ever hope to satisfy a depraved monster?"

Charlotte flinched as though his words were physical blows.

"For innocent is what you are," he murmured. "And you should value your innocence, for it is a prize without price, like your good and true heart. If you cast it aside to buy his love, he will view you as he does those who sell their bodies to him now and cast you off in the same manner as those unfortunate women. When he is finished with you, you will have gained nothing but his contempt."

He knew she'd heard tales in the powder room amid all the inane giggling, believing them nothing more than overblown gossip. Hearing it from a gentleman, however, was quite different.

Sensing that her will was about to crumble, Herrington pressed his advantage. "Should you somehow manage to force Pelham to the altar, you would be miserable, Miss Charlotte. You want love and fidelity from a man whose passion is for you and you alone, and Pelham is incapable of giving that to any woman."

She stared at him, visibly stricken.

He looked down and toyed with the hem of his silk jacket, feigning pained reluctance. "Much as I hate to admit it, I'm no better than you in where I place my affection. She will never care for me, especially now that she's taken up with that ridiculous Italian. I, along with everyone else, can see she has fallen prey to his wicked influence. She is lost to me forever. So you see, Miss Charlotte, we are both bleeding from wounds to the heart. We've loved those who never have and never will love us back."

Her tear-filled eyes lifted, full of despair, and Herrington squirmed inside. He'd justified his choice, but she'd done nothing to deserve what was about to happen.

It should never have come to this. Mélisande should have been his. She *would* be his! And she would pay for every sin he committed in making it happen. She would pay each and every night for the remainder of her life. His blood heated at the thought of how he would exact his revenge.

His thoughts must have shown in his eyes, for Charlotte froze.

Herrington cursed himself for his lack of self-control, shaking his head and looking down to cover his slip. "We are of a kind," he sighed. "You understand the pain in my heart, and I know yours as no one else can. Your sweetness and compassion have eased my heartache, Miss Charlotte. Our shared suffering has forever formed a bond of kinship between us."

He gave a weak laugh. "I should be content to name you friend and confidante after such commiseration, but instead, I am ashamed to say that, that...well, the truth is I'm afraid I find myself unexpectedly drawn to you, Miss Charlotte."

Shock wrote itself all over her face.

"I cannot help but wish she had a heart like yours, but she does not," he continued. "I see now that she is a fickle jade unworthy of my tender regard. It is strange, but in admitting so, I find her power over me diminished."

"I—I'm glad to have been a help."

"You have freed me, Miss Charlotte. You have freed me from her spell."

A bitter smile crossed her lips. "Truly, I *am* glad to have been a help to you, Your Grace. I wish you happiness in your newfound freedom."

"But I am not free."

Her cloud-colored eyes flicked up, wary.

"I find it ironic to be liberated from one bewitchment only to fall prey to another," he continued. "Your compassion has touched me in a way I had not thought possible, Miss Charlotte. After having been imprisoned in the dark with my own bitterness for so long, the warmth and light of your kindness is like the sun. And your purity and beauty are as a bright flame."

Charlotte jerked back as he reached for her.

"Forgive me!" Herrington dropped his hand. "I'm afraid I have simply lost all reason this night—leave me before I say any more!"

She started to obey, but before she could turn, he leapt up and grasped her wrist. He felt her pulse hammering beneath his fingers as she stared at him, trembling like cornered prey. Genuine excitement stirred in his loins.

She was confused and terrified.

*Perfect.*

"I beg one last word before you leave," he pleaded. "Tell me if you feel anything for me, anything at all. A simple yes or no will suffice, and I shall be satisfied."

"I, I don't—I don't know!" she quavered.

He leaned closer. "Tell me you feel nothing for me, Miss Charlotte, and I will leave you in peace. I swear it."

When she did not answer, he took her silence for a yes. Taking her in his arms, he pulled her close and brushed his lips against her mouth. When she shivered and softened, he parted them and plundered her mouth, enjoying the knowledge that he was stealing her from Pelham's unworthy grasp.

"Charlotte," he whispered, surprised at how much he actually desired the chit, even though he knew it was nothing compared to his lust for Mélisande. Still, he would be equal to the task of deflowering this gullible little nitwit, should the need arise.

Tilting her head back, Charlotte closed her eyes, opening to him completely.

A total surrender. Herrington smiled triumphantly as he leaned her back against the cushions of the settee.

# Chapter Twenty

## KEEP YOUR FRIENDS CLOSER

THOUGH SHE TRIED TO REMAIN CALM, MÉLISANDE WAS nearly ready to call a search of the grounds. When Charlotte finally resurfaced, however, her panic was only briefly relieved, for her face held a fresh glow that she immediately recognized.

Alessandro and several others within earshot looked askance at the colorful string of French invectives she released on seeing the cause of that glow hovering near Charlotte's elbow.

*Herrington!*

Mélisande made a beeline for David. "We must do something!"

"This is your fault," he said, his eyes hard. "If you hadn't set such a terrible example and then allowed her to mimic your outrageous behavior, this would not have happened!"

Anger made her bold. "I beg to differ. It is *you* who are to blame!"

"I beg your pardon?"

It was time to end this foolishness. "Charlotte has been in love with you practically since she was born, you idiot!" Mélisande hissed. "You cannot tell me you didn't notice."

He maintained an unblinking stare. "I'd rather hoped she would get over it, quite honestly."

"Yes, well, as you can see, she's over it," she replied flippantly.

"She deserves better, Melly. We both know it."

"And you think *that's* better?" she exclaimed, barely missing a passing footman as she flung an arm in the general direction of the dance floor. "*Look* at her!" she commanded. "She will ruin herself out of despair for love of *you*! If, *if* she hasn't already! And you don't care one bloody—"

"If he has touched her, I will kill him," David snarled.

The violence in his eyes silenced her. It was now quite clear that he more than cared for Charlotte; he loved her.

They watched as Herrington kissed Charlotte's hand and left to attend another guest.

Without another word, David stalked over and grabbed her by the arm, causing her to squeak in protest. Bending low, he muttered something in her ear, after which she fell silent and allowed him to escort her out of the ballroom.

Mélisande followed.

Opening the first door he came to, David pulled Charlotte in and slammed the door shut behind them.

Not to be deterred, Mélisande reopened it and slipped inside.

"Exactly what do you think you are doing?" David snapped, jerking Charlotte roughly toward him. "Dressing like a harlot and behaving like one, too—and with *Herrington*, of all people! If you'd chosen any other man upon which to hone your flirting skills, this would be comic, but *not* him. That man has a soul as black as pitch, Charlie! I thought you had better sense. Pick someone harmless, like Prewitt, if you want to practice playing grown-up games!"

Mélisande winced as the beginnings of a smile faded from the girl's face.

"Let me go!" Charlotte yelled, tugging her arm in an effort to break his hold. "You're one to talk of harlots and blackened souls. You should know!"

"*My* virtue isn't in question here," he said. "How far did he take it?"

"Enough, both of you!" Mélisande interrupted, stepping forward. "This is neither the time nor the place."

They ignored her.

"Why should it matter to you?" Charlotte spat at David, still struggling.

"How far?" he grated, tightening his grip.

"Far enough to know I want more!" she hissed. Clawing at his fingers, she tried to wrench free of his grasp. Finally, she tore loose, stumbling backward into a table. A delicate figurine fell, shattering into pieces as it hit the floor. Blindly, she reached behind her and grabbed the nearest object, a book, and hurled it at him with a shriek.

Her explosion of temper stunned Mélisande. This was not the sweet, mild young lady she knew! She watched as David ducked another missile, a small vase. It grazed his head and crashed into the wall behind him, sending shards of porcelain flying.

"Charlie, control yourself!" he commanded, flinging his arms up to protect his face as another object whistled past.

"I will *not*!" she shouted, casting about for something else to throw. "You've no right to question me. You're not my father or brother. You—you're *nothing*!" she wailed, tears streaming from her eyes.

The door burst open behind them.

Whirling, the three found themselves face-to-face with Herrington. Charlotte immediately rushed around David and into his arms.

Herrington held her to his chest as she sobbed. "There, there, my dear," he murmured, stroking her shoulder as he smirked at the other man. "Pelham, I think it might be best if you leave before there is any further unpleasantness."

"Charlie, he does not love you. He's only using you to get at Melly," David told her.

Charlotte turned, her storm-cloud eyes staring back at him with pure venom as she edged closer to Herrington.

"Come with me," David repeated calmly, holding out his hand.

"I think our host is right, *Lord Pelham*," she said, her voice thick with tears. "You should leave."

David shifted forward, but Mélisande placed a restraining hand on his arm. "You cannot," she murmured. If he called Herrington out, Charlotte would hate him, because Herrington would most certainly die.

His lips thinned, telling her he didn't like her advice.

"Not here. Not now," she added, fixing him with a hard stare. "David, you know I'm right. She'd never forgive you. Let us resolve this another way."

After a moment, he nodded. Without further argument, he turned and departed.

The instant he was gone, Charlotte burst into another storm of tears.

"Charlotte," Mélisande said with all the calm authority she could muster, "you will come with me immediately. We're leaving. Now."

Just then, Reggie burst into the room. "I just saw David. He said Charlotte was in…" His words died out at the sight of his sister in Herrington's arms.

Charlotte turned to Herrington, burying her face in his shoulder. After a moment, he pried her loose and cupped her cheek. "You must go. Do not worry; I will take care of everything. I'll call very soon. I promise."

"You will do no such thing," Reggie said, finding his tongue at last.

"Reggie!" Charlotte turned pleading eyes on her brother.

Mélisande stared at Herrington. "Reggie, I think you'd better take your sister home now."

"Come, Charlotte," said Reggie.

Having no choice, Charlotte went to her brother, who quickly escorted her out of the room.

"You will not see Charlotte again," Mélisande told Herrington. "As her chaperone, I forbid it. And I'm sure her brother will forbid it, also."

"You may forbid all you like, but I believe her parents will welcome my suit," he replied, clearly enjoying himself. "Indeed, they may wish us married immediately, under the circumstances. Completely unnecessary, of course. We've done nothing to warrant such hasty action, but nevertheless." His shrug was nonchalant. "I'm perfectly amenable to the idea—unless of course another, better option presents itself. You could take her place."

"Me?" she blurted, confused. "But you despise me!"

"Despise...desire." He shrugged. "They are but opposite sides of the same coin. You are a beautiful woman, Mélisande."

Alarm filled her. "I did not instigate this hostility," she retorted, taking a step back. "However if you wish a public apology I will gladly give one if it means saving Charlotte from a broken heart. But I will *not* become your whore."

Herrington smiled then, a terrible, slow smile that made the hair on the back of her neck stand up.

"You misunderstand my intent," he told her. "I wish to make you my *wife*. You see, by marrying the woman who spurned me, I shall be publicly vindicated, my humiliation erased. And if you refuse, I shall marry Charlotte."

"But you don't love her!"

He shrugged again. "I don't love you, either. But if I cannot have what I *want*, then I shall have her as consolation." His expression darkened. "And I will console myself with her every night for the rest of her unhappy life. And every time I use her body, every time I break her spirit to my will, know that I will be thinking of *you*. You will be to blame for all her woes. If you marry me, however, she can run back to Pelham, bear his brats, and live happily ever after."

Shock and horror permeated her. "I will *nev*—"

"I shall write to Charlotte's parents immediately," he cut in. "Expect me to call within the week." He paused, his strange, amber gaze resting on her. "Think on it. If you change your mind, you know where to find me." And with that, he strode past her and out the door.

Filled with worry, Mélisande immediately sought out Alessandro. "I cannot stop him from writing them," she told him after filling him in on the details. "Even if I told them the truth of the matter, he would only deny it. If only Reggie had heard him!" she said, frustrated. "What am I to do? This is an unmitigated disaster!"

"Come, let us leave," Alessandro said. "Once Charlotte has calmed herself, you can try to reason with her."

It was an uncomfortable journey home. Refusing to speak, Charlotte stared out the window until the house and its lights passed beyond view. Then she kept her eyes trained on the floor while Reggie plied her with questions she did not answer. She did not react even when he raised his voice.

Mélisande tried her hand after Reggie and Alessandro left.

When the clock struck three in the morning, the girl finally spoke, her voice cracked with fatigue. "You've been right all along, Melly. David isn't the right man for me. He will never love me. In his eyes, I'm nothing more than Reggie's annoying baby sister, and that's all I'll ever be to him."

"Oh, Charlotte, you couldn't be more wrong," Mélisande replied. "David *does* love you. He just refuses to admit it to himself. I know it for a certainty. And Herrington is nothing more than a vindictive, petty blackguard. He lied to you in order to get at me." Anger swept through her, hot and fierce. That he should bring Charlotte into their private disagreement was unconscionable!

Charlotte said nothing, but gave her a long, penetrating look.

At last, Mélisande gave up and went to bed, exhausted. In light of events, she and Alessandro had agreed to cancel this evening's rendezvous. She was too worried, in any case, to engage in pleasant diversion.

Reggie and David showed up the next morning to speak to Charlotte. Both looked absolutely haggard. Charlotte, however, would not come down as long as David was present, so Reggie went up to see her. Half an hour later, he came down, his face ashen.

"She's been compromised. She told me herself. And she wants to marry him."

## Chapter Twenty-One

### THE TRUTH WILL SET YOU FREE

*D*AVID SAT DOWN WITH A THUMP, HIS COLOR FADING TO match Reggie's.

"I don't believe her," Mélisande said. "Herrington told me himself that nothing happened. She has not been compromised, Reggie. And this has gone far enough."

She started to rise, intending to drag Charlotte downstairs and pry the truth out of her by whatever means necessary, but Reggie reached out and took her arm, eyes desolate.

"Melly, she's never lied to me before. She wouldn't. Not to me."

Her heart squeezed painfully. "There is a first time for everything, Reggie. Let me talk to her again."

David stood. "Reggie, if you'll allow it, I will go up and speak with her. I know why she's doing this, and I can put a stop to it."

Reggie eyed him. "What makes you think you'll have any influence on her decision?"

"Am I the only one here who takes note of the obvious?" Mélisande broke in, exasperated. "Because she's loved him since she was a child, Reggie. It is her love for him that has driven her to this folly. She will listen to him."

"I doubt she'll listen to him anymore," Reggie countered. "She's just now informed me that she's in love with Herrington and that she wants to marry him as soon as possible to avoid the shame of bearing his child out of wedlock."

Upon hearing these words, David rose and walked out. The front door slammed a moment later.

"Well, this is just a bloody catastrophe, isn't it?" Mélisande exclaimed. "I don't believe her—I don't!" she insisted. "Reggie, you didn't hear what Herrington said to me after you left. He's up to something awful!" *And it's all my fault. If I hadn't been distracted by Alessandro, I would have been paying attention.*

Reggie shook his head. "Unfortunately, if she is determined to marry him and he is willing, I'm afraid there isn't much we can do to stop it. My parents will be delighted she has caught a duke and will do everything in their power to ensure the match's success."

Mélisande's heart sank. When she went back upstairs, Charlotte's door was again locked. She received no response after knocking, but heard furtive movement within. Unable to persuade her charge to open it, she decided to let the girl think things through for a while in peace. Perhaps reason would return of its own accord once she calmed herself.

"I have missed you," Alessandro murmured as he held Mélisande. It had been nearly a week since the incident at Herrington's ball. "I would have come sooner, but the fool Jacobites kept me at the king's side night and day. He would not let me leave until he'd decided what to do."

"What happened?"

"Evidence has been brought to him that Charles is indeed fomenting another rebellion, trying to gather the support of the Scottish clans. I doubt he will succeed."

"I would have thought you'd be more supportive of his cause," she said, chuckling.

He shook his head. "I work for Rome, it is true, but even I know when a cause is hopeless. Even if he made it all the way to London, Charles does not have enough trained men at his disposal to take the throne. I told George this, but it made no difference. He was still all in a fury. The bulk of his army is still in Germany."

"Do you think Charles will actually try to invade?" she asked as they ascended the stairs to the bedchamber.

"I think he is fool enough to make an attempt, yes. But as I said, I doubt he will find much success. His forces are limited, and support for him here has grown increasingly thin since he fled into exile. People tend to support stability, and George has been here long enough to prove himself a capable ruler." He closed the door behind them. "Enough of politics. How are things with Miss Charlotte?"

"I was beginning to think she might never speak to me again," Mélisande replied, letting the robe slip from her shoulders as she approached the bed.

"She has relented, then?"

"Yes. Two days ago, she appeared at breakfast and began nattering on as though nothing untoward had occurred. It was most peculiar."

"And what of Herrington?" he prompted, his hand wandering down to follow the dip of her waist and the luscious curve of a hip. Though they'd been lovers for some time now, he still could not get over how glorious she was naked. "Has he followed through on his threat?"

"Indeed. I received a letter from Charlotte's parents late last week, informing me of the 'delightful news.' He's been given permission to call on her at my residence. Worse, they've asked that I facilitate the courtship."

She buried her head in the pillow. "I don't know how I'm going to get through this," came her muffled voice from within the depths. "The blackguard arrived unannounced for tea the very day I received the letter—almost as if he *knew*. And every day since, I've had to sit and watch him ply Charlotte with sweet words and false smiles."

Alessandro drew her back up and kissed her. "We will find a way to stop him, *amora*. I promise."

"The situation with David is degenerating, too," she added. "The rumors are terrible. Drunken rants, reckless gambling. He's always been wayward, but never out of control. I read in the papers yesterday morning that he'd fought a duel with Lord Chilton. David apparently walked away with a few minor scratches, while Lord Chilton very nearly died. David's second had to physically restrain him from running the man through. I pray he does not end up dead or in prison."

"The wound in his heart is driving him to commit such rash acts," Alessandro told her. "He will return to sanity again, in time."

"Time is a luxury we do not have," said Mélisande. "I'm convinced Charlotte still loves him. I sometimes hear her crying at night when I pass her door. But if Herrington is allowed to continue gaining ground..."

"Has he made any more mention of you taking her place?" he asked, his gut tightening unpleasantly.

"Not at all. He didn't even speak to me during his visit today. Not one word. He knows I'll never agree to it."

The look in her eyes reminded Alessandro of her father—her *true* father. The tension in his middle eased. "There must be a way to make her see the truth."

"If there is, I cannot think how to accomplish it."

"Perhaps we should try to make him show Charlotte his true nature, much as you had planned to do with Pelham?" he suggested.

"No," she replied, quaffing the last of her wine. "I dare not try to manipulate the situation like that again. My last attempt failed spectacularly."

"True, the strategy failed to achieve its purpose the first time, but that was due to Herrington's interference."

"No," she repeated more firmly. "It failed because I did not stay focused on the task at hand. I let myself become distracted."

"You had no way of anticipating his actions."

"If I had been watching her properly, he never would have attempted to subvert her!"

"Do not be angry, *amora*," he whispered, tipping up her chin so he could see her eyes.

Her shoulders slumped. "I am not angry with you, Alessandro. I'm angry with myself. I made a mistake, and I must rectify it."

"What do you propose?"

"I will try to reason with him directly. I'm sure we can resolve our differences in a civilized manner. He doesn't truly want to marry me; the man can hardly stand the sight of me," she told him, laughing a little. "This is purely a matter of tit for tat—his vanity was bruised, and now he wishes to bruise mine. If I *did* agree to marry him, he would only jilt me at the altar. I'm certain of it."

Alessandro wasn't so sure. There was more than animosity in the man's eyes when he looked at her. Still, he held his tongue. There was no point in causing her further distress. He would simply watch over her more closely from now on.

"The king's masquerade ball is in just two weeks. I'll speak with him then," she told him.

"And if he refuses to change his mind?"

"I don't know," she admitted reluctantly. "I'll think of something. I only know that I cannot let Charlotte marry him."

Alessandro knew of one solution. Tomorrow, he would be paying Pelham a visit.

"*Le Renard* indeed!" Mélisande clapped her hands in delight as Alessandro bowed. He'd come to pick her and Charlotte up for the masquerade ball wearing a russet coat trimmed with fox fur at the neck and cuffs, matching breeches, and a pair of brown leather boots also trimmed in fox fur. But best by far was his mask: a crafty fox's muzzle curved in a leering, ivory-toothed grin.

"Perhaps I ought to have dressed as a chicken," she teased.

Silently, Sir Fox raised a finger and spun about, eliciting further laughter—protruding from the rear split in the skirts of his coat was a large, white-tipped fox's tail. When Alessandro had revealed to her the comparison he'd made the first time he had seen her unclothed, she'd confessed her nickname for him, as well.

In honor of being dubbed Diana the Huntress, her costume was modeled on a statue of the deity she'd seen while visiting Versailles. It consisted of a long, sleeveless white silk tunic belted loosely about her waist, Roman-style sandals, a silver bow, and a small quiver filled with delicate, fletched silver rods. The mask she held was also silver, spangled with diamonds and framed by soft white feathers.

It was a beautiful costume, but she was almost afraid to wear it in public. The anonymity of the masquerade guaranteed immunity from criticism—at least openly—but it did not guarantee acceptance. The fabric was not *quite* sheer, and it was draped in a manner that prevented outright shock, but it still left little room for the imagination.

"You had best be cautious, lest you incite the goddess to jealousy." Alessandro laughed. "According to the old tales, the female deities have little liking for beautiful human women."

Mélisande snorted at his flattery but gave him an appreciative smile nonetheless.

The Season was nearly over, and while he had not yet evinced any desire to bring their arrangement to an end, in the back of her mind she knew it must be coming. Any day now he would begin to cool toward her. How she would bear it, she did not know.

No matter how hard she tried, she could not close her heart to him. Not even the knowledge that she was setting herself up for incredible heartbreak and misery could stop the tender ache he inspired. It was a sensation she'd begun to notice more and more whenever she was with him.

Every time he spoke, every time his eyes danced with laughter and mischief, every time they made love, the bindings that held her heart tightened a little more.

"I hope the king doesn't set his hounds on you, Your Grace," Charlotte laughed from the doorway. The "wood nymph" was covered in jeweled silk leaves in varying shades of green, beginning at the bodice and going all the way down to the bottom of her skirts. The slightest movement made her appear to be floating amid a whirlwind of spring foliage.

The crush when they arrived was incredible, as was the din. Typically staid individuals cavorted about in a wanton display of frivolity, their identities safely hidden behind their masks, their dignity and reputations protected by fanciful disguises. The atmosphere was one of unfettered gaiety.

Mélisande observed Reggie's scowl as he approached with Lady Angelica at his side. He was dressed as a Turkish sultan, while the Season's beauty wore the form of a butterfly, complete with a pair of bright, glittering wings and long, curled antennae.

"You look lovely, little fairy," Reggie told his sister.

"Thank you, O master of the desert, but I'm no fairy. I, sir, am a nymph," Charlotte replied pertly, spinning so that her leaves rustled.

"Oh, how lovely!" exclaimed Angelica. "Who designed your costume? Has Winifred seen it yet?"

"She has not," answered Charlotte. "We agreed to keep them secret and then to try to find each other during the ball without knowing ahead of time."

"Well, then. I shall *not* tell you which one she is." Angelica laughed. "Come, you must see Olivia and Mr. Kesselman." She smiled at Reggie. "I shall return before the first dance begins," she promised.

As the two chattering magpies departed, Mélisande edged closer to Reggie. "Is he here?"

"I don't know what convinced him to attend, but yes, he is here." His gaze flicked to Alessandro. "Pelham is dressed as Night, and Herrington's disguised as a satyr."

Mélisande's skin prickled with annoyance. Now she understood why Charlotte had insisted on a new costume, complaining that her Sun was old and tired. "I will make an effort to reason with Herrington once more. You two work on David and Charlotte," she told him and Alessandro. "Find a way to throw them together for a dance or something."

Reggie's face grew grim. "I don't know if that's such a good idea. Pelham's taken a rather unpleasant attitude of late, and he's been drinking today. Heaven only knows how he'll react."

"Well, things can't get much worse than our current predicament, can they?" Mélisande snapped. "We cannot allow this foolishness to continue!"

"Yes, but that's not all," said Reggie. "I suspect Herrington is waiting for him to make a move. He's been skulking about the edges of the room, watching us ever since we arrived. If Charlotte causes a scene, it will almost certainly end in a duel."

"I'll distract Herrington," Mélisande told him. "He won't be able to interfere with them if he's occupied elsewhere. I'll ask him to speak somewhere in private. He won't disagree, as the matter in question is not likely one he wishes aired in public."

She had to get to the bottom of this mess and set things right. Herrington had a grudge against her, and she was the only one who could make peace between them and save Charlotte. And David as well. If she could just bring them together and make them both see reason…

Such good intentions could not be acted upon immediately, however. As soon as Herrington spotted Mélisande, he came looking for Charlotte. Sneaking in behind the young ladies, he swooped down and tossed the sprite over his shoulder with a loud growl. Her squeals of delight could be heard across the room as he spun her about, then boldly kissed her full on the lips in full view of everyone.

A few partygoers raised their glasses at the sight, giving hearty cheers of encouragement. All manner of impropriety was sanctioned at a masque ball.

Charlotte, pink cheeked and grinning beneath her mask, introduced her friend Mistress Butterfly.

Angelica curtsied, looking as though she wished she was somewhere else.

Mélisande knew he'd been among the foremost of the contenders for her hand before she'd decided to follow her heart and accept Reggie's suit.

As politely as possible, the girl excused herself.

Mélisande watched as Herrington led Charlotte away, his hand resting boldly at the small of her back, propelling her forward. Helpless to prevent it, she joined her friend Mrs. Montagu while Alessandro went to find David.

The dancing began and the celebratory atmosphere heightened. There was food and drink aplenty for all, and as the sun set, the general mood grew more and more uninhibited.

At the height of the revelry, the king at last made his appearance. Resplendent in a costume of tawny amber velvet trimmed with a real lion's mane, his snarling, golden mask turned him into a ferocious caricature of the king of the beasts. At his side walked Spring, the Countess of Yarmouth, swathed in pale green silk and pink satin petals.

Alessandro reappeared just as His Majesty gestured to the orchestra. Everyone cheered as a waltz was struck and the king stepped out with the countess to lead the dance.

Mélisande and Alessandro joined them, along with a surprising number of others.

"I believe we started a trend," she laughed as they swept across the floor. "London's dance instructors must be making a fortune this Season."

She kept close watch on Charlotte, making certain there were no more disappearances while awaiting the opportunity to make her move. Much to her frustration, the besotted sprite remained at Herrington's side almost the entire evening, but at long last the girl finally deigned to dance with another gentleman.

"I must go at once," Mélisande whispered to her lover. "I fear there may not be another chance."

Alessandro made to come with her, but she stopped him with a gentle hand. "You cannot accompany me—I must speak with him alone," she said in response to his frown. "I'll suggest that we take a walk through the courtyard statuary. That should afford us a small measure of privacy without any real danger. People are wandering all over the palace grounds tonight; he won't risk exposing himself here."

He nodded, releasing her.

Approaching her mark carefully from behind, Mélisande touched Herrington's shoulder.

Startled, he turned, his hawk's eyes immediately narrowing. "If you are here to again try and dissuade me, you have come in vain—unless..." His gaze raked her costume. "Unless you agree to my terms."

Mélisande's flesh crawled, but she mastered her disgust and stared him down. "I wish to speak with you privately. Might I suggest we take a brief stroll through the sculpture gardens?"

Wordlessly, he held out his arm.

As Mélisande picked her way through the crowd, Alessandro signaled Pelham and then casually moved to a position where, between them, they could observe all the exits leading out to the gardens and statuary.

## Chapter Twenty-Two

### OF MONSTERS AND MEN

TOGETHER, Mélisande and Herrington wended their way through the jubilant throng and out into the night. Stars pierced the darkness high above, laughter echoed from within the garden maze, and the flickering light of the torches along the pathway caused their shadows to chase each other as they passed. It would have been very romantic had it been Alessandro at her side.

After several unsuccessful attempts to find a private corner, they at last found a small, unoccupied alcove. In it, standing between two low stone benches, a tall marble angel reached toward the heavens.

Releasing Herrington's arm, Mélisande moved in to explore, feigning interest in the statue as an excuse to put some distance between them. The angel wore a look of despair on its carved face; the stone tears welling in its eyes and streaming down its cheeks were exquisitely crafted.

Her enemy cleared his throat, removing his mask.

She followed suit and faced him. "I've come to make peace with you before it's too late," she stated, keeping her voice steady and low.

His strange eyes mocked her. "Then you agree to my terms," he murmured, taking a step forward.

Mélisande thrust out a hand to ward him off. "You misunderstand me, Your Grace. I am *not* here to offer myself as a sacrificial lamb."

His soft, malicious chuckle trailed fingers of ice down her spine.

"Did you know I visited Versailles recently?" he asked. "I wintered in France on the Crown's business last year. A bit indecorous, the French court, but all in all still a very pleasant, very *interesting* experience. While I was there, I happened upon the strangest thing in the king's private chambers: a portrait of *you*. I'm sure you can imagine my surprise at such an…odd happenstance."

Mélisande's pulse jumped, but she maintained iron control. "How very odd indeed, considering I have no memory of sitting for any portraits during my brief visit as a child. You'll pardon my rudeness for changing the subject, but I came here to discuss the conflict between us, not French art," she managed in a dismissive tone. *He cannot possibly know…*

His smile broadened and he moved closer, constricting the space between them.

Mélisande took an involuntary step backward and bumped into one of the stone benches. She should never have come out here alone.

"Oh, the woman in the painting wasn't you," he stated, coming closer still. "But the likeness was extraordinary. The resemblance was so striking that, at first, I simply could not tell the difference. It was only upon closer inspection that I was able to make the distinction. There were several remarkable similarities."

Mélisande searched for a means of escape as he drew nearer. The alcove was surrounded by four-foot-high walls topped by thick hedges, and there was only one point of egress. Herrington was blocking it.

He closed in. Reaching out a single finger, he touched the little mole above her heart.

Mélisande froze like a deer at the sound of a hunter's footsteps.

"For instance, the woman in the painting had the *exact* same little mark, just here," he said, circling it, taking the opportunity to caress the swell of her breast with his knuckles. His tone then shifted, taking on a menacing singsong cadence. "The lady in the painting also had the same...unusual...eyes." He reached up to grasp her jaw, turning her face this way and that. "The king said she was his mother. Naturally, I couldn't help but wonder..."

With a sudden movement, he sprang forward, pinning her against the wall. His other hand reached down, slipping beneath her tunic.

Mélisande clawed at his hand. "Lord Wilmington knew my mother was with child when he married her!" she spat, her tongue loosed by rage. "He claimed me as his own! You have no right to—"

"I was right," he breathed, eyes ablaze with triumph. "You *are* the daughter of the French king and his whore. The moment I saw that painting, I knew the similarity could not be coincidence. And you've known all along."

An unnatural, icy calm settled over her. There was great deal more at stake here than Charlotte's future now. Drawing herself to her full height, she found her voice at last. "What is it you really want from me, Herrington?"

The torchlight reflected eerily in his amber eyes as he cocked his head. The guttering flames cast his features into sharp angles of light and shadow, making him look demonic. "Why, the same thing I have always wanted. You, of course."

He grinned, a vicious expression devoid of any warmth or humor. "I've wanted you since the moment I first saw you, my dear little impostor. You saw fit only to humiliate me, and thereafter your constant taunting turned us into bitter adversaries, but it doesn't have to be that way between us."

His finger traveled the line of her neck and shoulder and down her arm, raising gooseflesh. Feeling ill, Mélisande shrank from his touch, repulsed. Like a snake, he struck out and captured her wrist in a viselike grip, eliciting a gasp of pain.

"So very lovely," he murmured as he slowly forced her hand up to his mouth and kissed the inside of her wrist.

Squirming, Mélisande tried to jerk it away, but he only gripped it tighter. Prying open her clenched fingers, Herrington kissed her open palm, flicking his tongue across the sweaty flesh.

"You can end this by becoming my wife," he whispered. "You will, of course, pay the price for the constant torment you have visited upon me these last few years, but your penance can be a private matter, just between us. And I promise I shall not remain angry forever. Once you have paid for your sins, I shall be merciful and forgiving, the very best of husbands."

She ceased her struggles. He was much stronger than she was, and she needed to save her energy to run at the first opportunity. "What of Charlotte?" she gasped, trying to distract him. "She thinks you're in love with her—you're practically engaged—it will destroy her!"

Cruelty played at the edges of his harsh laughter, and his lips curved in a crafty, unpleasant smile. "The girl is of no consequence; she was merely one means of securing your cooperation. One I no longer require."

Mélisande's panic subsided, a strange peace settling over her. "You, sir, belong in Bedlam," she said with as much scorn as possible. "I will hear no more of this lunacy. I will not allow you to harm Charlotte, nor will I take her place. You will cease your pursuit of her immediately, and I *never* want to see your face again!" She wrenched her arm as hard as she could, but Herrington's grip remained firm.

He dragged her closer. "You have no choice," he hissed, his hot breath fanning her cheek as she turned away in disgust. "If you refuse me now, I'll reveal your true lineage to the king. I will, of course, also present him with a ready solution to the nasty little problem you represent. I shall generously offer to make you my wife in order to prevent a public scandal, as well as to provide His Majesty with *true* English guardianship of the *stolen* Wilmington title and lands. He will gladly accept my offer," he told her smugly. "I have you neatly boxed, my little French dove."

Mélisande smiled through her fear and raised her chin defiantly. "There is one tiny, yet *very* important detail you seem to have forgotten," she informed him. "I am already engaged to Lord Gravina."

He let out a bark of laughter. "That seducer has no intention of ever marrying you, and you bloody well know it! Even if he did, the king will never allow it, now. Gravina is a foreigner, which means he cannot assume the title—even if it *did* rightfully belong to you. He is of no use to England. If anything, he would be an incredible liability, as his loyalty is to Rome."

Mélisande opened her mouth to reply that no husband of hers would ever take the title anyway, but Herrington spoke over her.

"And don't think to escape by marrying Pelham, either," he said slyly, his eyes narrowing to golden slits. "If such even remains an option. He's in love with that miserable little twit who belongs to *me*, now. He's become a worthless, drunken fool ever since she spurned him!" He cackled in delight as Mélisande again attempted to free herself in vain. After a moment, his laughter ended abruptly, cut off as if with a sharp knife.

"You should be glad I am willing to bargain, for by marrying me you will ensure that the secret of your traitorous birth will be safe. And you will eventually find your way back into my good graces—provided you are sufficiently obedient. That is my offer. More than fair, considering the circumstances, I should think."

The man was a beast in human guise. Mélisande could not allow him to prevail. It seemed Alessandro had been right after all. If she could make him angry enough, she might force him to expose his true nature now, publicly, before it was too late.

"You leave me little choice," she whispered. His gaze flared with unholy desire as she leaned in, at last giving way to the pressure on her wrist. Pressing herself firmly against him, she stretched up on her toes to whisper softly in his ear. "I will marry you when the fiery lake freezes and devil skates upon it."

She braced herself.

Herrington roared with rage. Jerking her arm nearly out of its socket, he twisted her wrist and slowly forced her to her knees on the gravel, his smile ugly as she gasped in agony, tears streaming down her face.

Gathering her breath, Mélisande shrieked and struck out at him with her free hand, aiming for his most sensitive manly parts.

His knee rose to block the blow as he raised his hand high.

Mélisande had only a fraction of a second to shut her eyes before the back of his hand landed across her cheek with a crack that echoed across the courtyard. Black spots swam before her vision as she reeled from the impact. As she tried to regain equilibrium, Herrington used the opportunity to grab her other wrist and yank her to her feet. His amber eyes were bright with fury and lust as he pulled her in and ground his mouth against hers. She thrashed and kicked, biting down on his lip with all her might, tasting the iron tang of blood.

Again, Herrington roared, withdrawing to swipe a hand across his torn lip, chuckling at the dark, vitreous smear on his fingers. "Ferocious little bitch!" He grinned and lashed out with the speed of a whip to again grab her by her arms, laughing aloud at her whimper of pain as he dug his fingers deep into her flesh. He crushed her against the stone wall. "Yes, fight me!" he hissed. "Once we are wed, I will relish taming you!"

"I will *never* submit to you!" she bit out, glaring at him with hatred.

"You should be grateful for my attentions!" he rasped. "No matter. You'll soon learn proper appreciation for my favors."

Mélisande let out another terrified shriek. It was suffocated by his mouth. Heaven help her, the lunatic was going to rape her right here in the king's own garden! She tried to bite him again, but he withdrew just in time, chuckling as he again twisted her wrist until the pain caused her knees to buckle beneath her. A sweaty palm was clamped over her mouth, preventing her from screaming, while his other hand held her wrist in agony.

Footsteps crunched around the corner, coming to a halt in a skittering of gravel.

Herrington had only an instant's warning before he was knocked sprawling to the ground by a powerful blow to the side of the head. When he looked up, the Duke of Gravina was standing over him.

"Get up," Alessandro grated, death in his smoldering, black eyes.

"Alessandro!" Mélisande gasped in a breathless sob, rushing to his side.

Herrington, in no hurry to rise, braced himself on one elbow. "You have no authority here," he said, taunting him with a serpent's smile. "This is English soil and you are a foreigner."

"No matter, I will still see you brought to justice!"

Herrington grinned. "It might interest you to know that your hellcat fiancée is a foreigner as well," he said, wiping at his lip and flinging a bloody hand in her direction. "She's no countess—she's nothing more than a bastard! The illegitimate get of yet another worthless foreigner!"

"I challenge you!" Alessandro said just as Reggie and David rounded the corner, Charlotte hard on their heels.

"And I accept," said Herrington with a sleek look of triumph.

Charlotte, taking in the scene and seeing the blood on Herrington's face and hand, rushed to his side, falling to her knees. Her face contorted in a mask of cold fury. "How *dare* you!" she raged at Alessandro. Rising, she strode across the alcove, fists clenched.

Mélisande backed into the shadows as she approached, shocked at the hatred in her friend's eyes.

"You couldn't leave well enough alone, could you?" Charlotte snapped coldly. "You have your happiness, yet you would deny me mine. You have no right!"

"You don't underst—"

"I've heard enough of your lies!" Charlotte yelled, stepping back from Mélisande's outstretched hand as though it were a snake. "He has tried to make peace with you for years, and you've done nothing but fling it back in his teeth and treat him with contempt! You made *him* out to be the villain when it is *you* who are to blame!"

David stepped forward. "I can promise you that this man has made no attempts at peace," he interjected. "He is using you, Charlie."

Charlotte's eyes were slits of pure hatred as she walked over to stand before him, trembling with rage. "Don't call me that anymore! Don't even speak to me!"

"He doesn't love—"

"You fornicate with women *paid* for their affection and *dare* talk of love? Do you really think you have the love and gratitude of your whores? Given a choice between performing vile acts with you for money or dying of hunger in the streets, they've merely chosen the lesser of two evils. Or so they think!"

"I understand how you've come by your opinion of me, but if you will just hear me—"

"Why? Why should I listen to you? Any of you?" she said with a sneer. "You've insulted this man for years, refusing to hear his side of things. He's done nothing to earn your contempt, yet you've given him yours in full measure. And now you've determined *me* worthy of your contempt, as well."

"Charlotte, that isn't so," Mélisande interjected. "You are a sister to me—don't be fooled by this, this deceiver! Come with me. Please. I beg you."

"It is you who are the fool and the deceiver!" Charlotte said, pointing a shaky finger at her. "You pretend to be my friend and call me sister, when the truth is you've done nothing but feed me lies! I know what you are!"

Mélisande blanched. Had Herrington revealed his suspicions to Charlotte? Was her secret about to be shouted to the world?

"You've done nothing but lie to me, Melly, as you've lied to everyone else," Charlotte said. "But your time is coming. Soon, your sins will come to light and everyone will see you for what you are: a liar and a fornicator just like him." She jerked her chin at David. "You deserve each other."

"Charlotte!" Reggie thundered. "That's quite enough!"

Mélisande saw that people had begun gathering along the path behind them, drawn to the disturbance. Their view was blocked by Reggie and David, but Charlotte's voice had carried clearly on the night air.

Without another word, Reggie stepped forward and clasped his hand over her mouth. She bit him as he attempted to drag her from the alcove. Finally, he was forced to pick her up off the ground, sling her over his shoulder, and haul her away like a sack of flour. She protested, kicking and screaming curses as he pushed his way through the spectators.

Herrington shook with silent laughter as he rose. He smiled at Mélisande, then turned to Alessandro and bowed. "Dawn. Tothill Fields."

"If he does not kill you, I most certainly shall," David growled as he stepped aside to let him pass.

Like reeds before the wind, the crowd parted for Herrington, closing ranks behind him, waiting to see what would happen next.

Retrieving his mask from where he'd tossed it before knocking Herrington to the ground, Alessandro helped Mélisande replace hers. Then they, along with David, departed.

A silent sea of curious eyes glittered from within the dark holes of countless masks as Mélisande passed, some beautiful, others grotesque, all unnervingly surreal in the flickering torchlight.

The susurration of whispers following their passage made the hair on the back of her neck rise. She longed to break into a run and escape the hollow stares, but gritted her teeth and walked at a stately pace, back straight, head high.

David rode home along with them, as Reggie had taken Charlotte home in his carriage. Once safely away, Mélisande told them everything.

"He is a dead man," Alessandro stated, the chill of the grave in his voice.

"You'll need a second," David offered quietly.

In the light of the lamps lining the Row, Alessandro nodded acceptance, his face unyielding.

"I beg you not to do this," Mélisande beseeched him. "You swore never to duel again over a woman, remember?"

"I made no such vow," Alessandro answered. "I merely chose not to fight good, decent men over the honor of women who, in truth, had none. This is different. That man is neither good nor decent, and you, *amora*, are worth fighting for."

"There is no need to do so! I will go to Uncle George tomorrow morning and petition against Herrington. He has no real proof!" She looked to David for support. "Tell him it isn't necessary!"

David looked at her with sympathy. "It is absolutely necessary. He cannot be allowed to go unpunished."

Darkness fell over the three as the carriage made the turn. Beneath its cover, Mélisande allowed herself the luxury of tears. Alessandro was going to leave England eventually anyway, but she would much rather it be later rather than sooner. If he killed Herrington—and she was sure he would—he would have to do so immediately.

There was also a risk that Herrington might kill him.

Either way, this duel meant that Alessandro would be taken from her far sooner than she was ready to accept.

When they arrived at her residence, the butler's shocked exclamation made her run for the entryway mirror. For a long moment, she stared in frank dismay at the image in the glass before turning to face her companions.

Both men swore vehemently.

Her swollen cheek bore a small cut and a darkening bruise where Herrington's ring had struck it high on the bone. It was plain to see where the beast had gripped her arms, as well, for his cruel fingers had left plum-colored, crescent-shaped marks in her flesh, and one of her wrists was ringed in deepest violet.

Alessandro held her in his arms as she wept. "Tomorrow morning, I will have satisfaction and make certain the bastard never strikes another woman again."

A message arrived. Reggie had taken Charlotte to the house and requested that David delay his return until he could either make her see reason or arrange for other lodgings. The girl was hysterical and refused to calm herself.

"She was right," David muttered. "How could I speak to her of love? Look at the way I've lived my life."

Mélisande took pity on him. "Stay," she offered, blotting her eyes and gathering her composure. "And you as well," she told Alessandro firmly. "Please. I do not feel safe here alone with that animal on the loose," she said for the benefit of the servants.

Wordlessly, David nodded.

Later that night, she tried to persuade Alessandro to retract his challenge, with the reasoning that revenge against Herrington wasn't worth the risk of death. There had to be another solution.

Alessandro refused. "The man dared to lay violent hands upon you. How can I not demand satisfaction? I could never show my face in public otherwise." He paused, caressing her hair. "Come, let us make the most of what is left of this night."

She pushed his hands away for the first time since they had become intimate. "I will not be distracted!"

"*Amora*, do not deny me now," he whispered, kissing away her objections.

He made love to her with tender skill, slowly building the fire between them. With adoring hands and lips, he erased one by one each of the hurts Herrington had inflicted upon her, replacing the memory of pain with fresh delight. The inexorable pull of desire dragged her toward release, and when the conflagration at last engulfed Mélisande, she welcomed its healing ecstasy.

"My heart!" he whispered, kissing her tears away. With a shudder, he buried himself within her and gave way before the storm.

With desperation born of both love and fear of loss, Mélisande clung to him. This man was part of her very soul. He could not, *must* not die!

As they lay drifting back to earth, utter peace filled Alessandro. His breathing grew deep and even, his mind clearing of everything but this moment. He remained so for hours, hovering just at the edge of slumber, savoring the quiet of the predawn hours.

Just as he was beginning to contemplate getting up and leaving for his own bed before the servants awakened, he heard a whisper.

"I love you," Mélisande breathed.

Knowing she thought him asleep, he remained unmoving, a tender smile spreading across his face. At last. Elation mingled with dread. He'd faced death a dozen times, each with a fatalistic attitude. This time, however, he fervently prayed he survived.

# Chapter Twenty-Three

## DOUBLE DECEPTION

NNOYANCE FILLED GEORGE. THIS WAS SUPPOSED TO BE A night of revelry, damn it all! Matters of state could wait until tomorrow. *Late* tomorrow. He waved the messenger away, returning his attention to his mistress.

Upon receiving a second urgent message, one stating that it was a vital matter affecting England's security, however, he agreed to receive Lord Herrington. After all, he was a trusted counselor to the throne. If he said it was of vital importance, then it must be serious.

Herrington entered the private chamber, bowing and scraping. All in a rush, he proceeded to explain how he'd stumbled upon a Jacobite plot involving the Countess of Wilmington during his last diplomatic visit to France. Evidence of the lady's true ancestry had been discovered: a portrait of the king's mother that had looked exactly like Lady Wilmington, right down to the mark on her breast—the same mark borne by the Bourbon king. She was *his* get, brought up by a Frenchwoman who'd surely instilled French Catholic loyalties in her child. She could only be a Jacobite spy.

George kept his expression placid. He'd known Melly her entire life. She'd been born in Kensington House, and he'd seen firsthand Wilmington's excitement at her arrival. His had certainly not been the reaction of a man greeting a cuckoo.

His thoughts ranged back to that day. It had been a little over seven months after Isabelle had first arrived. At the time, he'd thought nothing of it. But if Melly *was* the French king's bastard...

Did she know it? Had Wilmington known? He gestured at Herrington's face. "How did you come by your wound?"

Herrington looked him directly in the eye. "I inquired of the lady regarding the matter, seeking only to ascertain whether or not she was aware of her lineage, and I'm afraid she took it rather badly. She became violent," he said, touching his lip with a look of chagrin. "She knew, Your Majesty. It is the only possible explanation for such a reaction."

George chuckled drily. "In the midst of a public celebration, you informed a woman that you believe her to be illegitimate. Her less than favorable response seems quite reasonable to me."

Frustration flickered across Herrington's face. "Your Majesty, even if she turns out not to be a Jacobite spy, the fact that an English title has passed into her hands by subterfuge cannot be overlooked by your beneficence, especially given her lineage."

George could not help but snort at the preposterous idea. "What can she possibly do?"

Herrington drew himself up importantly. "I assure you her ladyship is *quite* aware of her origins, Your Majesty—and that puts her loyalty in question. One also cannot help but note how frequently she associates with foreigners like Philipp Stamma and Friedrich Kesselman—both Papists. And now she is in league with that Gravina fellow, of whom we know very little, save that he is an Emissary of Rome and welcome in Versailles. It all seems rather suspicious to me, Your Majesty. You must admit it is not inconceivable that she could be spying for the rebels, gathering and passing along sensitive information to her contacts."

"I see. And where is your supposed spy now?" George inquired.

Herrington shrugged. "I know not. She fled the palace after striking me. She could be anywhere by morning, Your Majesty."

George eyed him circumspectly. There were at least two layers to this conundrum. The man had withheld his suspicions for months following his return from France. If he'd been truly concerned about Melly supporting an uprising, he should have brought it to his attention immediately, allowing the Crown to take charge and place watchful eyes on her. That the fellow was only just now experiencing a patriotic impulse told him that he'd failed to gain her cooperation in some other matter and was now resorting to another means.

George did not like the idea of being used. Still, he had to at least consider the possibility that the man had stumbled upon *something*. With the French supporting the Stuarts' claim and Rome watching England's every move, he would be a fool not to look into every potential threat.

"Treason is a serious charge." He pinned Herrington with his gaze. "One which would require significant and irrefutable evidence to substantiate. Until such evidence is produced, I should be quite cautious in whom I spoke with regarding this matter. Much unnecessary damage can occur due to an unfounded rumor. We certainly hope no such gossip causes damage to the countess's good name."

"Of course not, Your Majesty," Herrington replied with haste.

*Things are not unfolding according to his plan,* George thought, noting his nervous fidgeting. He decided to draw him out a bit further: "We shall investigate your claims—quietly. If she turns out to have aided the rebels, we will deal with her according to the law. If not, and it turns out that only her legitimacy is in question, we expect you to provide adequate evidence to support your claim. In the event you *are* able to produce it, we should like your recommendation as to how the matter might be resolved."

Herrington's eyes brightened. "It *might* be possible to solve the dilemma with a strategic union," he ventured. "What she needs is an English husband to provide legitimacy for the next Wilmington heir."

"Mmm, a sort of restoration of pedigree." George nodded, humoring him. "And whom would you recommend for such a task?"

Herrington pursed his lips. "The man who weds her will be tied to her for life, bound to her tainted blood and required to watch her at all times lest she act treacherously. I'm loath to suggest that another man sacrifice himself. Thus, I can only offer myself." He kept his eyes downcast.

"How altruistic of you," George commented, not buying into the humble martyr act. "But why should you be willing to do such a thing? Was it not you who suggested she might be part of a long-range plan to subvert England's throne by infiltrating the peerage?"

Herrington paled slightly. "I cannot hide the truth from you, Your Majesty. I must confess that I find her desirable. For all her tainted blood, she is a beautiful woman. I desired her before I discovered her true identity, and it is with great shame that I admit to still desiring her. If I were a man ruled purely by logic and reason, I should be glad to see her stripped of her ill-gotten gains and thrown into gaol. But as a man of flesh and blood, I find myself unable to make such a recommendation. Thus, I propose to become her guardian and sentinel, and to forever relinquish my line's claim to England's throne."

"You would give up your peerage?" George asked, surprised. "Are you immune to corruption, then? Do you not fear she might seek to subvert you with her feminine wiles?"

Herrington squared his shoulders. "I shall never be ruled by a woman, Your Majesty. A wife submits to her husband, and I assure you that as *my* wife she will know her place and obey me in all things. My vigilance will know neither sleep nor rest."

"And what of young Miss Stanton?" George countered. "Word has reached me that the two of you are very nearly engaged. And, speaking of engagement, the countess is already engaged to the Duke of Gravina."

"A farce, Your Majesty!" Herrington scoffed, indignant. "The man has made several offhand comments insinuating that his time in England is drawing to an end. I myself heard him say this very night that he would soon cut his ties to this 'dismal place' and return home—likely to deliver information *she* has given him to aid the Pretender."

He couldn't resist. "And how do you explain their engagement if she turns out not to be a spy?"

"If such is the case, then one can only surmise that Gravina has duped the countess and is using her as a means of gathering information. Even if *she* is not a spy, *he* most certainly is."

George searched the duke's peculiar eyes for a long moment. There was something very disturbing about Herrington's fascination with Melly. He resolved to get to the bottom of this mystery. "We will take your information and recommendations into consideration. In the meantime, you are not to discuss this matter with anyone."

"Of course, Your Majesty," replied Herrington.

George watched as he bowed and departed, noting the man's thinly veiled excitement. As for Melly, he doubted she was a spy, but if the strange tale of her ancestry *was* actually verified, it presented a real problem.

The sound of giggling awakened Alessandro. He smiled at the warm weight on his shoulder, turning his head to nuzzle the mass of soft, inky hair. His bedmate stirred at the motion, groaning just as another titter floated on the air.

The laughter had not come from Mélisande.

Cracking open a bleary eye, he saw a maid standing beside the bed, a lamp in her hand. He flinched, causing Mélisande to let out a muffled sound of protest as her head rolled off his shoulder.

"M'lady," called the servant softly.

"Mmm. What is it?" Mélisande flung an arm over her eyes to block the unwelcome light.

"You gave orders to awaken you at the fifth hour."

Alessandro, now fully awake, gently shook his fiancée.

Shoving aside the thick, straggling locks of hair obscuring her vision, Mélisande stared at the maid in confusion.

"It's the fifth hour, m'lady," the girl repeated. Her gaze was now respectfully aimed at the floor.

"Thank you, Martha. I shall dress myself this morning. You may return in half an hour to arrange my hair. And Martha, understand that you'll be dismissed at once, should you speak to anyone regarding what you have just seen."

"Yes, ma'am," the girl answered, again ducking her head.

Alessandro waited until the door closed before he began chuckling.

Mélisande shot him a black look. "I fail to see the humor in this situation, especially at such an ungodly hour," she snapped sourly. Then her expression became contrite. "Oh, Alessandro, I can't bear it! There *must* be another way!"

"I must, *amora*. I will come for you as soon as it is finished," he promised, holding her tightly.

Pulling back, she regarded him with flinty eyes. "I'm coming with you," she insisted. "This duel is being fought on my behalf and I *will* witness it, whatever the outcome."

He shook his head, but she cut him off.

"No! I refuse to be left behind! If you won't allow me to go with you, I'll follow on my own. You cannot force me to remain."

Arguing with her was pointless. Alessandro sighed, releasing her. "Very well," he conceded. "But you will stay in the carriage," he ordered firmly, staring at her until she nodded agreement.

The air outside was heavy as they departed. Every sound seemed magnified in the predawn hush: the horses' hooves against the cobblestones, the occasional rumble of a cart as the morning deliverymen went about their rounds. A morning mist rose from the ground in hazy wisps as they neared Tothill Fields. The first rays of sunlight caught in it, making it appear flame-like amid the dew that shimmered on each blade of grass.

Herrington's carriage had already arrived.

"I will return as soon as it is done," Alessandro again promised her as the driver opened the door.

Pelham took up a leather satchel, two sheathed rapiers, and a flat wooden case. "Let us get this over with."

Alessandro kissed her once more, and then followed his second out onto the wet grass.

Mélisande watched from the window as the two men crossed the silvered green, the golden mist swirling at their feet.

Herrington and his second, a slight, pale-haired gentleman named Sir Charles Bittle, waited.

With grim determination, Alessandro unfastened his cloak, handing it to his second. A familiar, detached calm washed over him as he observed his enemy. Emotions receded as his mind flowed into a state of hyperawareness. Every flicker of the eyelids, every facial twitch, every tiny tremor of his opponent's fingers seemed etched in clear light. Breathing deeply, Alessandro relaxed, focusing solely on bringing down his adversary in order to survive.

Pelham brought forth the weapons and presented them. "Choose," he commanded.

Herrington tapped the wooden case and Pelham opened it, revealing a pair of finely crafted Jover pistols.

Bittle, as the challenged party's second, bent to examine them. Carefully, he lifted each by its grip and inspected it. Proclaiming the weapons satisfactory, he then took one, loaded it, and handed it to Herrington. Pelham removed the other and loaded it, then passed it to Alessandro.

"Six paces," Alessandro said. Turning his back, he cocked the hammer, waiting.

On Bittle's count they measured out their steps, the distance between them widening with each pace. Birds sang from the trees surrounding the peaceful meadow, unaware that violence was about to erupt.

When the two men stopped and turned to face one another, Pelham raised a silk kerchief high in the air and released it. With the speed of lightning, both combatants raised their firearms. Two shots rang out almost simultaneously, startling the birds into panicked flight.

A sharp pain lanced Alessandro's left arm, but he kept his eyes trained on his opponent. Herrington crumpled to the ground, clutching his midsection. In his hubris, the Englishman had faced his enemy full on, not turning to the side as he ought. A foolish mistake.

The instant he saw the scarlet blossoming across the man's belly, Alessandro knew the man did not have long. A gut wound almost always assured an opponent's demise either through loss of blood or infection. It would be a miracle if he survived. Fast footsteps approached, and he turned to see Mélisande running toward him, her face ashen. He dropped the now useless pistol to embrace her.

Pelham ran over to where Herrington lay on his back, still gripping his spent weapon. Shouting for Bittle to come quickly, he took off his jacket and pressed it against the wound.

Releasing Mélisande, Alessandro ran over to help, though he knew it was no use. It would bleed out internally and nothing could be done to stop it. Still, he must make every effort, even if only for appearance's sake.

Herrington coughed, spewing pink froth as he brought up a hand to clutch his enemy's where it pressed down into his midsection.

Before Alessandro could react, Herrington's other hand, which had lain concealed, lifted. In it was another pistol.

"I shall n-not go to hell alone," Herrington whispered, a malicious grin stretching his bloodied lips. "I'll take the bastard with me."

With a shout of alarm, Alessandro flung himself aside at the same instant Herrington shifted his aim and squeezed. Even as the fire in his enemy's eyes died, a high, sharp cry sounded from behind Alessandro and something heavy fell against him, sliding down his back. His heart contracted in terror as he turned to see Mélisande sprawled on the grass. Crimson bloomed from her right shoulder, rapidly spreading across her bodice and down the sleeve of her gown. "*Amora!*" he whispered, peering down at her bewildered face. *Dio, no! Please...*

"Alessandro?"

Before he could answer the weak inquiry, Mélisande shuddered, her eyes rolling as her body went slack.

A wordless bellow burst from his throat as sudden tears blinded him. Dashing them away, he shouted for Pelham. He must work quickly.

The moment Pelham arrived, Alessandro grabbed the satchel out of his hands, thrusting it at Bittle, who stood close by. "Make yourself useful and find the bandages!" he barked. As Pelham knelt down, Alessandro gently transferred Mélisande's limp body into his grasp. Turning her on her side, he produced a small knife and used it to cut the cloth at her shoulder, peeling back wet silk to expose pale, bloodied flesh. The bullet had ripped through her right shoulder just below the collarbone and passed out the other side.

"Come and stanch the wound," he commanded Bittle. When the little man did not move, Alessandro reached up and tore the sack from his limp hands. At last he found a wad of clean cloth. He used it to sop up the blood welling from the wound, and then bade Pelham press down on it while he again looked in the satchel.

Drawing forth a small glass bottle filled with a dark liquid, he tipped some of the fluid into the wound.

Mélisande moaned, her dark brows drawing together. Before she could rouse completely, Alessandro had Pelham press a fresh bandage to the wound while he turned her over to repeat his ministrations on the side from which the bullet had emerged.

Mélisande again groaned before slipping back into oblivion.

"Help me wrap it—tightly," Alessandro ordered.

Together, they swaddled her shoulder and upper arm. It was appalling how quickly those immaculate white cloths turned red.

Alessandro looked down at the blood drying on his hands and swallowed, suddenly ill. He'd seen far more horrific wounds, witnessed firsthand the stinking fields of war, waded through knee-deep bodies, bathed in mud mixed with the blood of dying men. He'd been covered from head to foot in blood, but this was somehow different. This was the lifeblood of his beloved drying on his hands.

"It looks a lot worse than it is," Pelham muttered. "The bullet passed through cleanly and the bleeding is not as bad as it appears. We must get her to a doctor immediately. Help me lift her and move her to the carriage."

Alessandro tried and winced at the sudden burning in his arm. Glancing down, he saw his sleeve was drenched in blood— his own.

Pelham looked up and swore.

Alessandro gritted his teeth against the pain as he let the man pour the remaining fluid from the bottle over his arm and bandage him up. It would have to do until he could get proper treatment.

With Bittle's help, he and Pelham carried Mélisande to the carriage. Alessandro got in and they laid her across the seat with her head cushioned on his lap.

"Go to my house," Pelham advised. "It is the closest. I will be there as soon as we take care of Herrington's body." His jaw tightened. "I would leave the refuse for the thieves and crows, but that would only do you ill when the king heard of it."

Bittle finally broke his silence. "Take one of Herrington's horses," he told Pelham. "I'll follow behind with the body. You'll go much faster on horseback. I think it far better for the dead man to arrive late rather than the doctor, do you not?"

Pelham agreed. Closing the door, he shouted instructions to the driver. A moment later, the conveyance jolted forward and began its slow journey.

Not too long after, Alessandro heard the approach of rapid hoofbeats from behind. Peering out the window, he saw a flash as Pelham thundered past at an all-out gallop. The man rode as if the devil were at his heels.

He peered down at Mélisande's ashen face. How he wished they could make such speed! But without a saddle, it would have been impossible to stay astride with her before him, even uninjured. There was nothing for it but to wait—and pray.

The doctor, a small, bespectacled gentleman named Burroughs, emerged from the bedroom, his expression grave.

"Will she recover?" Alessandro asked.

"She'll be fine, provided there is no infection," Burroughs responded. "The bullet passed through the tissue cleanly, just missing the bone, so there were no fragments to contend with. Be sure she gets plenty of rest. She should not be moved from this room until she's able to stand on her own and walk."

The doctor peered at him over the rims of his spectacles. "My compliments to you, Your Grace, for your excellent battlefield care. Your immediate cleansing and binding of the wound may very well have saved her life. Now, if you will come with me, I'll have a look at your arm."

"I want to see her. At once," demanded Alessandro.

"Very well. My instruments are already in the room with her. You may see her while I treat your wound."

Entering the chamber, Alessandro saw Mélisande's pale form propped up against a pile of pillows. A sheet was draped across her chest and held in place beneath her arms, exposing both shoulders. One was hidden by the dark tangle of her hair, the other was swathed in bandages. Upon close inspection, he saw her chest rising and falling beneath the sheet, though only shallowly.

"I've given her laudanum to help with the pain and allow her to rest," Burroughs said, leading him over to a chair. Carefully, he removed the layers of blood-soaked bandages. "The bullet only pierced the outer flesh, a minor wound that will heal well, as long as it is kept clean. It has already stopped bleeding. May I assume the same treatment given the lady was also given to you?"

"Yes," Alessandro replied absently, all his attention focused on the supine form in the bed. She was pale, so pale.

The physician rewrapped Alessandro's arm with clean strips of cloth. "I shall give Lord Pelham instructions for her care and return in the morning to check the wound. If at any time it should begin bleeding again, or if she begins to grow feverish, send for me and I will come immediately, whatever the hour." Packing up his instruments, he departed.

Alessandro sat beside the bed, his face bleak. *Provided there is no infection...* He'd endured the horrors of an infected wound twice, both times barely surviving the ordeal. His tired eyes roamed aimlessly about the room, coming to rest on a pile of scarlet-stained cloth in the corner. He blanched anew. She'd lost a great deal of blood. He began to pray. He'd not sought divine intervention this much since he was a child.

"Take some rest, I'll keep watch," Pelham promised.

Alessandro did not even flinch, though he'd not heard the man come in. "I will not leave her."

"It could be days, even weeks," Pelham objected. "You yourself must rest and recover."

"I will not leave her," Alessandro repeated.

"Will she truly recover?" Reggie asked, eyes dark with worry as he entered the room, Charlotte at his side.

"As long as there is no infection," Alessandro echoed the physician's words, unwilling to feel any sense of relief. The danger was still very real. If the wound festered, Melly would likely not survive. "He said the same of me."

"Bittle told us what happened," Reggie murmured, awkwardly patting his sister's arm.

"You were right. He never loved me," Charlotte said quietly, her red-rimmed eyes brimming with tears. "Sir Bittle told me what he said just after—after…" Her hands flew to her mouth as she turned into Reggie's shoulder.

"Charlie, it's not your fault," he said gently.

"He *lied* to me," she sobbed bitterly, "and I believed him rather than my own brother and m—my dearest friends! I'm sorry, sorry for the h-horrible things I said!"

"I'm sure she knows you didn't mean it."

She shook her head. "You tried to explain why His Grace challenged Herrington, but I didn't believe you. I called you a liar, my own brother! Then I saw the bruises when they brought Melly in, and I heard Sir Bittle say to the doctor that she'd been shot, and"—she gulped air for a moment—"that *he'd* done it and—and what he said!"

Fresh tears flowed from Charlotte's miserable eyes. "If I'd only listened to you and trusted you, she wouldn't have confronted him, she wouldn't be dying. *None* of this would have happened! I beg your forgiveness. I'll ask hers, if I'm ever given the chance."

"There is nothing to forgive," Alessandro told her. "You were deceived. You could not have known what would happen. Please don't blame yourself. She wouldn't want that."

"I shall help care for her," she announced, swiping at her eyes. "You have also been injured and cannot stay with her the entire time. You *must* let me," she begged. "She's my best friend, and after what has happened, it's the least I can do. Please…"

"She will need your help as she recovers, certainly, but not tonight," Alessandro said, looking at Bittle, who'd quietly come in behind the brother and sister. "We'll see what the doctor says in the morning. In the meantime, let us all pray there is no infection and that she rests well."

Bittle stood there, looking awkward. "I should be leaving." He paused, shuffling his feet. "But first, I want to apologize," he stammered, flushing. "Please believe me when I say I would never have agreed to second Herrington had I known the truth."

"I hold no complaint against you, for you were also deceived," Alessandro told him. "Indeed, you have only my gratitude for your assistance."

Bittle nodded, clearly relieved. "It was the least I could do. I will also speak on your behalf when the time comes," he promised. "You should not be condemned for what happened."

"It will be greatly appreciated," Alessandro answered, nodding at Pelham, who, taking the hint, proceeded to clear the room.

After a moment, quiet footsteps retreated and the door closed, leaving only the sound of Mélisande's shallow breathing to break the silence.

Just before dawn, she began to burn with fever.

# Chapter Twenty-Four

## TO RUN THE GAUNTLET

*O*N LOOKING AT THE PATIENT, BURROUGHS SHOOK HIS HEAD. "I'm afraid there is nothing more to be done except watch, wait, and use the laudanum to help make her ladyship comfortable."

Refusing to accept this, Alessandro had Pelham dispatch a runner with an urgent message to His Majesty, begging assistance. Two hours after Burroughs pronounced doom, the runner returned with Sir Hans Sloane, the king's own physician.

Alessandro watched intently as the ancient man examined Mélisande's wound.

"No sign of infection," muttered Sloane. "The fever is likely due to something else. But the wounds will fester if left open." He dug in his case for a moment and retrieved a bottle, then lifted her eyelid to peer beneath it briefly before slipping another spoonful of laudanum between her cracked lips.

Not a drop was spilled. In spite of his age, Sloane's movements were precise, his hands steady as stone. Removing several cauters from his case, he prepared for battle, moving to the hearth to position their tips among the hot coals. While they heated, he methodically cleansed the wound with strong spirits, reopening it and causing it to bleed afresh.

Mélisande did not even stir.

"You"—Sloane gestured to the men—"make certain she cannot move."

Alessandro and Pelham each took a side while Burroughs lay across her feet. All watched in horrified fascination as Sloane retrieved one of the cauters and carefully inserted its glowing tip into the entry wound.

Mélisande, though heavily drugged, let out a ragged cry of agony and attempted to rise up off the bed as her flesh was seared by the red-hot metal. The three men held her down through her brief struggle until she slipped back into unconsciousness.

Alessandro fought down nausea as he watched a wisp of smoke rise, filling the room with the stink of charred meat.

Sloane tipped another few drops of sleep between his patient's lips and waited.

When the physician repeated the process on the other side, where the bullet had exited her body, Mélisande remained quiescent. She was beyond the reach of all pain, slumbering peacefully in the arms of the laudanum.

Sloane redressed the wounds and bade the gentlemen keep her as cool as possible until the fever passed. *Now* there was nothing to be done but wait.

Alessandro remained at her side as she raved incoherently in her delirium. He held her hand as she shook with chills until her teeth clacked violently and a cloth-wrapped stick had to be inserted between them. He spooned laudanum and water between her cracked lips, rubbing them with grease to keep them from bleeding. He plied her face and body with damp cloths to keep her temperature down, to stop the burning of his beloved.

It took two days. Two days of hanging between hope and despair. At last, on the morning of the third day, she burned no more.

Mélisande opened her eyes to the beams of an unfamiliar ceiling. Someone breathed softly at her side. Turning her head, she saw Alessandro fast asleep, his head resting on his arm. Smiling, she lifted her hand to touch his hair and winced at the sudden fire that erupted in her shoulder.

Memory flooded back.

"Alessandro?" she croaked. The ragged sound surprised her.

He stirred, his eyes blazing back to life at the sight of her awake. "*Amora!* How do you feel?"

Mélisande observed the deep violet bruises beneath his eyes, the hollows in his unshaven cheeks, and thought him the most beautiful man she had ever seen. "I've been better," she whispered, giving him a weak smile.

On the far side of the room behind her, a chair scraped across the floor. "Herrington is dead," she heard David say.

She shifted slightly as he came into view, closing her eyes against the pain. "How long?"

"Three days," answered Alessandro. "Try not to move. You don't want to reopen your injury."

"I'm thirsty," she whispered from parched lips. Alessandro brought her a glass of water and held it to her mouth while she drank.

A short while later, Charlotte peeked around the door. "Melly?"

"It's good to see you, Charlotte," Mélisande said, smiling before she thought about it. If Herrington was dead, then that meant… "Are you all right?" she inquired.

"Oh, Melly! Can you ever forgive me?" the girl pleaded. "I've been such a fool!"

Mélisande's eyes stung. "The fault was mine. I should have told you everything from the beginning."

"And how is the invalid?" Reggie chuckled from the doorway, somber eyed despite his cheery smile. "You certainly gave us a good scare. What were you doing out on the field?"

"I should have listened when you told me to wait for you in the carriage," Mélisande replied. Guilt filled her as she looked at Alessandro. "I thought Herrington was already dead when I saw him fall."

"Well, he's dead now, and good riddance," said Charlotte.

Mélisande's heart wrenched at the bitterness in her voice. "I'm so sorry. I never meant—"

"Don't be," the girl urged. "The man was a blackguard. He never loved me. I know that now, and I'm glad he can no longer hurt us."

David moved to stand beside her. "I've some news to tell you, Melly. I've spoken with Reggie and asked for Charlie's hand."

"Oh, David! How very wonderful!" Mélisande exclaimed. "When?"

"Would you object to a double wedding?" asked Charlotte.

Mélisande's smile faded only slightly. "I think that would be grand."

"You must recover first," David admonished. "And then there is the small matter of the king's inquiry to get through before anything else can happen."

Mélisande looked to Alessandro, worry creasing her brow.

"I must answer for Herrington's death," he explained. "All will be well, I am certain. I had just cause for my action. In any case, I possess diplomatic immunity," he assured her. "The worst that can happen is expulsion."

Her heart did not grow any less heavy at his words. Perhaps she might be able to intervene on his behalf, especially since the entire debacle was her fault.

"It will be several weeks, at least, before we can see the king," David informed her. "I'm certain we will be able to win his favor, given the situation."

Exhaustion suddenly swept through Mélisande. *So tired…* The bedroom door opened, admitting a servant. The tantalizing scent of chicken broth filtered throughout the room. Her stomach growled audibly, causing Charlotte to giggle.

"I guess it's been a while since I last ate." Mélisande chuckled, her smile returning.

"Then you'd best have something immediately," replied Charlotte, taking the tray and moving toward the bed.

Mélisande first became bored and then cantankerous in very short order.

Two weeks had passed when Sloane began receiving his patient's first complaints. A week of bed rest had done her a world of good; her surface wounds had closed and the scabs looked healthy—and she was weary of her confinement.

"Things are progressing quite nicely indeed. Just a few more days in bed, I think," Sloane muttered as he examined her, nodding in satisfaction. "Then we'll see about walking—gentle, *slow* walking, to begin with," he added.

Mélisande let out a sigh. "It's my shoulder that's been hurt, for heaven's sake," she groused, "not my legs! I don't see why I can't go down to the gardens now and sit *there* doing absolutely nothing!"

"Dear Countess"—the doctor smiled benignly—"I know you grow weary of this room, but you must be extremely careful not to jostle the injury, lest it begin bleeding internally again. I'm afraid there will be no trips to the garden just yet."

"I shall have someone carry me down."

Sloane met her glare with a stern eye. "Madam, you may walk about up here as long as you are cautious, but *no* stairs. Not yet. You must wait at least another week."

It was pointless to argue. David and Alessandro would have her hide if she didn't follow Sloane's orders. "Fine." At least she'd won partial freedom.

"We can finalize the plans for the wedding, perhaps even have a dressmaker bring some cloth for you to look at," offered Charlotte.

"Yes, of course," replied Mélisande, maintaining a bright smile even as her gut twisted. The king had forbidden dueling within the city of London and, although they had observed His Majesty's command by leaving it, the fact remained that Alessandro had killed a peer of the realm.

*We have so little time. And here I am, helpless to do anything but watch it slip by.*

Word of the duel had spread like wildfire, and suddenly everyone wanted to see the woman who'd cheated death. The sheer drama of it made all other gossip seem dull.

"How tiresome!" Mélisande grumped at the breakfast table after accepting yet another tray heaped with correspondence. Many had asked to see her during her convalescence, most of them not even friends or acquaintances.

"Relax," David told her, peering over the top of the latest edition of *The Gentleman's Magazine*. "It'll die down soon enough, and then you'll complain of boredom."

"Not likely." She sipped her tea, feeling awkward and imbalanced with her arm in a sling. Sir Sloane had been most adamant about her keeping it immobilized, and she knew better than to disobey his orders. "I'm sick to death of your house. I want to go home."

*I want to be where I can at least speak with Alessandro privately.*

David's prediction was correct, however. Demand for her company quickly diminished as the novelty wore off, especially since she was unwilling to discuss the event in any kind of satisfying detail.

Stamma came and played chess with her every other day, and Elizabeth begged David's leave to host a small literary meeting in his home since Melly could not visit her salon. Lady Angelica visited frequently as well, but everyone knew whom she truly came to see. It made Mélisande smile to see her and Reggie together.

Perhaps a double wedding wasn't to be ruled out after all.

Except when it rained, Mélisande and Alessandro walked in the gardens every day. Though she longed to do so with increasing intensity, she knew it was impossible to resume their physical relationship while she remained in David's house. She had to content herself with talk and the occasional kiss beneath the arbor in the orchard.

If the kisses were a torment, the talk was even more so. The more they talked, the more she grew to love him. She'd given up trying to stop it. All she could do was try not to let it be obvious.

Though she knew he was fond of her, Alessandro had made no mention of love.

Maman had been "fond" of Papa, too. And she'd broken his heart.

Eight weeks later, His Majesty's summons finally came.

Though she'd just been pronounced fit for travel by Sir Sloane, there was an ache Mélisande feared would never leave her, and it had nothing to do with the ugly pair of puckered red scars she now bore. Those marks and the occasional twinge of discomfort were all the physical evidence that remained of her brush with death. But in her heart, she'd already begun to mourn the loss of the man she'd grown to love more than she'd ever thought possible. During her confinement, she'd come to see him not only as her lover but as her dearest friend.

How would she bear it when he left?

Mélisande chose her gown carefully for the audience with the king, making certain the neckline was low and wide enough to reveal her scars. Most women would have hidden such blemishes, but she showed them proudly, knowing it would be to Alessandro's advantage for the king to see for himself what she'd suffered.

When they were summoned into His Majesty's receiving chamber, they found several members of His Majesty's council present, including David's uncle, the Rt. Honorable Henry Pelham, Sir Hans Sloane, and the Duke of Devonshire. Sir Charles Bittle, as promised, was also present.

"Melly," King George greeted his goddaughter, blanching slightly when his gaze lit upon the sling and the angry red welt marring the skin of her right shoulder. "Sloane tells me you've made a remarkable recovery. I am truly glad to see you well."

"Yes, Your Majesty," she answered. "I am well enough now to leave Lord Pelham's. In fact, I had only just begun to make the arrangements when your summons arrived."

He beckoned her closer and lowered his voice. "The reason I waited so long was because I wished to see you as well. Herrington came to me with a rather strange tale the night before the unfortunate incident that claimed his life. As he can no longer answer my questions, I must seek answers elsewhere."

"I shall, of course, answer as best I am able, Your Majesty." Mélisande struggled to keep from showing her fear.

"I should very much like to know why the challenge was issued to begin with," he asked.

Relieved, Mélisande told him of the bizarre conflict. When she came to Herrington's seduction of Charlotte, Charlotte came forward to deliver her part of the story herself. Each of her friends gave their testimony, filling in the pieces. When Alessandro finally spoke of his challenge and the circumstances under which it had been issued, George's face grew grim. Bittle and Pelham then described the duel and Herrington's final, dishonorable act.

When all fell silent, Mélisande watched as her king's eyes flicked to the puckered scar on her shoulder, then back to Alessandro. "I believe your cause was just. However, I must tell you that a great many members of my council have already advised your expulsion. They believe allowing a foreigner to kill a peer with impunity sets a bad precedent, regardless of the justification."

Mélisande's stomach clenched.

"We shall not command your expulsion," George continued. "However, we *request* that you leave as quickly as possible."

At his gesture, the Duke of Devonshire stepped forward.

"I've been informed that several of Herrington's friends plan to avenge his death," Devonshire addressed the entire group. "I know not how the man managed to gather so loyal a following, but until they are convinced of the truth, the Duke of Gravina is in grave danger of assassination."

Mélisande glanced at Alessandro, her heart beginning to break.

"There is another matter about which I must inquire, Melly," said George. "Before his demise, Herrington spoke to me privately regarding your claim to the earldom."

Her spirits sank yet further. *Damn you, Herrington. I hope you are in the hottest part of Hell...*

"I'm afraid I have no choice but to ask you some difficult questions, my dear," George told her. "However, this matter pertains to you and you alone," he added. "If you wish, we will clear the room so that we may converse in privacy."

Mélisande nodded. "I wish Lord Pelham, Miss Stanton, Mr. Stanton, and my...fiancé to remain."

When the door closed, George spoke plainly. "I see no delicate way to address such a matter; thus, I shall come right to the point. Herrington claimed you are not of Wilmington's blood-line, and that you are a Jacobite sympathizer and spy. He alleged that your mother and the French king were lovers before she met Wilmington and that Spencer unknowingly raised a Bourbon bastard. The man vowed to have seen a painting bearing your likeness in Louis's bedchamber. He also said you both bear a shared birthmark. I was loath to believe such a preposterous tale, of course, but..."

Mélisande looked down at the ruby on her finger and again cursed Herrington. Raising her eyes, she faced her king. "First, allow me to address the first accusation and say that I have never been anything but your loyal subject. The idea that I would ever support the Stuart claim to England's throne is an insult." She took a deep, steadying breath. "Secondly, there are two birth-marks, Your Majesty. One here"—she pointed to the one on her breast—"and another that cannot be seen."

# Chapter Twenty-Five

## OF LOVE AND SACRIFICE

ÉLISANDE WATCHED HIS EXPRESSION TRANSFORM TO one of shocked disbelief.

"I have no cause for shame," she continued with quiet dignity. "I did not choose the circumstances of my birth. While it is true that my mother was the French king's mistress, Papa met and fell in love with her before she knew she was to bear the king's child. When she revealed her condition to Louis, he decided to make arrangements for her. Knowing that Papa was taken with her, he told him of her situation and asked him if he wanted to marry her. Papa agreed."

"Why in heaven's name would Wilmington do such a thing?" George asked, incredulous.

Mélisande blushed. "Because of an accident in his youth, Papa was unable to sire a child. He needed an heir. The fact that his bride was already with child was a happy solution to his problem."

Profound silence followed her revelation.

After a moment, Mélisande came forward and fell to her knees before him. "Your Majesty, I did not meet the man who sired me until I was fourteen. Until then, I had no knowledge that I was anything other than the English daughter of an English earl. When Louis heard about Papa's impending visit, he requested that he bring his family along—in order to see me, if only once. He surprised us all by offering to acknowledge me. I declined out of love for Papa. Spencer Compton was and always will be the father of my heart."

George came forward and placed a gentle hand on her bowed head. "Wilmington was my friend. When he asked me to be your godfather, I was honored and shared in his joy. I did not believe Herrington." He shook his head, his sadness evident. "I was prepared to dismiss his claims and consider the matter closed. Why did you not simply deny it?"

"Because I'm tired of living in fear," Mélisande told him. "Herrington discovered the truth and told you. God only knows whom else he might have told before he died. It matters not, in any case. What matters is that I made my choice long ago. As far as I'm concerned, I am Mélisande Esmée Compton, the daughter of an English earl, not a French king."

"I'm afraid others will not see it that way," said George. "If Herrington did indeed expose your secret, which I suspect he has, the peerage will be beating down my door demanding that you be stripped of your title and lands, perhaps even imprisoned for fraud."

Mélisande's face hardened. "You have known me since the day I was born. You cannot possibly question my loyalty."

"No, *I* do not," he said. "But the fact remains that you are a Bourbon and we are about to be at war with France. If you were of *any* other lineage, I could gladly overlook it. As it stands, however, I have no choice but to act. It is a matter of perceptions, and I cannot be seen to put personal desires above England's needs."

"So, because of politics, you will punish me for an accident of birth over which I had no control?" she asked bitterly.

"It is not my desire to 'punish' you, Melly. You must understand that my hands are tied. I cannot risk losing the confidence and support of the peerage." He let out a long sigh. "Much as I

dislike acknowledging it, Herrington actually made a suggestion that would provide a way to salvage this situation and prevent your losing everything. We can arrange for you to marry an
Englishman so that your children will have a legitimate, English
claim to the earldom, which I will bestow upon your husband."

The blood whistled in Mélisande's ears as she processed this.
She had no choice. Her engagement to Alessandro was a sham,
anyway, a foolish fantasy that was now over. He was leaving
England. Quashing the impulse to rage and weep, she instead
focused on keeping her spine straight.

"Whom would you have me marry?" she inquired, unable to
keep her voice from trembling. She dared not look at Alessandro's
face lest she break down.

"You were once engaged to Pelham, here," said the king.
"Why not simply reinstate the arrangement?"

"Because he is in love with someone else, and I will not have
him," Mélisande replied firmly.

"Since when is love a concern in matters of marriage?"
George said dismissively. After a moment's pause, he looked to
Alessandro and raised a brow.

Taking the cue, Alessandro stepped forth. "It is a concern
when it involves me, Your Majesty. Let it not be forgotten that
Lady Wilmington is already engaged to be married to me. If your
intent is to withdraw the blessing you bestowed upon me regarding our union, I fear I must strongly object."

Mélisande whirled to face him. "What blessing?"

"This man requested permission to marry you several
months ago," George answered.

She stared at Alessandro, unbelieving. "But I thought—"

He took up her hand, the one bearing his ring. "Our engagement stands, if you will have me. For five years I searched for you,
Mélisande. And now that I have found you, I do not want to lose
you again. I love you."

It shone from his warm cinnamon eyes, naked and powerful, and her heart beat faster, causing her shoulder to throb. She
ignored the pain.

*He wants to marry me!*

A cloud passed over her joy. "But I'm illegitimate," she
blurted, terrified he might reconsider. He was, after all, a duke in
his own country.

Alessandro laughed, drawing her close. "I care nothing for
the blood in your veins, *amora*. You could be a milliner's daughter and still I would marry you. I have seen the painting in the
French king's chamber, as well as his—*your* birthmarks, for I
also attended Louis at his morning dress and saw the mark upon
his hip."

George cleared his throat. "Am I to understand that you
have already consummated your relationship with this man?" he
inquired lightly.

Alessandro flashed her a knowing smile.

Realizing what he'd done, Mélisande reddened. "Your
Majesty, I—"

George held up a hand for silence. "The decision is made.
You will wed your fiancé before you depart England."

Mélisande was torn between joy and misery. The man she
adored beyond all reason was to become her husband, yet it had
cost her the only home she'd ever known. She had to know...
"And who will assume my"—she paused and swallowed—"the
Wilmington title?"

The king's gaze moved to David. "I'm of a mind to make
young Pelham here the next Earl of Wilmington. Despite his
prodigal behavior, he is extremely intelligent and capable. His
uncle spoke of him frequently in favorable terms. And I know
you trust him."

David's head snapped up, along with everyone else's. "I—I
beg your pardon, Your Majesty?"

"We shall make it plain," the monarch said with good humor. "The current countess has chosen to wed a foreigner and abdicate her position. Immediately upon her marriage to Lord Gravina, she will forfeit the earldom. As the Wilmington title has no other heir, we will create you the new Earl of Wilmington. It is as simple as that."

George glared at each of them in turn. "We see no need to expose the real reason behind our decision. In fact, we hereby command that this matter never be spoken of again outside this room." He looked to Mélisande and smiled. "I assume this meets with your approval?"

Mélisande nodded, dumbstruck. The tumultuous emotions of the past several months slowly gave way to a new feeling of lightness. Turning to Alessandro, she smiled, tears stinging her eyes. The warmth of his gaze reached out to envelop her, immediately followed by his arms.

After a moment, she turned to David. His face was, for once, easy to read: he didn't know whether to feel sorrow for her loss or joy for his gain. "You are the best possible choice," she told him quietly. "All my life you've been like a brother to me. You love the Wilmington lands just as Papa did. You know them. And now they are yours to care for. Take the gift with my blessing, and be happy."

"Melly," he croaked. "I cannot—"

"You can," she cut in. "And for my sake you must. I could not ask for it to be given into better hands." She raised her palm to forestall any further objections. "I have but one condition: that you marry Charlotte *before* I leave England. She will make a fine countess, and one day, a fine duchess!"

Wedding invitations were sent out a week later, causing tongues to wag at the indecent haste of it all, for the ceremonies were to happen a mere month hence. Even so, not a single person declined, for the Countess of Wilmington was to marry the most infamous seducer in all of Europe, and England's most notorious rake, her former betrothed, was to marry as well. It was scandalous, and therefore not to be missed.

The weddings were held at Kensington House, and the king himself gave away Mélisande. The avid crowd watched as she became the Duchess of Gravina and Miss Stanton became Lady Pelham. Immediately following the ceremony, Mélisande relinquished her English title. In the next breath, Pelham and Charlotte became the Earl and Countess of Wilmington.

It was a momentous event indeed.

People lining the streets cheered as the carriages bearing the newlyweds at last rolled away from the palace grounds, away from the ongoing celebration fête, away from the well-wishers and joyful pandemonium.

Mélisande sighed in contentment as she leaned against Alessandro. Though she was leaving England's shores tomorrow, never to return, she was truly happy. *No more lies, and no more fear.* It was intoxicating, this freedom.

With a wicked little laugh, she arched a brow and slipped eager hands beneath the skirts of her husband's jacket. "I have a confession to make," she whispered into Alessandro's ear.

"Another? What is it this time? Are you related to the Russian Empress? I assure you I would not recognize any shared birthmarks, if you are."

She could not help but giggle, despite how her blood was heating as he dropped little kisses down her throat. "I instructed the driver to take the long way back."

"Did you? But why would you wish to prolong our journey?"

She leaned back and smiled down into his twinkling eyes. "Because your shameless wife has a rather shameless proposal for you to help pass the time."

It was an invitation no former *roué* could refuse.

# *Epilogue*

## *ITALY, 1757*

LESSANDRO ROLLED OVER TO GAZE AT HIS WIFE. HER beauty and grace had only deepened in the nearly seven years that had passed since their wedding day, and still she consumed and fascinated him.

As though she'd felt his stare, Mélisande smiled. He watched the slow, sensuous curling of her lips. It was the same siren's smile that had intoxicated him the day he first saw her. Leaning over her, he kissed it, the beginnings of desire stirring in him once more, though they had made love only a few hours ago.

Releasing a throaty laugh, she withdrew to stare at him, her eyes sparkling.

He gazed back at her with growing suspicion. "And what mischief do you hide behind those jewels this morning, *amora?*" he asked. "Come, you know you cannot keep a secret from me. I know how to get it out of you," he teased, reaching for her again.

"Well, I should hope it isn't *too* much mischief—we certainly have enough of that already," she quipped, batting at his hands. "But I can't imagine having much choice in the matter, especially given the impish nature of our other two…"

His heart began to beat a little faster. "You are with child?"

"Sometime in the spring," she whispered back, her smile broadening.

The door to their bedchamber opened, and a pair of large, forest-shade eyes peeked around its edge. A moment later, another pair the color of warm earth appeared just below them.

"Come in, darlings," Mélisande beckoned.

A dark-haired little girl dressed in rumpled nightclothes revealed herself. At her side, chubby fist held firmly in his sister's hand, was a merry-eyed little boy of nearly four. Shuffling up to the edge of the bed, they looked up hopefully.

Alessandro patted the coverlet. "Come! I have a secret to share with you," he whispered with excitement as they clambered up onto the bed, the girl helping to haul her little brother up beside her.

"A secret! Tell, Papa! Tell!" the girl begged, bouncing.

"Yes, Papa. Tell us," echoed the little boy, his demeanor far more serious than his sister's, despite her being nearly two years his elder.

Alessandro grinned, his heart swelling with pride. "Well, your mother is actually the one with the secret," he informed them. "Perhaps I should let her tell you?"

Expectant eyes swung over to Mélisande. She smiled over their heads at him. "Oh, I don't know. I think it would be all right for your Papa to reveal this particular secret," she teased.

Pleading eyes again swiveled back to Alessandro.

"Do tell us, Papa," beseeched the girl, squirming with anticipation.

Laughing, he beckoned them closer until their heads nearly touched. "All right," he whispered, "I shall tell you, but you must promise not to yell and wake the house." His manner was stern, but his smile belied his ominous tone.

"We promise, Papa," swore his daughter. She turned to her brother, wearing a perfect copy of her father's severe expression. "*Don't* we, Aldo?" she prompted.

"I promise, Bella," he replied, his face somber.

Beroaldo might appear serious in comparison to his big sister, but Alessandro knew he was at the root of the recent spate of pranks played on the household staff.

"Very well. But know that I shall hold you to your vow," he said, eyeing them fiercely until they giggled. "The secret is that you are going to have a new brother or sister sometime next spring."

The anticipated explosion was not long in coming.

Simultaneously, Isabella and Beroaldo sucked in a deep breath, looking first at each other and then at their father, who'd begun to quake with silent laughter. Squeals of delight erupted as they began jumping up and down on the bed, holding each other's hands while crowing at the tops of their lungs.

Mélisande reached across the coverlet and took his hand.

Fate had brought them into each other's lives twice. Now, they would never be apart again.

*Fin*

# GLOSSARY OF TERMS & PHRASES

(F) = French          (I) = Italian          (E) = English

*Ah, pardon, mademoiselle! Je m'excuse!* (F) – Ah, my apologies, miss! Excuse me!

*Benissimo* (I) – Very good
*Bête noire* (F) – A person, object, or abstract idea that is particularly disliked or avoided
*Bistre* (F) – A rich, deep brown pigment. Many of the Old Masters used bistre as the ink for their drawings.
*Bragg* (E) – An early version of poker
*Brocade* (E) – A class of richly decorative shuttle-woven fabrics, often made in colored silks and with or without gold and silver threads. Often called "embossed cloth," ornamental features in brocade are emphasized and wrought as additions to the main fabric, sometimes stiffening it, though more frequently producing on its face the effect of low relief.

*C'est un vrai coureur de jupons, ma fille! Ne pas aller près de lui!* (F) – This is a seducer of women, my daughter! Do not go near him!
*Calèche* (F) – A wired hood worn by women to protect high hairstyles
*Cendrillon* (F) – Cinderella
*Cochon* (F) – Pig
*Corna* (I) – A hand sign thought to ward against the evil eye

*Décolletage/Décolleté* (F) – The female chest area or cleavage
*Deshabillé* (F) – A state of undress

*Fête champêtre* (F) – Outdoor party/country feast
*Fichu* (F) – A lace neckerchief worn to cover the low décolleté, more for modesty than for warmth, usually tucked into the bodice or held with a clasp in front
*Fin* (F) – The end

*In flagrante delicto* (I) – In the act

*Jamais!* (F) – Never!
*Je ne suis pas aveugle, Maman!* (F) – I am not blind, Mama.
*Jover* (E) – A London manufacturer of fine dueling pistols
*Jupe* (F) – Skirt

*Kensington House (Kensington Palace)* (E) – A royal residence set in Kensington Gardens in the Royal Borough of Kensington and Chelsea in London, England. It has been a residence of the British Royal Family since the seventeenth century. The last reigning monarch to use Kensington Palace was King George II.

*La marque de la coeur* (F) – The heart brand, or mark of the heart
*Le Renard* (F) – The fox
*Les engageantes* (F) – Long lace flounces at the lower end of the sleeve

*Mais, Louis a insisté* (F) – But Louis insisted
*Malocchio* (I) – The evil eye
*Manteau/Mantua* (F) – Generic term for the coat-like, open-fronted female garment worn from the late seventeenth century

until the French Revolution. The front of the bodice was worn wide open to reveal a richly embroidered stomacher. From the short sleeves protruded those of the chemise, decorated with lace.

***Merde*** (F) – Excrement

***Mes amies, préparez à jouer la valse maintenant*** (F) – My friends, prepare to play a waltz immediately

***Minuet*** (F) – A social dance of French origin for two persons, usually in 3/4 time

***Molto bene*** (I) – Very good


***Panniers*** (F) – The hoop skirt typical of the eighteenth century involving two baskets, one over each hip, to dramatically exaggerate the flare of the hips, allowing for wide lengths of cloth to be displayed

***Paste*** (E) – Simulated gemstone made from rock crystal or glass. Often used to decorate clothes or as a substitute in jewelry.

***Primero*** (E) – A popular sixteenth-century gambling card game


***Quadrille*** (F) – A French square dance in a lively duple time, popular in the eighteenth and nineteenth centuries, danced by four or more couples


***Rotten Row*** (E) – A broad track running along the south side of Hyde Park in London, leading from Hyde Park Corner to the west, it was established by William III at the end of the seventeenth century. Having moved court to Kensington Palace, William wanted a safer way to travel to the previous St. James's Palace. He created the broad avenue through Hyde Park, lit with three hundred oil lamps in 1690—the first artificially lit highway in Britain. In its heyday in the eighteenth century, Rotten Row was a fashionable place for upper-class Londoners to be seen.

***Roué*** (F) – Lecher or rake; seducer of women; a man who is habituated to immoral conduct

***Sans*** (F) – Without

***Sciocchezze!*** (I) – Nonsense!

***Stomacher*** (E) – A piece of stiff fabric, roughly the shape of a long, narrow triangle and sometimes boned, that covered the gap of the *manteau* over the stomach and chest. It was covered with fine fabric and often heavily embroidered and/or decorated with lace. The fronts of the robe were pinned onto it to hold them in place.

***Tesoro*** (I) – Darling

***T'es mon coeur*** (F) – You are my heart

*Read on for a sneak peek of Liana LeFey's next seductive romance!*

**To Wed in Scandal**

*Available May 2013 on Amazon.com.*

**For Lady Sabrina Grayson, it's a case of too many suitors...**

NOTHING WOULD BRING SABRINA RELIEF SAVE HENRY'S removal from this house. She knew he slept somewhere in the opposite wing, but that mattered not. He might as well have been in the next room, as far as she was concerned.

It was going to be a long night.

A faint rustle at the door drew her attention, and Sabrina watched as something slid beneath it. The moment the messenger's footsteps retreated, she tiptoed over and snatched up the note. She frowned. It was probably another hideous poem from Chadwick.

"I should never have come to this damned house party," she muttered sourly as she tore off the wax and opened it. The writing jumped at her from the page:

*Forgive me. H.*

Her traitorous heart pounded as she refolded it. Padding to the desk, she picked up a quill, hesitating, uncertain whether to respond or to simply ignore the communication.

Nib touched paper.

*Forgiven. Now, I beg you to forget me! S.*

Half an hour later, she still lay awake, unable to sleep after having sent her reply. A soft knock startled her from her reverie. Flinging off the coverlet, she rushed across the room, hoping to catch the messenger and tell him to bear the letter back to its author unopened. She jerked open the door and gasped in surprise.

"I cannot," said Henry, his voice hoarse, his face haggard.

Sabrina's whole body quaked at what she saw in his eyes.

"May I come in?"

"No," she answered.

"Sabri—"

"No!" She tried to close the door, but his foot was wedged in the opening.

"Sabrina, I must speak with you."

"Do you think I've forgotten what happened the *last* time you managed to get me alone?" she hissed, pushing against the door in vain, terrified of the heat already unfurling in her belly.

"I swear I shall not lay a hand upon you. Not even a finger. Upon my honor."

She snorted, unable to contain her censure. "What honor?"

"I wish only to speak with you, and then I shall trouble you no more this night. You have my word."

After a moment, she reluctantly stepped aside.

Henry slipped past, carefully avoiding her person.

Sabrina followed, leaving the door unlocked. As long as he didn't get between her and that door, she was safe. Shivering, she moved to the fire's warmth. "Have your say, then, and begone," she commanded, ignoring the strangled sound that issued from her uninvited guest.

Striding over to her bed with a curse, Henry yanked off the heavy down quilt and held it out to her. When she made no move to take it, he shook it, turning his face away. "Take it, damn it! Or I won't be responsible for what happens."

The shriek she'd been preparing to release died in her throat, suffocated by mortification. Snatching the blanket, she quickly pulled it around herself, grateful for the warmth as well as the concealment it provided.

With a sigh, Henry sank into one of the chairs before the hearth, gesturing for her to do the same.

Sabrina perched on the very edge of the seat opposite him and waited.

"I wish to marry you," he said at last. He looked at her then, and his eyes revealed the depth of his turmoil. "I can find neither peace nor joy in the things that once brought me pleasure. You are all I think about, night and day. Please."

"That is not possible," she managed, shaken by his bluntness.

"Why?"

"Because…" Her parched tongue would not form the words. Every fevered dream she'd had during the past week was sitting right here in front of her, living and breathing. In her room. He wore his shirtsleeves with the neck open, and she could see his throat as it worked when he spoke. Her fingers longed to trace the line of it, to feel his voice vibrating beneath them.

*Sweet heaven help me…*

"Why?" he demanded. "Why won't you consider me?"

"Because you're not the right man!" There, she'd said it.

One brow rose. "And might I inquire as to whom you think that is?"

She answered him with stubborn silence.

"Who, Sabrina?"

"I don't know—but it *isn't* you!" she burst out, releasing some of her frustration. She saw him flinch, and shame gnawed at her. "I'm sorry!" she wailed, fighting the urge to go to him and soothe away the hurt she'd just inflicted. "I just…" She took a deep, steadying breath. "It was like this between my parents, and my mother was miserable because of it. I cannot endure what she suffered. Please understand."

"We are not our parents."

"No, but I'm not so foolish as to think history cannot repeat itself. I want a marriage that does not include this, this...emotional upheaval!"

"Sabrina, I can assure y—"

"No!" she yelped, jumping up to put her chair between them as he rose. "And you swore you wouldn't touch me and that you'd leave me alone once you said your piece! Well, now you've spoken. Please go. Now. Before something terrible happens."

His brows crashed together. "And by *terrible*, I suppose you mean my making love to you?"

Sabrina looked down to where her toes curled into the rug. Heat suffused her at his bold words. It was both humiliating and utterly debilitating, her reaction to him. He had to leave. Immediately.

Her head snapped up, eyes widening in alarm as Henry slowly advanced toward her. She took a hasty step back.

"I swore not to lay a hand on you, and I shan't," he said in response. "I never break my word, Sabrina."

Even so, the look in his eyes made her take another step back. Panic fluttered in her breast as her backside bumped into something behind her, the wardrobe.

"I promised I'd leave you alone for the remainder of the night when I was done," he continued.

"Yes, you did—now leave!" she choked. Fumbling behind her, she searched for the edge of the obstacle, not daring to take her eyes off him.

"Ah, but I'm not finished, Sabrina. In fact, I'm far from through with you."

Moving with astonishing swiftness for so large a man, Henry trapped her in the corner between the wardrobe and the wall, bracing his hands on either side of her, blocking her escape.

Squeezing her eyes shut, Sabrina prepared to scream. But instead of kissing her as she'd anticipated, Henry merely stared down at her. The heat of his nearness twisted her insides. What was he waiting for?

Slowly, deliberately, Henry removed his hands from the wall beside her and clasped them behind his back.

The scream died in her throat, lost along with the breath that rushed from her lungs as he leaned in to trace the delicate line of her jaw with a feather brushing of his lips. "Kiss me, Sabrina," he whispered, the ache in his voice tearing at her defenses.

Longing exploded across every inch of her flesh. In an involuntary reflex, she turned her face upward, shuddering with hunger as he took the offering.

Henry held true to his word, keeping his hands behind his back. He did not break his promise, even when she released the quilt to twine her arms about his neck and draw him close.

# About the Author

An exciting new voice in historical romance, Liana LeFey loves to tell stories that capture the imagination and bring to life the splendor of the Georgian era. Liana lives in Texas with her husband/hero, two spoiled-rotten "feline masters," and several tanks of fish. She has been devouring historical romances since she was fourteen and is now delighted to be writing them for fellow enthusiasts. To learn more or drop Liana a line, visit www.facebook.com/writerliana.

15549120R00173

Made in the USA
Charleston, SC
09 November 2012